By Victor LaValle

LONE
WOMEN

LONE WOMEN

a Novel

Victor LaValle

ONE WORLD

NEW YORK

Published in the United States by One World, an imprint of Random House, a division of Penguin Random House LLC, New York.

ONE WORLD and colophon are registered trademarks of Penguin Random House LLC.

Hardback ISBN 9780525512080
Ebook ISBN 9780525512097

Printed in Canada on acid-free paper

oneworldlit.com
randomhousebooks.com

9 8 7 6 5 4 3 2 1

FIRST EDITION

Book design by Barbara M. Bachman

To Paul, my brother

"Wanna fly, you got to give up the shit that weighs you down."

—TONI MORRISON, *Song of Solomon*

ONE

1

THERE ARE TWO KINDS OF PEOPLE IN THIS WORLD: THOSE WHO live with shame, and those who die from it. On Tuesday, Adelaide Henry would've called herself the former, but by Wednesday she wasn't as sure. If she was trying to live, then why would she be walking through her family's farmhouse carrying an Atlas jar of gasoline, pouring that gasoline on the kitchen floor, the dining table, dousing the settee in the den? And after she emptied the first Atlas jar, why go back to the kitchen for the other jar, then climb the stairs to the second floor, listening to the splash of gasoline on every step? Was she planning to live, or trying to die?

There were twenty-seven Black farming families in California's Lucerne Valley in 1915. Adelaide and her parents had been one of them. After today there would only be twenty-six.

Adelaide reached the second-floor landing. She hardly smelled the gasoline anymore. Her hands were covered in fresh wounds, but she felt no pain. There were two bedrooms on the second floor: her bedroom and her parents'.

Adelaide's parents were lured west by the promise of land in this valley. The federal government encouraged Americans to homestead California. The native population had been decimated, cleared off the property. Now it was time to give it all away. This invitation was one of the few that the United States extended to even its Negro citizens, and after 1866, the African Society put out a call to "colonize" Southern California. The Henrys were among the hundreds who came. They weren't going to get a fair shot in Arkansas, that was for damn sure. The federal government called this homesteading.

Glenville and Eleanor Henry fled to California and grew alfalfa and wild grass, sold it to cattle owners for feed. Glenville studied the work of Luther Burbank and in 1908 they began growing the botanist's Santa Rosa plums. To Adelaide the fruit tasted of sugar and self-determination. Adelaide had worked the orchards and fields alongside her daddy since she was twelve. Labored in the kitchen and the barn with her mother for even longer. Thirty-one years of life on this farm. Thirty-one.

And now she would burn it all down.

"Ma'am?"

Adelaide startled at the sound of the wagon man.

"Good Lord, what is that smell?"

He stood at the front entrance, separated from the interior by a screen door and nothing more. Adelaide stood upstairs, at the threshold of her parents' bedroom. The half-full Atlas jar wobbled in her grip. She turned and called over the landing.

"Mr. Cole, I will be out in five minutes."

She couldn't see him, but she heard him. The grumble of an old Black man, barely audible but somehow still as loud as a thunderclap. It reminded her of her father.

"That's what you said five minutes ago!"

Adelaide heard the creak of the screen door's springs. A vision flashed before her: Mr. Cole coming to the foot of the stairs and Adelaide dumping the remaining gasoline right onto his head; Adelaide reaching for the matches that were in her pocket; lighting one and dropping it right onto Mr. Cole. Then, combustion.

But she didn't want to kill this old man, so she called out to him instead.

"Have you got my trunk into the wagon yet?" she called.

Quiet, quiet.

Then the sigh of the screen door being released. He hadn't stepped inside. He called to her again from the porch.

"I tried," he said. "But that thing weighs more than my damn horse. What did you pack inside?"

My whole life, she thought. *Everything that still matters.*

She looked to the door of her parents' bedroom, then called down one more time.

"Five minutes, Mr. Cole. We'll get the trunk in the wagon together."

Another grumble but he didn't curse her and she didn't hear the sound of his wagon's wheels riding off. For a man like Mr. Cole, that was as close to an "okay" as she was going to get.

Would she really have set him on fire? She couldn't say. But it's startling what people will do when they are desperate.

Adelaide Henry turned the handle to her parents' bedroom and stepped inside and shut the door behind her and stood in the silence and the dark. The heavy curtains were pulled shut. She'd done that at dawn. After she'd dragged the bodies of Glenville and Eleanor inside and put them to bed.

They lay together now, in their marriage bed. The same place where Adelaide had been conceived. They were only shapes, because she'd thrown a sheet over their corpses. Their blood had soaked through. The outline of their bodies appeared as red silhouettes.

She went to her father's side. The fabric had adhered to his skin when the blood dried. She'd pulled the sheet up over his head. Better that way. She didn't want to see what remained of him. She poured gasoline over his corpse, from his forehead to his feet.

Now Adelaide moved round to her mother's side.

She'd pulled Eleanor's side of the sheets up only to her chin, hiding the damage done to her throat. She hadn't felt able to pull the shroud over her mother entirely. Strange to get squeamish about that part considering all the other damage done to Eleanor's body. Adelaide tilted the jar above her mother's head but found she couldn't pour out the last of the fuel. She held it over Eleanor and stared into her mother's opened, empty eyes.

She couldn't bring herself to do it. She set the jar down and crouched by the bed. She whispered into Eleanor's dead ear.

"You kept too many secrets," Adelaide said. "Look what it cost you."

With that, she rose and reached into her pocket. The matchbox bore the symbol of the African Society, a silhouette of a Black man driving a plow. She struck a match and watched it burn. She flung it at the bed, where it landed on her father.

She turned quickly so she wouldn't have to see the bodies catch, but she heard it. As if the whole room took a single deep breath. An instant later she felt heat across her scalp and neck, but when she stepped out of the room the flames still licked at her skin. She realized it hadn't been the fire that burned at her but the guilt.

On the upstairs landing her right knee buckled and she nearly went down. Kneeling with one hand on the railing. She'd done it. Behind that door her parents were burning. Maybe she should stay with them. That's what she considered. Enough gasoline had spilled on her hands, her dress, that it wouldn't take long for her to burn. Step back inside the bedroom and kneel at the foot of their bed and be engulfed. End the family line. That's what she deserved. What kind of daughter would do the things she'd done in the last twenty-four hours? A foul and terrible daughter.

Soon Adelaide rose to her feet but hardly recognized she'd done it. As if her body wanted her to survive even if her soul felt differently. She rose and put one foot forward. Then the next. She'd be leaving, it seemed. *Who decided that?* she wondered, even as she held the railing and descended the stairs.

"Well, there you are," Mr. Cole said when she stepped out from the screen door. He looked from her to the house. Did he see smoke yet? Could he hear the upstairs bedroom walls starting to crackle?

His buckboard wagon sat by the porch; horse nearly as malnourished as the man. Adelaide stood six inches taller than Mr. Cole and outweighed him by forty pounds. No wonder he couldn't lift the trunk.

There were handles on either side of the Seward steamer trunk. Adelaide grabbed one end and Mr. Cole took the other. She bent her legs and lifted. Mr. Cole huffed with the strain.

"Quick now," he said. Though he wasn't doing much work, he still felt happy to give commands.

She yanked the trunk toward the bed of the wagon and Mr. Cole was pulled along.

They reached the wagon and with one last effort they set it down in the bed. The wagon sank inches and all four wooden wheels creaked. Mr. Cole's horse took a step forward as if trying to flee the burden. When they stood straight both Mr. Cole and Adelaide were breathless.

Adelaide climbed into the wagon. The only other item she'd brought—besides that trunk—was her travel bag. It had been packed already, sitting right at the threshold inside the house. Mr. Cole got in beside her on the spring seat.

He looked back at the house. "Where's your people?" he asked.

"My parents," she said softly.

"They don't come out to see you off?"

She looked at the house as well. The bedrooms lay at the back of the structure. Even if there was smoke, it probably wouldn't be seen from the front of the house for a little while. Maybe she had a bit more time before the fire became obvious.

"They're resting," she said.

Mr. Cole kept any further questions to himself. He held the reins and gave two clicks with his tongue and his poor horse pulled and pulled until, finally, the wagon moved.

Adelaide was leaving California with $154, a large sum of money and still hardly enough for an entirely new life. But that was all she had. That, and her travel bag, and her trunk.

The farmhouse would burn. Eventually their neighbors—the closest farm lay nearly a mile away—would notice. They would sift through the damage and find only two bodies inside. They would ask where Glenville and Eleanor's daughter had gone.

On Tuesday, Adelaide Henry had been a farmer.

By Wednesday she became a fugitive.

2

"I KNOW YOU."

Adelaide and Mr. Cole were an hour into their trip before he said these words. The first ones spoken since Adelaide's farmhouse disappeared behind a bend in the road. She hadn't minded the quiet.

"Queer folk," Mr. Cole continued. "That's what they say about the Henrys."

Mr. Cole's horse had become accustomed to the weight. Not comfortable, but accustomed. The bed of Mr. Cole's buckboard wagon wasn't large, which meant the trunk hardly had room to shift even as they went uphill or down; a small blessing for the animal. Adelaide wondered at her sympathy for this horse when she had so little for herself.

"Oh yes," Mr. Cole continued, feeling bolder. He cut his eyes in her direction. "I'm not just talking about round here. They know y'all in Victorville and Allensworth."

She'd hired this man to take her to the Port of Los Angeles. A twenty-four-mile ride south. And when she got there, she meant to board a ship. She guessed they had another five hours to go. Five more hours of this. The weariness is what made her speak; it certainly wasn't curiosity.

"And what do they know?" she asked.

He grinned, began a recitation: "Keep to your property. Don't visit with others. Never speak a word in church."

"We bring plums every Sunday," Adelaide offered.

Mr. Cole pinched his lips, but nodded finally. "I'll give you that much."

Adelaide thought her father would've been pleased. She could tell Mr. Cole wasn't the type to give credit for much of anything.

Adelaide looked at her hands. The cuts ran along her palms and most of her fingers. Some of the gouges were quite deep. They'd stopped bleeding but she hadn't bandaged them. Her hands must've looked nearly inhuman. She turned them back over, palms down, when she understood Mr. Cole had glanced her way. The cuts wouldn't heal for days. Somewhere along the journey she'd better buy gloves.

She tried her best but she couldn't picture exactly how she'd got the wounds. Not to say she didn't know the cause—of course she did—but the moment when any one nick or scratch appeared had been scrubbed from her mind. There was dinner yesterday evening and the sun coming up at dawn. The time in between had disappeared. It was as if she had materialized in the kitchen, her hands covered in cuts, and on the counter there were two jars filled with gasoline. She didn't even remember filling them.

I burned the evidence.

Adelaide caught herself, a hand literally thrown over her lips. For a moment she thought she'd said the words out loud. But no, she hadn't, she could tell because Mr. Cole still sat there jawing about her family and their reputation in the Valley. His lips were moving—no doubt he felt bold enough to insult her family openly now—but she couldn't hear him. Instead she heard only herself. *Every tongue shall confess.*

She kept her hand over her mouth because she wasn't sure what might come out. The words, or the last meal in her stomach.

"You feeling sick?" Mr. Cole asked.

She nodded and looked to him with a tight grin.

"Well, if something comes up," he said, looking toward the horizon, "make sure you spill over the side. I keep my wagon clean."

———

TWENTY-FOUR MILES TOOK HALF a day. Half a day with Mr. Cole. Imagine how tedious that sounds. Then double it. A funny thing happens when a man thinks he has a woman's company all to himself. He may show a face to her that he would keep hidden if there were even one more person around. He speaks from his secret self.

And even though Adelaide had been part of a family that largely kept to itself, she'd gone back and forth to Victorville and Allensworth, hauling plums to be sold. At the markets, or along the roads, she'd encountered many men by herself. The things they said. When she began making the trips alone, she wouldn't recount the words to her mother or her father. They became like a small bag of stones she carried in one hand. A bother. A nuisance. They made it more difficult to do the necessary things, big or small. She'd travel farther just to avoid certain roads. So Mr. Cole spent much of the journey talking badly about her family and did it with impunity because who else was around to shame him?

As the trip continued, Adelaide wondered what it would feel like to bring a bag of rocks down on this old man's head. By about the fourth hour, she passed the time casually imagining all the ways she might murder this spiteful man. Like right now, one hard push off the wagon and he might break his neck. She watched him and the fantasy made her grin.

But then he looked directly at her and said, "What you smiling about, girl?"

And the moment passed.

That's twice she'd contemplated killing him. There were people who would judge her harshly for her thoughts. Those people, she felt, could fuck themselves.

The wagon ride continued.

There was some confusion as they approached Los Angeles. Turns out the Port of Los Angeles was located in a town called San Pedro.

Mr. Cole learned this at a feed store along the way. His exact words were, *Well, that's some foolishness.*

If the door to the feed store hadn't been open, Adelaide wouldn't have overheard the news about the error. Mr. Cole got in the wagon and pretended like he hadn't made any mistake at all. Every tongue shall not confess, apparently.

Mr. Cole backtracked for half an hour and soon set them on the proper road. Adelaide said nothing. Getting to the Port was all that mattered. She had a ship to catch, and now she worried she might not make it.

When they finally reached San Pedro, the city shrank them. Both Adelaide and Mr. Cole felt reduced. On Beacon Street they passed the San Pedro Bank Building; its clock tower stood four stories tall. It cast a shadow that crossed the road. It seems foolish, but when they rode through the shadow, Adelaide shivered. Even Mr. Cole stopped talking. She'd seen plenty of grain silos that size, but never a clock.

The whole town was wired for electricity. A streetcar rumbled through the intersection carrying twenty-five people, maybe more. Adelaide and Mr. Cole sat in the wagon and watched the streetcar rattle past. A few of the passengers looked at her without seeing her. They looked through her, past her. They didn't know her. Didn't know her family. She was unknown. To some this might sound terrible, but that moment was the first time Adelaide Henry realized she might escape. What if she skipped all the rest and settled here?

But six hours from Lucerne Valley wasn't hardly far enough to go. And besides, Mr. Cole, this mouthy coot, he'd know where she'd settled. A man like this savored gossip the way others did her father's plums. When the streetcar passed, Mr. Cole looked to her.

"Keep going?" he asked.

For him, the Lucerne Valley was welcome, and welcoming. Had she ever felt that way?

"We're almost there, Mr. Cole." Adelaide gestured forward. "Let's keep on."

He studied her face, as if memorizing something.

He clicked his tongue and with a snort his horse took two steps forward.

The wagon wheels creaked. The trunk shifted as much as it could in the small space behind the spring seat. Adelaide reached back and placed a hand on the trunk as if it might leap from the wagon and flee. As if her touch could calm it.

3

THE PORT OF LOS ANGELES, WHAT A MESS. THOUGH OTHERS would call it progress.

The Port ran riot with industry. Steamships and sailing freighters sat so close in the harbor that a person might hop from one to the next and never risk getting wet. The steamships coughed out clouds of smoke and the railway engines did, too. Railroad tracks ringed the docks like manacles.

As soon as they arrived, Adelaide felt a fine layer of soot settle over her skin. It was as if she'd hadn't lived her entire life in the clean desert air of Lucerne. And, in fact, she would never live there again.

Mr. Cole's wasn't the only horse and wagon moving through the Port, but his was certainly the most cautious. Wagons and pedestrians weaved around them. Trucks threatened to smash right through them all.

To approach the ticket booths, they had to cross two sets of railroad tracks, and Mr. Cole prayed aloud as his wheels bumped over them. Adelaide asked Mr. Cole to wait while she went into a booth. Then, she said, she'd need him to ride her to her ship's berth so she could board. He demanded she pay him before stepping off the wagon. She felt insulted—did he think she'd leave her trunk with him and flee?—but she said nothing and simply paid him. Five dollars.

She bought a ticket to Seattle on the S.S. *Queen*. Eight dollars and thirty-five cents one-way, which included her berth and meal, leaving

from Pier 9 at four. Because of Mr. Cole's earlier mistake, they'd arrived at the Port with only twenty minutes to spare.

When she stepped out of the booth, she found Mr. Cole tossing
her trunk out of his wagon. He didn't have the strength to pull it out,
so the man grabbed one handle and flipped the trunk onto the ground.
The thing went upside down and landed with a crash so loud it could
be heard over even the whistles of the nearby trains.

"Mr. Cole!" she howled, running toward him.

Now she would kill him. No gasoline, no bag of metaphorical rocks,
just her two bruised hands. She'd throttle this old motherfucker right
here in public. She'd serve the jail time so long as she enjoyed the satisfaction of watching the Judas take his last breath. She'd—

But by the time she reached the trunk, the wagon man had already
rolled off. Without the burden of Adelaide and her cargo, that skinny
horse made top speed in a snap. Mr. Cole didn't look back once, not
even to gloat. Just left her there with her heavy-ass trunk.

A moment of rage and shock rose and passed, and only then did
she think to make sure the trunk hadn't been split open in the fall. The
body seemed intact and then she checked the brass padlock. It held.
She grabbed the top end of the trunk and, gently as she could, turned
it right side up and set it down flat on its bottom again.

She looked for Pier 9 and, good luck, it sat only twenty yards away.
She caught the eye of the ship's superintendent, who'd just checked a
couple against his manifest, then waved them up the ramp. He saw her
and she saw him and before he could look away she raised her arms
and waved for him.

He frowned at her. What was she trying to say?

She waved her ticket, then pointed at the ship. He gestured for her
to come to him. After all, he couldn't bring the ship to her. She pointed
to her trunk and now he seemed to understand but only shrugged,
pointed at the space beside him, and looked away. That was it.

You and that trunk need to get *here*.

And now she only had fifteen minutes.

Chivalry is not an entitlement, but a gift, apparently. One that not a single man offered Adelaide as she was forced to drag that trunk all twenty yards, right to the superintendent's feet. And when she reached him, out of breath, sweat making her scalp itch, the superintendent said, "Nearly too late."

And that's all this man said.

Then, after checking her ticket, he gestured to the stevedore on deck, who ordered his men to haul the Seward steamer trunk up. Two men came down, but even working together they couldn't quite lift it. They had to call a third man in. Hearing them grunt, watching them tremble as they inched up the ramp, Adelaide did take some pleasure in that. Halfway up the ramp they stopped and looked back at her, seeming to wonder how she'd dragged the trunk more than an inch.

Desperation, that's how. And a lifetime working the land.

She boarded the S.S. *Queen* wanting to hide away in her berth, not appear again until they reached Seattle. But when she boarded, a steward told her the vessel had been oversold and that her ticket would provide her meals and passage, but there were no free cabins left, no empty beds. She'd have to stay on deck for the duration.

He said it so casually, maybe that's what made her angriest. No, it was definitely paying for a room and then not being given one that set her off the most. But the offhand way the steward shared this information, not even with a tone of apology, was hard to accept. But what could she do? Already the anchor was rising from the waters, spilling foam that resembled popped champagne.

Passengers gathered along the deck to watch the steamer swing away the pier. Adelaide moved among them, knowing no one and catching no one's eye. As far as she could tell, she might be the only Negro woman on the ship. Certainly the only one who was a passenger at least. She saw two men talking closely by the railing; they weren't white. She had never seen Japanese people before. Nevertheless, she felt jealous they were paired.

She found a deck chair and pulled a book from her travel bag. *The*

Tenant of Wildfell Hall by Anne Brontë. She'd read it so often the cover threatened to fall off. This book, and a few others she'd packed, would be her only companions.

As the ship reached open water she felt no sense of ease or safety. She had much farther to travel before she might truly disappear.

4

A WOMAN IS A MULE.

Adelaide's mother used to say this to her. Those might've been the first words Eleanor Henry ever shared with her daughter. If not, they were certainly among the ones she used most often.

A woman is a mule.

It's how Eleanor explained the toil of life. Waking before dawn with Glenville, laboring inside the home while he planted or plowed in the field. Working the fields herself when the times demanded it and staying up through the night preparing for the next day's labor even as Glenville fell into bed. Eleanor meant to prepare her daughter, train her up in endurance and acceptance.

My burdens will be your burdens; I am a mule and you will be, too.

And Adelaide had been a dutiful daughter—what choice did she have?—but that shit wears you down. The reward for sacrifice is simply more sacrifices.

So it shouldn't be all that surprising that Adelaide had been pining to get away ever since she was old enough to understand there was an outside world to get away to. She'd always felt a fondness for Montana in particular. They shared the same birthday, for one thing. November 8. Though Adelaide was born in 1883 so she was actually six years older than Montana. A fact that made her mother laugh.

Hearing her mother's voice made her sit straight in her deck chair. They were in open water, but it was as if Eleanor had been sitting right beside her, whispering in her ear.

How long had passed? The sun was nearly down.

Now Adelaide heard it again: the splash of the gasoline on the wood floors of the farmhouse; the softer sound as the gasoline soaked into the sheet that shrouded her father; her mother's eyes looking up at the ceiling, her throat torn open so she would never speak again.

"A woman is a mule."

Adelaide whispered these five words to herself, as if her mother's mantra would help dispel the memory of the massacre back in California.

A mule can kick backwards and sideways.

Adelaide rose from her deck chair, packed her travel bag, and walked inside, then below deck. It would be dinnertime soon, but so far she felt no hunger. What was the word for what she felt? Abandoned? No, that couldn't be right since she was the one who'd fled.

Isolated. Forsaken.

Bereft.

Yes.

Adelaide wound her way below deck to where the baggage had been stowed. So dark in here. She moved through the rows of cargo, seeking out the one thing she had: that trunk. There were plenty others down here, but she recognized hers by the big brass lock and, perhaps, its scent. It still smelled like the Lucerne Valley. At least that's how it seemed to her. There was only one key to this lock and she wore it on a length of twine tied around her neck.

Adelaide planned to travel by ship all the way to Seattle. And from there catch a train heading east, to Montana. Still a long way to go. She sat down in the dark beside the trunk; the feeling of it against her back was the closest she might ever come to an embrace again.

If a crew member had come down here at some point in the journey, he might've stumbled across this odd sight: a Negro woman sitting in the dark. Strange enough, yes, but if he'd gone still and slowed his breathing, he might've detected something even less ordinary: in the dark, that Negro woman, the side of her face pressed to the trunk. It would've looked like she was praying, perhaps. Or whispering.

5

JUST TWO YEARS EARLIER, IN 1913, A WOMAN NAMED MATTIE T. Cramer caused a lot of conversation when she published a letter in the Great Northern Railway *Bulletin*. A testimonial from Montana published under the headline "Success of a 'Lone' Woman." Adelaide had a copy. Back home she'd hidden it under her mattress like a child.

In this letter Cramer explained she'd left Iowa City, Iowa, with her little boy in tow and moved to Montana, near a town named Malta, arriving on May 4, 1908. Mattie went because the federal government had been giving out 320-acre plots of land for homesteading, only requiring a "person"—that wording was vitally vague—to live on the land for three years, making it habitable and cultivating crops. If, at the end of those three years, the *person* had done all this, then the land would become theirs forever. Completing the three-year bid was called "proving up."

Mattie T. Cramer went out to Malta with plans to do just that.

When she went, she had less than one hundred dollars to her name. By the time she'd published her testimonial in 1913, Mattie had built a two-story frame house on the property. Also "a barn, chicken house, dug a well, fenced all the land, and 21 acres of the plot is under cultivation. Besides, I bought two lots in town and built a five-room cottage which I rent. I consider this the land of unlimited opportunities."

Crouched below deck, in the dark, Adelaide repeated those last two words as her ship arrived in Seattle.

"Unlimited opportunities. Unlimited opportunities."

She spent three nights in Seattle, the time it took to track down a real estate salesman who offered her a bargain on a property that had been abandoned.

A map of Montana had been pinned to the wall of his office. Beside it maps of Wyoming and North Dakota. He marked each claim he represented with a nail on the map. There were forty-nine, spread out among the three states.

Mattie Cramer had chosen Montana, so Adelaide would, too.

"This one," she said, pointing to an area not far from the Canadian border. A single nail, far from everything.

"Not much up there," the salesman said.

"That's all right," Adelaide told him.

"There's a town, I guess. Big Sandy. But even for Montana it's small."

He thought he was scaring her with these words, but she didn't shiver.

"Won't be anyone to come save you if you get in trouble." He said this with such urgency that it almost made her think he was worried.

"And if you die up there before proving up," he said, "the property reverts to my office."

She nodded and grinned at this. Just business, that's all this was to him, and she didn't mind. Adelaide touched the nail again. "This one."

The salesman made a big show of pulling a hammer with a nickel-plated head and ebonized handle from his desk drawer. He let her yank the nail from the map. She pulled it with such force that it came out looking more like a fishing hook. He dropped it in her palm.

"The last homesteader built a shack on the property and dug a working well," the salesman told her. "Those'll cost you one hundred dollars, payable now. It sounds like a lot, but I promise you it's a leg up that you won't have to worry about building yourself a home or having drinkable water."

Was it true? Suppose she got there and the cabin had been pulled up from the ground by now? Or a creature of the wild had made the place its den? For a moment she felt the strongest desire to consult with her mother about this decision.

What would Eleanor suggest?

Nothing, now.

Adelaide paid the property agent one hundred dollars; in return he gave her the claim number and coordinates to the property. The agent filed her name on the contract, and it was only after she saw her name written in black ink that she realized she'd made her first mistake. She could have given this man any name she liked. Why had she made the error of honesty? It's just how she'd been raised. Instead of fussing over this misstep, she left the property agent's office and busied herself with more immediate needs: a railway ticket to Montana.

After stowing her steamer trunk in the luggage car, she boarded the train headed east toward Big Sandy. As they steamed out of King Street Station, she felt the grief and the worry and sickening uncertainty, yes to all of that, but could she be forgiven for also feeling anticipation? Excitement.

What would she make of the town? And what would they make of her?

Unlimited opportunities, she told herself.

6

FRED HARNDEN ARRIVED EARLY TO GREET THE ARRIVING TRAINS. He worked for the *Bear Paw Mountaineer,* the local paper of Big Sandy and its surrounding territories. Meeting the train counted as his job, but more than that, it felt like a calling. He thought of himself as an ambassador. The first local face many new arrivals would see. He didn't have a great smile and he knew it, but his eagerness and excitement to meet people often won them over anyway.

He wasn't the only person waiting for the three o'clock out of Seattle. There were a dozen others waiting on the Great Northern, too. But most of the other people were looking for their kinfolk, or were employers come to greet a new employee. Fred had a higher purpose, he felt. And he came out every day, notepad and pencil in his right coat pocket. Only one other person came to meet the train as often as him.

Today's train was about two hours late, but this surprised no one. The only constants about trains were that they were loud and they were late. Folks enjoyed speculating about what might've slowed the rail. A game locals played to make the time pass.

Once a train had been delayed by five hours because a stubborn flock of sheep would not be scattered from the tracks. Antelope could be a problem, too, though they were more skittish.

"What's your bet then?"

Fred Harnden started with surprise. He'd thought he was alone and had been enjoying observing the others around him. When he got lost in his own thoughts, it was easy to forget he, too, had a body taking up space. He turned to find one of his favorite residents by his side.

"Mrs. Reed," he said, softly, the way you might to a beloved aunt.

Mrs. Jerrine Reed, wife of Jack Reed, though she would never introduce herself that way. President of the local chapter of the Busy Bees *and* the Big Sandy Suffragettes; now, those were titles she embraced.

The top of her head reached Fred's shoulder, and Fred was not a towering figure. She wore a bluebird pin for happiness, attached to the lapel of her coat, and a black Mary Pickford cap. She was the second-best-dressed woman in town.

"Sheep," Fred said. "That's my guess."

She slapped his arm. "No likely guesses, please. Those are dull. Only the least likely."

"Well then," Fred said, tilting his head as if to catch a better idea falling from the sky. "Idaho has declared war on Montana. The train is a spoil of war."

Mrs. Reed lost her smile and Fred knew he'd made a mistake.

"Idaho afforded women the right to vote in 1896, Mr. Harnden. Eighteen years before the people of Montana saw fit to do the same. I won't hear any jokes about that fine state."

Fred looked to his feet. One other thing worth knowing about Mrs. Reed: she and her husband were the richest people in Big Sandy. They donated funds to the *Bear Paw Mountaineer* every year and threw parties for the publisher; when Fred took the job on the paper, they'd bought him a typewriter, an Oliver Batwing that he used to this day.

"I didn't mean," he began, looking up from his feet to the bluebird pin.

"Oh, Fred, look," she said, before he could stammer out the rest of an apology. "The train is here."

He looked to her face and she pooched out her lips. *Look at that, not at me.* A playful gesture, and he did look to the train and immediately felt better. The train arrived at five.

Beside him, Mrs. Reed applauded the train's arrival. She was the other person who came to greet the train each day that it arrived. If Fred Harnden felt like the town's ambassador, then Mrs. Reed, it was no exaggeration, counted as its queen.

As the train slowed to a stop, Fred practiced the kind of copy he'd be running in tomorrow's paper:

J. P. Smith from Flaxton, N.D., is here for a while visiting Fred Curtis near Virgelle and incidentally assisting him in making some repairs with his gasoline engine.

L. R. McKenzie, a former Big Sandy boy, was a caller from Havre Saturday between trains, having a little business to attend to in regards to the erection of the new Clack elevator.

Fred Harnden would file twenty or thirty such updates in the paper each week, greeting arrivals, newcomers and returnees, and logging the information they shared. For *Mountaineer* readers it was nearly as good as checking in with your neighbors personally.

As the passengers were helped off the train by porters, Fred pulled out his notepad and pen.

"I'm off to work now," he said to Mrs. Reed, and took two steps toward the arriving passengers, but then turned back to her.

He made a show of flipping his notepad open, gripping his pencil theatrically.

"I realize that *you* always greet arrivals, Mrs. Reed, but I should still ask, is there anyone in particular you're hoping to see today?"

Mrs. Reed said, "Not who, Fred. *What.* The theater organ is arriving."

"For the opera house?"

"For the opera house," she agreed.

Fred put pencil to paper, excited in an entirely new way. An organ for the opera house.

She gestured with her hand, turning him back toward the crowd forming on the platform. Did she mean to dismiss him or was he being too sensitive? Both, probably. Nevertheless, what could he do? He turned back toward the train.

Immediately he met two Big Sandy residents returning from out of town: Bernhart Sonkson and his mother. The boy had broken his arm by falling off a roof and now proudly displayed his plaster-of-Paris cast. Why had he been on the roof? Harnden asked, and the boy looked at him with surprise, even disgust. As if Harnden were a fool for not knowing that the job of any boy was to gain access to roofs.

Harnden continued interviewing arrivals for the next hour. At one point he encountered a tall Negro woman who asked him where she might hire a wagon. He'd been in a hurry, rushing to get to three more Big Sandy residents who'd also returned on the train. He turned to the tall Negro woman and quickly gestured toward town. He never thought to ask her name. He assumed her to be a domestic, come to work for one of the local families.

Welcome to Montana, Adelaide.

7

BIG SANDY.

A town of five hundred or so. About half lived in the town itself and the other half farther out on the plains, on tracts of land they hoped to homestead. But even those numbers far outdid what Adelaide had been used to back in the Lucerne Valley. There had been five neighboring families within the vicinity of her family's farm. Add up all the children and parents and you might've had forty people, give or take. More livestock than people by a factor of one hundred. So even Big Sandy's numbers might've made Adelaide feel small, as she'd felt in San Pedro, to say nothing of her short time in Seattle.

But as she walked from the train station toward Main Street, which was really the *only* street, it seemed as though the town was hardly there. This wasn't the fault of the place. Blame the sky. The largest hotel, the sole hotel, the Gregson Springs Hotel, was downright palatial by Adelaide's standards, and yet it hardly troubled the horizon. Fifty miles east lay the Bear Paw Mountains, but from here they registered as little more than mounds of dirt. The flat expanse of Montana had floored her as she scanned the state from her train. But the flatness felt majestic now, with a whole town laid out to offer some perspective. Maybe this is how Moses felt as he walked between the parted waters of the Red Sea. *Look at God.*

This is why she quickly forgot the slight she felt when she spoke to the hurried little white man who she'd passed on the platform. She'd seen what he did with each passenger he encountered. They exchanged a few words, then the man took out his notebook and wrote down whatever the newcomer said next, then the little white man moved on. But each person he spoke with strode off seeming to feel welcomed. An actual change in their stride. So when she got to him and asked where to find a wagon driver, she expected him to ask, *And where are you arriving from?* But he didn't. He only pointed her in the right direction and scuttled off to flatter someone else with his attention.

Now, here's the funny part: Adelaide Henry came out here hoping to disappear. She didn't want to be found, meant to be hiding, so if the man had asked her name, what would she have done? Lied, maybe, though she'd never been too good at that. Instead, she might've made the mistake of telling him her true name and hometown. Then she would've needed to go off running once again, north to Canada or some such. But Canada didn't allow single women to own their land outright, and certainly not a Negro woman, so what good would that have done? Which is all to say, the little white man ignored her and that was both the best thing for her *and* it hurt her feelings.

So now she moved toward town, wondering if wagon men were all the same. If she was about to encounter another version of Mr. Cole—nosy and noxious—she'd have to steel herself this next leg of her journey. The questions and the cruelty.

But that's not what happened. Instead, before she could go searching for a wagon man, she felt a hand tugging her coat. A tiny little woman stood there smiling at her. She wore a bluebird pin and a hat that was meant to be stylish, though Adelaide never had an eye for such things.

"Yes, ma'am?" Adelaide said.

This woman still hadn't let go of Adelaide's coat. It was as if she was trying to stop her from entering the town altogether. Denying her entry. One more barrier in a journey that had already been full of them. But then the woman spoke.

"You're looking for a wagon man?" the woman asked.

Adelaide watched the woman warily.

"I'm sorry," she said. "My name is Jerrine Reed. Welcome to Big Sandy."

What that did for Adelaide Henry can't be overstated. The woman seemed to grow in direct proportion to her generosity of spirit, until it almost felt like she and Adelaide were standing eye to eye.

"Ask for Mr. Olsen," she said. "He's the only honest wagon driver we've got." She looked left and right, playful. "But don't tell the other drivers I said so."

And off she went, toward the train. She waited at the platform for a moment, and Adelaide watched her. Mrs. Reed raised her arms, and, as if by this motion, an enormous item appeared on the platform, rolled into view by six men, all working at great effort. It came crated up, but Mrs. Reed pointed to the box and waited as one of the men ran off for a bar and when he returned she made them pry the face of the crate open. Every passenger, every townsperson, even animals stopped moving and gave Mrs. Reed their full attention.

The sides of the crate were yanked apart and the back of the crate fell backward and now on the train platform sat a Model 190 Wurlitzer. A theater organ built by the Rudolph Wurlitzer Company of North Tonawanda, New York, and eventually shipped by train all the way to Montana; fifteen feet wide and thirteen feet deep; 584 individual pipes organized into eight ranks; nearly four hundred pounds. Two more even larger crates still sat in a freight car on the train, carrying the organ's pipes and instruments. Mrs. Reed would inspect each one there on the platform, work that would take hours but better to have it done here than to get everything hauled to the opera house only to find any part of it had been damaged. Mrs. Reed approached the theater organ and rested her hands on one of the organ's keyboards. Under that endless sky, it looked as if she was going to play a melody for God. Then she clapped and waved the workers into action.

Now Adelaide finally turned away from the spectacle of Mrs. Reed and walked into town, a matter of only ten yards' distance from the train platform. There were a few wagon men milling around before their wagons, each one making his living by delivering the new and hopeful homesteaders out to their tracts of land. But Adelaide had been told who to look for, Mr. Olsen. She went from one man to the next until finally she found him.

Talk about a big fella. And that meant something coming from Adelaide Henry, who tended to dwarf most women and men. From where she stood, he seemed about as large as those Bear Paw Mountains in the distance. Had a warmer smile, though. You know who else had a good smile? Her father, Glenville. Even though a few of his teeth were crooked, he offered it to everyone he met. Unabashed. It might've been his finest feature besides those Santa Rosa plums.

"I might have room," Mr. Olsen said, his voice rumbling like a railroad engine. "Though it depends on what you're bringing."

"Just me," she said softly. "And my steamer trunk."

He looked back to his wagon, which sat half full. "I got one family who already hired me. But if all you have is a steamer, then I'm sure you could fit."

He said this, then narrowed his eyes. "And that really is all you're bringing?"

"Does that seem foolish?" she asked him. Looking into his face, she saw something else she hadn't enjoyed in a while: concern.

"It's not for me to judge," Mr. Olsen told her. "At least not till after you've paid me."

He smiled again and then something even more unexpected happened.

For the first time in a long time, she smiled, too.

8

"IT IS QUESTIONABLE IF ANY STATE IN THE UNION HAS BETTER climate."

Adelaide said these words to herself in the back of a wagon crossing the Badlands of Montana as a spiteful wind blew so hard it nearly snapped her spine.

"The winters are less severe than in areas further east and the cold spells of short duration," she continued.

The wind.

How to comprehend it? Nothing in her life had prepared her. It had the churning quality of an ocean, a similar strength, but felt more deadly because it remained unseen. She'd gotten into this open wagon an hour ago and been pummeled by the wind for sixty minutes straight, chipped at and smoothed. Montana was already sculpting her.

She looked to the other side of the wagon, to the family who'd hired Mr. Olsen. A woman and four boys. The boys ranged from about twelve to seventeen. All of them—mother and children—slimmer than a sliver, but they looked rugged, not weak. Adelaide's strength came from decades of working the plow, threshing the soil; this family came from some other line of labor, but she couldn't guess what. They hadn't spoken to her once. Nor to Mr. Olsen, not in her presence. Mr. Olsen had made the introductions.

These are the Mudges.

As Adelaide had climbed into the wagon, she'd looked to the mother and nodded, but all the woman did was stare back. Adelaide

ignored the whole family for quite a while after that, didn't pay attention to the boys until they'd started off from town. She'd seen them, of
course, but hadn't registered one particular element: all four boys wore
handkerchiefs over their eyes. Now, an hour into the journey, they still
hadn't removed the cloth or peeked out from underneath. It took some
time before Adelaide understood: all four boys were blind.

These are the Mudges.

A mother and four blind boys, off to homestead in Montana.

Once she fully grasped the situation, Adelaide nearly fell backward
out the wagon from the shock of it. And immediately she forgave the
fact this woman hadn't returned her greeting. Imagine the stress and
worry that must have been tumbling through Mrs. Mudge's mind. A
mother and four blind boys. Out here.

My goodness, Adelaide thought. *My God.*

To steady herself, she closed her eyes and once again recited lines
from the pamphlet written by Mattie T. Cramer. Adelaide hadn't realized she'd memorized the full text until she'd begun chanting lines to
herself in the wagon.

If Mattie T. Cramer could do it, then Adelaide could do it.

If Mattie T. Cramer could do it, then Mrs. Mudge and her boys
could do it, too.

"In summer, hot winds that wither vegetation are but little known,"
Adelaide continued. She curled forward in the bed of the wagon, trying to hide from the stinging wind, but it hardly helped.

"Bunk!"

Adelaide opened her eyes. She looked to see who'd spoken. Not
Mrs. Mudge. Not the boys. Mr. Olsen. Driving the wagon up there on
his California seat, looking back over his shoulder.

"That stuff you're saying is pure hokum," he told Adelaide.

She couldn't guess how he heard her over the roar of the wind.
Maybe he was well used to tuning out that sound. Or maybe she'd
been shouting.

"Shouldn't have believed in no railway rag!" he hooted.

Railway rag? Mattie T. Cramer's article? It had first seen print in the Great Northern Railway *Bulletin*, but that hardly invalidated the woman's testimony, did it?

He laughed now, up there in his wagon seat. He must have been buffeted by the winds, just like her, but he hardly seemed to move. Steady and smug. She'd felt warmly toward Mr. Olsen in town; now her feelings developed a sharp chill. But before Adelaide could say anything, Mrs. Mudge rose from *her* seat. She placed one hand on the shoulder of her youngest son to steady herself.

"My boys don't need to hear from cynics!" Mrs. Mudge shouted toward the driver. "And neither do I!"

Go ahead, Mrs. Mudge! That's what Adelaide thought. She even smiled at the woman, not that Mrs. Mudge noticed.

"We've come too far," Mrs. Mudge said. Those words were quieter. Adelaide barely heard them. Mrs. Mudge spoke to herself then, not to Mr. Olsen. *We've come too far.*

Me too, thought Adelaide.

The road—such as it was—dipped and the wagon tipped to its side just enough for Mrs. Mudge to lose her balance. It almost seemed intentional on Mr. Olsen's part, but probably just seemed that way because of the heated feelings of the moment. After all, this wagon had been rising and falling, dipping and slipping, the whole way since they'd left town.

But when Mrs. Mudge lost her balance, her free hand fell hard on Adelaide's steamer trunk. Slamming it as if knocking at a door.

Instantly Adelaide's eyes fell to the brass lock on the trunk. Was it the dip in the road that suddenly made it rattle or was it something else?

Adelaide jumped from her seat, throwing a shadow across Mrs. Mudge.

"Get back!" Adelaide shouted. "Get off!"

She pressed one hand against the slim woman's shoulder and gently pushed. She meant to be gentle, anyway.

But Mrs. Mudge's small frame slammed down with such force that maybe Adelaide hadn't been so gentle after all. And then a remarkable thing happened: those boys moved.

Mrs. Mudge went down hard in her seat, and all four young men rose. They tilted their heads, seeming to *listen* for Adelaide's position. They crouched into grappler's poses, each one facing her exactly, prepared to pounce. The coordination of it, the silent efficiency, thrilled and terrified Adelaide. She felt foolish for assuming their blindness meant they were helpless.

Those four boys were ready to kill.

"Quit," Mrs. Mudge said. She spoke softly and yet the reaction was immediate.

As one, the boys fell back into their seats. It was as if they'd never moved at all.

Mr. Olsen, the cause of all this sudden chaos, said nothing now. He drove his wagon and didn't look over his shoulder and kept his eye on the path ahead. Maybe he'd been intimidated by those four boys as well.

Mrs. Mudge stared into the distance, too, ignoring Adelaide with a muted fury.

Only Adelaide remained on her feet in the wagon. Suddenly she felt the cold again, the wind rocking her. She looked down at the trunk, then back to Mrs. Mudge.

This old feeling; oh yes, Adelaide knew it well. The spectacle; the overreaction; the shame.

Queer folk. That's what they say about the Henrys.

Should she apologize? Probably.

Did she apologize? She did not.

Instead, she shrank. She knew how to do this. A lifetime of practice. Big as she was, she shrank down to the size of something you might slip inside your coat pocket.

Queer folk. That's what they say about the Henrys.

Adelaide tugged the brass lock once. It remained intact. It remained secure.

They rode silent within the roar of the wind.

9

"YOU ALL HAVE TO GET OUT OF MY WAGON," MR. OLSEN SAID firmly.

The youngest Mudge boy shouted, "Like hell!"

Adelaide looked up sharply. It was the first time she'd heard any of the Mudge children speak.

Mr. Olsen stopped the horses, set the reins in his lap and lifted a lash. He hadn't used it on the horses yet. Was he about to beat the child? When he lifted the lash, it bent like a dowsing rod discovering water. Montana wind wouldn't let anything stay straight.

"Got a coulee ahead," Mr. Olsen said calmly. "Easier for the horses if we take out some of the weight."

Adelaide climbed out. Mrs. Mudge stepped down next and helped the oldest boy, holding his hand. He then turned and helped the next oldest down, and on like that until they'd all come down. They worked with precision, a sign of routine.

Up ahead the road dropped into a deep bowl of earth. This, apparently, was a coulee. A steep drop in and then, on the other side, a steep rise to get out. Bigger than a gulch, not as grand as a valley. The passengers would cross on foot while Mr. Olsen got the horses and wagon through.

The earth in the coulee was muddy and sucked at their shoes. Adelaide and Mrs. Mudge wore dresses; the Mudge boys wore suits. All hems were dirty by the time they'd taken twenty steps.

Mr. Olsen lashed the four horses and they trod down into the coulee, the loaded wagon bucking behind them. They hit the muddy bottom and the horses' power seemed halved. Mr. Olsen's lash finally got used, driving them harder, and soon he moved to the back of the wagon and pushed as well.

But it became clear, quite quick, the wagon wouldn't make it out.

"Well, shit," Mr. Olsen said, nearly as breathless as the horses. Adelaide only heard him because she'd been standing nearby. She'd been about to volunteer to help push.

He went to the horses to calm them and let them catch their breath. By now, the Mudges had reached the other side of the coulee.

"I suggest you climb the rise with them," Mr. Olsen told Adelaide.

She peeked at her trunk only once, then climbed the slope and found her place near the Mudges. The winds that had been so powerful during the day only picked up as night approached. And now they were even colder. The Mudges huddled together.

Adelaide, having no one, crouched low and crossed her arms. Hugging herself.

Mr. Olsen soon climbed the slope and called his passengers together. He'd brought a Dietz kerosene lantern with him from the wagon. Not a one of them, not even Adelaide, came up to Olsen's shoulder. Two women and four boys stood in the shelter of the wagon driver.

"I'm going to unload the wagon and haul your things up here one by one. Empty it enough to get the team up. Then I'll reload everything."

"But it's almost night," Adelaide said.

He nodded, but didn't look at her. She thought that if he'd looked her in the eye, he might've shivered at the specter of all the labor he was about to do.

"Nothing for it," he said, swallowing hard.

"And what about us?" Mrs. Mudge asked. "My boys can't help you. They're not fit for the task."

Mr. Olsen gestured northeast. "I'm going to get you all to shelter. Then I'll come back."

Mr. Olsen turned and walked east. As soon as he moved, Adelaide felt pummeled by the gales again. She'd left warm nights in California for this? She walked beside the big man if only for the feeling of company.

The Mudge family trailed behind them, Mrs. Mudge in the lead and her oldest boy just behind her, his hand set on her right shoulder. The second youngest set his hand on his older brother's right shoulder. As did the third boy and then the youngest. Obviously, Adelaide understood the hardship of their circumstances, but her gaze lingered on their hands, the unbroken family chain.

"I'm embarrassed," Mr. Olsen told Adelaide. "And confused. My team has hauled much bigger loads than this one. I don't understand what could be weighing it down so bad this time."

Adelaide walked along, nodding her head as if she, too, were confused. Of course, she was not. She could have answered the man's question easily. After all, she'd packed the trunk herself. Adelaide had brought her burden with her. She knew exactly how heavy it was. Those horses never stood a chance.

10

THE TEMPERATURE DROPPED MORE THAN TWENTY DEGREES without the sun. Early September and Adelaide, spoiled by a childhood in the Lucerne Valley, felt crippled by the chill. She limped alongside Mr. Olsen. He asked if she felt all right more than once and she lied, told him she felt fine.

The Mudges had come from rural Washington and seemed better suited to the relentless chill. Blindness or not, those boys looked heartier than her right now. With the daylight gone, the night enveloped them like a shroud, and Mr. Olsen lit the lantern. Any landscape more than ten feet from them had been erased. If not for the light in Mr. Olsen's hand, the night would've gobbled them up altogether.

"Have to spend the night at the old hotel," Mr. Olsen told them, his voice somber, almost apologetic.

"When will we get there?" Mrs. Mudge shouted.

"There it is," Olsen said.

And suddenly, as if dreamed up by the plains, the old hotel appeared.

Two stories and derelict and every window dark. Ugly as a rotted tooth. The whole structure leaned to one side, near ready to collapse. Would it be safer inside or outside?

"Used to be a town here," Mr. Olsen said as they approached the front steps. "I can't recall its name. The land took it all back. Except this place."

"Are there beds?" Mrs. Mudge asked, looking back at her sons.

"Nothing inside but the floors and walls," he said. "Some of the rooms still have a ceiling. You all get yourselves in. Take any room you want. I won't get sleep tonight."

Mrs. Mudge climbed the stairs and tried the front door. When it opened, the door damn near fell off the one good hinge that held it. The woman turned and guided her sons up the front steps, one by one. They entered the hallway and were lost to the darkness. Adelaide wouldn't even have known they were inside if not for the sounds of their boots scuffing the floors.

She looked back toward Mr. Olsen to thank him, but who had time for courtesy? He'd already started back. She watched him go. The light of his lantern remained visible for a long while because the land was so flat. She couldn't make out the silhouette of the man, so it seemed as if only the light traveled across the plains, a spirit in search of rest. Adelaide wondered if Mr. Olsen would return.

Eventually the chill forced her inside. She wrestled the front door back into its frame and even the scant moonlight of the plains disappeared. She stood quietly at the entrance for who knew how long until she could see, faintly, because of the moonlight pouring through the broken slats of the walls.

One empty entranceway, one empty parlor, ten empty bedrooms. Adelaide had expected to find a few strips of cloth, a broken chair or two, but everything had been sold, stolen, or withered away. Adelaide carried a box of matches in her bag. A match from this box had burned down the farmhouse in California. Turned her mother and father into ash. But she hadn't brought a lamp, not in her travel bag. So she struck a match and held it in two fingers and made her way through the fathomless dark.

She heard Mrs. Mudge on the flight above her. Cursing as she reached the top of the stairs, guiding her boys by the sound of her frustration. Adelaide followed the beacon, too. She might never have discovered the stairs otherwise.

As she climbed she felt a tickle at the base of her scalp. She told herself it was only the wind. More than enough cracks in the walls for it to sneak inside. And yet she couldn't escape the feeling of someone behind her on the stairs, blowing at the back of her neck. When her match flame died, she rushed to light the next, spilling one or two matches out of fear.

The Mudges entered the first room at the top of the stairs. Adelaide knew this because there were windows in that room and moonlight illuminated the interior. Adelaide stumbled toward the open door, but Mrs. Mudge held her back. She pulled the door closed so Adelaide could hardly see inside.

"Doesn't seem fitting," she said. "My boys sleeping in the same room as an unmarried woman. What would people say?"

"But we're the only people here," Adelaide replied.

Adelaide heard the Mudge boys bedding down. She wanted to plead with Mrs. Mudge—woman to woman—promise she'd make no noise; she'd sleep facing the walls. Just to be in a room with others rather than by herself.

"It would make a difficult night less difficult," Adelaide said softly. "If you let me in."

Mrs. Mudge cleared her throat. "Difficulty?" she asked. The slim woman opened the door a bit more, called out. "Joab. Come close."

The floor creaked faintly and, in a moment, the youngest boy appeared by his mother's side.

"This woman is suggesting that sleeping alone in a hotel room is a difficulty she can't manage."

Adelaide leaned back. It sounded so silly when Mrs. Mudge said it out loud, and yet, it was how she felt. Why make a show of it to her child?

"I didn't know I was blind until I turned six years old," the boy said. His voice trembled in that place between childhood and early maturity. He might've been twelve or a small thirteen-year-old.

Joab.

"I mean to say," the boy continued, "I didn't know anyone else considered my lack of sight a problem. Our mother never let us think of it as an affliction. We worked our land, walked to and from school without her once we knew the path. She taught us to persevere."

Mrs. Mudge looked at the boy, nearly as tall as her, and placed a hand on his shoulder, and Adelaide felt an ache. That simple touch, from mother to child, she would never know it again.

"A boy finally made me realize my circumstances," Joab said. "My *difficulty.* He started to follow me everywhere singing 'Three Blind Mice.' He made a game of it, I can tell you. One day, on the walk to school, I led him to an old well. Then I pushed him in."

Adelaide bolted upright. Dropped her match, which died on the floor. *What did this boy just say?*

Mrs. Mudge frowned, huffed once.

"Well, the boy didn't die," Mrs. Mudge said. "Did he, Joab?"

"No, ma'am," the boy agreed. "But he never sang that song near me again."

Mrs. Mudge nodded, looked back to Adelaide. "Difficulties are to be overcome, not indulged."

Well, what the hell was Adelaide going to say to that? She reached down and lifted her travel bag, placed a hand against the wall, and patted along as she searched for the next room. Behind her, she thought she heard the Mudges' door shut. But when Adelaide looked back over her shoulder—she couldn't be sure because of the utter darkness—she swore she saw the dark figures of Mrs. Mudge and Joab still out there on the landing. Watching her as she pawed through the shadows alone.

11

SHE ENTERED THE NEXT ROOM AND, MERCIFULLY, THE DOOR
shut tight and its lock still worked. Inside she unfurled a flannel blanket she'd kept in her travel bag, expecting the beds out here to lack
such luxuries. Instead the room lacked the luxury of a bed. She folded
the blanket over to double the comfort, such as it was.

She lay down but found it impossible to sleep.

If she'd had a lantern, she would've read through the night, but she
could hardly even make out the shape of the travel bag right beside her
head. She had to remind herself that's all it was—a travel bag—or her
imagination would turn it into a living thing, a wild creature snuck
into her room to feed. It didn't help to hear the coyotes out on the
plains now. They cackled and cried in a nearly human tone.

Glenville Henry had a terrible reading voice, but Adelaide adored
the sound of her father reading to her. If she closed her eyes, she could
hear that voice even now, and so, in a way, her father kept her company
through the night.

For a moment she felt herself between her mother's knees, hair
being combed and set with firm delicacy, oil rubbed into her scalp with
a forefinger. Her mind took her back to Lucerne Valley. Her mother's
fingers in her hair, listening to her father reading Anne Brontë's *The
Tenant of Wildfell Hall*.

"'You must go back with me to the autumn of 1827,'" Glenville read,
the opening lines of the novel. How many times had he read that book

to her and Eleanor? No other book had been studied more by the Henry family, not even the Holy Bible.

"'My father, as you know, was a sort of gentleman farmer in-shire; and I, by his express desire, succeeded him in the same quiet occupation, not very willingly, for ambition urged me to higher aims, and self-conceit assured me that, in disregarding its voice, I was burying my talent in the earth, and hiding my light under a bushel.'"

Queer folk. That's what they say about the Henrys.

Maybe that's why the rumors began. Because they attended church but half-heartedly and, eventually, not at all. Because the family prayed but without fervor. As if the three of them were unconvinced that anyone or anything was listening.

Instead, when the evenings were free and the family had eaten, they opened other books. *The Hound of the Baskervilles* and *Up from Slavery;* Helen Keller's autobiography and *Iola Leroy.* Eleanor insisted Glenville read books like these, stories, otherwise he would've happily read to them from the seed catalogs he collected.

And from the first day her father read them *The Tenant of Wildfell Hall,* that was a wrap for Adelaide. Could her parents have understood why this had been her favorite novel in the world? How the first lines of that story weren't about some British man, but about her?

My father, as you know, was a sort of gentleman farmer in-shire; and I, by his express desire, succeeded him in the same quiet occupation, not very willingly, for ambition urged me to higher aims, and self-conceit assured me that, in disregarding its voice, I was burying my talent in the earth, and hiding my light under a bushel.

On the last day, the very last one they'd ever share, Glenville had been the one to volunteer a reading. This time, Adelaide sat in the chair and Eleanor on the floor. Her mother's hair had been thinning. Going gray for years, but this time, as Adelaide combed it, she realized her mother's hair was falling out.

In seeing the passage of time written across her mother's scalp, she also felt her own. Her father read from the novel and she rubbed oil into her mother's skin as gently as she could and Adelaide Henry realized she was thirty-one years old. Of course, she knew this, but this time it registered differently, like taking in too much air all at once.

Her mother's hair was gray and her father's reading voice sounded feebler than it ever had before and when they died she would inherit this farm and the family responsibilities and she would never leave this place. She would be shackled to this farm until she, too, passed on.

She'd had a strange sensation—impossible but it was there anyway—that her mother *understood* what Adelaide had been thinking just then, as if the message had been transmitted through her fingertips and into her mother's mind. Eleanor reached up just then and patted her daughter's wrist as if to say, *A woman is a mule. Remember. I told you. A woman is . . .*

By the next morning Eleanor and Glenville were dead.

A day after that Adelaide set their bodies on fire and fled.

12

DAWN APPEARED SUDDENLY, QUICK AS SNAPPED FINGERS. HAD she slept? She couldn't say. Last night she heard her father, felt her mother's hair, and now she was awake. The sunlight came bright through the cracks in the walls, and Adelaide became aware of herself again. *Here I am.* She must've slept, but it didn't feel like it.

Outside, Mr. Olsen's horses snorted, and she rose to her feet, walked to those windows, and peeked outside. He'd done it, like he said he would. There was the wagon; there was her Seward steamer trunk.

There it was.

Four horses, a wagon, Adelaide's trunk, all the Mudges' things, everything accounted for. But the wagon driver himself? Nowhere to be seen.

He'd tied the lead horse to the railing by the hotel. If those horses had simply tugged their heads, they would've torn the rotted wood from the ground. They were well trained to stay in their place. Now she looked at the trunk more closely. Even from here, something about it seemed wrong, but she couldn't be sure at this distance. Her shoulders stiffened and her throat closed.

Adelaide tore open the door and moved down the hall, down the stairs so quick she almost fell. The hem of her dress spun around her ankles and she slammed against the wall at the bottom of the stairs. She felt no pain, didn't register it yet, though later she'd have a bruise on her left shoulder.

Out the door and straight to the wagon. She didn't climb into it; she leapt. The wagon jerked as she landed. A sturdy woman, Adelaide Henry. Her mother took pride in the strength of the Henry women. *A woman is a mule.* This saying had its positive connotations as well. On days when Glenville had to travel, away overnight, Eleanor and Adelaide made sure their farm ran right. At ten years old Adelaide could already control the plow. By the time she was grown, Adelaide found there were many advantages to being a big woman; you'd best believe it.

Now that she was in the wagon, she could finally understand what had seemed off. The brass lock. It was still attached to the trunk, but it had been unlocked.

It was open.

She grabbed for the twine around her neck, the only key. It still hung there.

"Know what happened at this hotel? Before the town shut up for good?"

Mr. Olsen stood beside the wagon now, talking to her.

"Man named Vardner got hanged right on the front porch," Mr. Olsen said.

In her surprise, Adelaide fell backward, away from the trunk, causing the whole wagon to shake. She looked to Mr. Olsen, trying to understand the words, but the brass lock hung loosely and it drew her attention and her breath.

"Vardner rustled cattle and got himself caught by the local Vigilance Committee," Mr. Olsen continued. "Thieving is serious business around here."

Mr. Olsen patted the side of the wagon to draw her attention, but that hand was so big the sound came on like thunder. Now she looked to where he was pointing, the front steps of the old hotel. The porch where a man had been hanged for stealing.

Adelaide's confusion made her look from the porch to Mr. Olsen's face. Then back to the trunk.

"I wasn't . . ."

Mr. Olsen nodded, though his eyes showed he wasn't listening. "You climb on down now."

"You're talking to me about theft," she said. "But the lock on my trunk has been opened."

Mr. Olsen leaned against the wagon to see it.

"Look at that," he said softly.

"Yes," Adelaide agreed. "Look at it."

Mr. Olsen sighed, staring at the trunk. "That is the heaviest piece of baggage I have ever had the misfortune of carrying. Had to use two of my horses to haul it out. The lock must've been knocked open."

Adelaide pursed her lips and furrowed her eyebrows. Was that the best he could do?

"Well, I'm not a thief," he said, raising his voice.

Now he stared back at her, face going red as if he'd been slapped.

Adelaide raised her eyebrows. "Oh? Did I insult you? Imagine how I felt when you suggested the same of me."

Mr. Olsen stepped back from the wagon, nodding his head.

"Can we make peace?" he asked. "Are you hungry?"

She looked at the trunk and pressed against it with her hands. Testing it for weight. It hardly budged, which meant it remained full. She couldn't open it to look inside, not with Mr. Olsen standing there, so she closed the lock, then pulled at it twice. Secure.

"I made breakfast," Mr. Olsen said. "Come eat, Mrs. Henry."

He'd made a fire along the western wall of the old hotel. Sheltered behind the building, it was easier to keep a flame alive. He had beans cooking. She ate quickly even though the beans were hot enough to scald her tongue. Mr. Olsen nodded as he watched her.

"Out here you'll be earning your hunger every day."

"Did you sleep at all?" she asked.

"Me?" he said with feigned nonchalance. "I'm feeling good."

Looking at the man's face proved the lie; his eyes were as purple as Santa Rosa plums. She finished her beans and wanted more. She wanted to ask again about her trunk, the lock that looked as if it had been picked. But what if he felt so insulted that he just unloaded the trunk and left her here? Took the Mudges but abandoned Adelaide? Mr. Cole the Wagon Man, the superintendent of the S.S. *Queen*, each had been happy to be callous, seemed to take pleasure in being cruel to her, so who could guess if Mr. Olsen would be the same.

Better to discuss something else. One question of great importance did occur to her. "Mr. Olsen," Adelaide said. "Let me ask you this straight."

"Go ahead," he said. He eyed the beans, bubbling on the fire. Had he eaten any of the meal yet?

"Am I going to find any other Negroes out here?" Adelaide asked.

Mr. Olsen coughed with surprise. Not the question he'd expected.

"My home," Adelaide continued. "We were all Negro farmers there. Twenty-seven families. Lucerne Valley, California. You heard of us?"

Mr. Olsen thought on this, looking toward the distance. "Can't say I have," he finally admitted. "But I've never been to California."

She felt disappointed. Just slightly. They'd thought of themselves as big news, in their own way. But what had she known of Montana before Mattie T. Cramer? A front-page story in one person's life might not even rate a line in the next person's newspaper.

"As for Negroes," Mr. Olsen continued. "Since you're near Big Sandy you'll meet Bertie eventually."

"Bertie," Adelaide repeated.

"Bertie Brown," he said. "Annie Morgan used to be on the land, but she died, I think it was last year. She was farther south, down at Philipsburg."

Adelaide patted her thighs. "Two Negroes. And one of them is dead."

Mr. Olsen laughed at this. "I guess you're right." He watched her a moment. "You're worried about it?"

She sat quietly, watching Mr. Olsen's face. She knew that to reveal one's fears is to make oneself vulnerable. Finally, he spoke when she didn't.

"It's really the Chinese who get the horns out this way, Mrs. Henry. Lotta people don't like them. And the red man has few friends."

"I see," she said quietly.

"I'm not helping your peace of mind, am I?"

"I wouldn't say so."

He spooned more beans out of the can for her and she ate them from her cup. They were protected from the direct winds by the wall of the old hotel, but they would have to leave the shelter eventually. Adelaide let the beans sit on her tongue rather than swallow them right away. When would she have beans again? She couldn't be sure. She meant to savor these.

"When people need one another, they find ways to be good," Mr. Olsen told her. "I wish I could say better of the human animal, but I can't."

He reached to his side and revealed a tin of dried peaches.

"This land is trying to kill every single one of us, let me tell you. And we keep each other alive. Your neighbors might not all welcome you, but I promise you they will help you if you need it. Because they will need you to help them eventually. For better or worse, that's the best I can give you."

Mr. Olsen swung the tin of dried peaches toward her. Adelaide took only two.

"You can have more than that."

"Those Mudge boys will want some," Adelaide said.

Mr. Olsen looked up at the hotel. "The Mudges are gone."

Adelaide stopped chewing. She didn't look at the hotel, but back toward the wagon, the trunk. The lock had been open. But the weight remained inside.

"Gone where?" she asked, her voice sounding shaky.

"I don't know. Went ahead, my guess. Wagons come through all hours, from different parts. If there's space, a driver will give a ride."

"To five people? And they just left all their goods behind?"

"Does seem like a lot. But anyone would have sympathy for a mother and four blind boys. Since they left their things in the wagon, I'm bound to finish the job. But I'll take you to your claim first."

He shook the can. Now the dried peaches, wrinkled and gummy, took on a horrifying appearance, like cured flesh. She declined.

She had slept, hadn't she? Why couldn't she remember it? Why didn't she feel at all rested?

The Mudges are gone.

Olsen put out the fire, kicking dirt over the embers. A strong wind could easily toss even the smallest one against the walls of the old hotel and start a fire that would burn down the last evidence of this former town.

Adelaide watched him put out the fire, but if she was standing or sitting she couldn't say. The lock had been open, and now. And now.

The Mudges are gone.

She went back into the hotel to get her things. With the daylight on her side, she checked the room where the Mudges had bunked, but it lay empty. She checked every room on the second floor, hoping she might discover the family, fast asleep in some hidden room.

But no.

The Mudges were gone.

13

THERE WERE NO NEIGHBORS. NOT IN THE SENSE THAT ADELAIDE was used to. On the farm the nearest neighbors, the Gaines family, were two miles away. At the time she'd thought she lived in isolation, but out here, to say it again, there were no neighbors. There was only land.

When Mr. Olsen pulled his wagon up to Adelaide's cabin, she laughed.

This couldn't be it.

Her closest company, as far as she could see, were the Bear Paw Mountains. Even with Adelaide's strong eyesight she found herself squinting to see them.

Mr. Olsen helped her haul the trunk out of the wagon; they had to work together to push it inside. Before he climbed back into the wagon, Adelaide touched his hand and he turned to her. Either her hand lingered there, or his did.

"Do you really think the Mudges will be waiting for you at their claim?"

He looked at their hands again, still touching.

"That wasn't what I thought you were going to say."

She knew what he meant, but feigned ignorance. Better that way. Safer. Instead she crossed her arms and spoke quickly.

"What if you get all that way," she began, and stopped. Took a breath. Was she really going to say this? "What if they aren't there? What will happen to their supplies?"

Mr. Olsen looked up at the wagon, then back to her. "By rights I'd get to sell them. Though I doubt I'd make all that much."

Adelaide didn't look at Mr. Olsen when she spoke next.

"If you get there and they don't turn up, please come back. I'll buy what they left behind."

Just saying the words made her feel like a scavenger.

Even more so because it might actually be her fault the Mudges weren't there.

"I understand," Mr. Olsen said.

Then he climbed into the wagon. Right before he got the horses going, he reached below his seat and held his hand out to her.

"Take these," he said.

The tin of dried peaches. With that, he rode off.

She stood at the doorway and watched Mr. Olsen go. She wanted him to turn around and say something, absolve her of her guilt. Her shame. But how could he do what she couldn't do for herself?

Finally, she had to turn away from Mr. Olsen and his wagon. The land here lay so flat—and so empty—that she probably wouldn't lose sight of him for miles. He might ride for an hour and it could still look like he'd barely moved. This made her feel lost, trapped, marooned. She focused on her new home just so she wouldn't scream.

The cabin was twelve by twelve, a single room, with an outhouse already built out back. The shack had been built with no foundation, plain boards for siding, then black tar paper to cover that. All of it held in place by lath that had been nailed in. The shack had a roof, but no ceiling. Adelaide could already foresee nights when the wind would creep up under the roof and settle down on her. In true winter the temperature promised to plummet below zero. She'd need an oven and firewood or coal. But right now, all she had inside the cabin was that steamer trunk.

Behind the cabin, the outhouse sagged like the old hotel. One of her first jobs would be to fortify it. A well had indeed been dug nearby, but when she tested it, it only brought up alkaline water. Animals might drink it, but not people. She wondered if the salesman knew it was unusable when he sold her the claim. The promise of the well had added twenty-five dollars to the price.

An empty cabin, no food, a well that didn't work, the utter emptiness of the landscape, and that wind, which never seemed to stop. Adelaide walked back into the cabin and sat on the trunk and wondered how she ever thought she would survive.

And then, for more than a moment, she wondered if she even should.

She had no people left, so what exactly was keeping her alive?

The only thought that brought her back was imagining Mr. Olsen arriving at her cabin door, meaning to sell her the Mudges' goods and finding Adelaide dead by her own hand. Then he wouldn't be able to stop himself, becoming curious about the steamer trunk. He would open it. And that would be the end of him.

How many more would die after that?

Adelaide Henry had a responsibility. One passed down from her parents. Caretaker? Jailer? What was the difference here, really? For her whole life—thirty-one years—she'd been preparing for this role. Some part of her had prayed that it would never come. But here it was.

Queer folk, that's what they say about the Henrys.

That might've been true enough, but one thing they never said is that the Henrys shirked their responsibilities. They weren't people who asked others to carry their load.

She took one deep breath sitting there on the trunk.

And then Adelaide Henry rose.

14

WHILE ADELAIDE FELT CHEATED BECAUSE OF THE WELL, THERE were some pleasant surprises. A root cellar beside the cabin, for instance. The former owner had stored almost one hundred lightning jars filled with preserves, though most of them had cracked. Adelaide felt disgust when she wrenched open the root cellar's door and smelled all the sweet rot. The odor was bad, but the waste of so much food was truly terrible. She spent a day clearing the space. If Mr. Olsen hadn't left her those dried peaches, she might've risked eating those spoiled preserves.

Mr. Olsen did return to her cabin. Took three days. When he arrived, the bed of his wagon remained full and Adelaide almost cried. She'd run through those peaches, and sleeping on only her flannel blanket was already fucking up her back.

Adelaide bought everything. Didn't ask after the Mudges and Mr. Olsen offered no word. If he didn't sell this stuff, he'd eat the cost. He charged her five dollars for everything, which was an act of profound generosity from him. Though it also meant his tired horses had far less to carry on their return, so it helped him, too. After her Seattle expenses, the train ticket to Big Sandy, and Olsen's wagon ride, she had twenty-seven dollars and sixty-five cents left. Winter hadn't even begun.

Though they were both relieved by the exchange, the scent of grave robbing still remained. They did what they must, but both felt shamed while they did it. When they'd offloaded the items, and Olsen had been paid, he rode off without even a goodbye.

But . . .

Now Adelaide had a wicker rocker and a great chair. She put up flowered wallpaper and replaced the old lace curtains with ones that looked new.

Adelaide now owned a single frame bed.

She assumed the boys would've bunked on the floor of their cabin, at least until they could afford to build a bigger home. Adelaide kept experiencing moments like this. Where her mind wandered to questions best left unasked.

She'd brought six books in her travel bag and turned one corner of the twelve-by-twelve cabin into her parlor, stacking the books here between the rocker and the great chair. Adelaide had brought her Bible, but also *The Secret Garden* and *A Little Princess* by Frances Hodgson Burnett. *Journey to the Center of the Earth* by Jules Verne. *The Testimony of a Blind Prophet* by Judah Washburn, and, of course, *The Tenant of Wildfell Hall*.

There was a two-lid iron stove. She set it in a corner and called that the kitchen. She hung the cooking pans on the wall above the stove. The pans didn't match, much like the curtains and the plates and so much else of the Mudges' things. She imagined they'd gathered these things step by step, buying what they could and making do. The Mudges had been magpies.

She hammered a nail into the wall by the oven and, for the first time since she'd left California, she took the length of twine from around her neck and hung the key for the trunk's lock there. She felt a thousand pounds lighter.

One corner for Adelaide's bedroom, one for her parlor, another served as her kitchen. And in the middle of the cabin sat the Seward steamer trunk. She dragged it so it lay at the foot of her bed. Each night, before sleep, she would check the brass lock to be sure it was secured.

And now Adelaide Henry had a home. With everything in place, she had time to wonder why she hadn't brought any of these items herself. How had she expected to survive? Was it just that she'd fled the farm in a panic, or had there been some deeper, bleaker plan for what she'd do once she got here? The items she'd acquired from the Mudges served like a second chance.

Too late in the season to break ground, but along with the Mudges' furniture they'd packed preserves, tins of pumpkin, squash, even salted pork; dried apples and beans so dry they would taste like leather once cooked, but they would still be edible. That's what mattered. There was enough to last her a few weeks, if she ate carefully. Still, she'd have to figure out some way to get back to Big Sandy, which lay sixteen miles southeast of her claim. She couldn't just walk.

One small gold-plated jewel box had been among the Mudges' effects. Inside she found photographs. As soon as she realized what lay within, she shut it back up, walked out to the root cellar, and tucked it away. She couldn't bring herself to destroy them, but she couldn't look at them either. *If the Mudges come back, I'll return their photographs.* Even as she said this to herself, she felt ridiculous.

On an exploratory walk she discovered Eagle Creek, where she could secure fresh water, a four-mile hike there and back. Nearby the creek she found lignite—brown coal—soft, combustible sedimentary rock; since she had no wood, she'd use that to heat the stove for now.

In the evenings she read. She often did so out loud. It's what she was used to and there was comfort in the routine. Listening to her own voice at night almost drowned out the wind and the coyote calls. Most nights she read the Brontë. And as the first week in Montana passed, Adelaide considered that perhaps she'd done exactly what she claimed she wanted to do: started again.

15

END OF SEPTEMBER, FOUR WEEKS INTO HER NEW LIFE, AND THE winds stayed cold. Good Lord, how bad would it get when winter began? Maybe it was better that she had no idea. If she knew the kind of winter Montana had in store, she might've died of fright.

This land is trying to kill every single one of us, let me tell you. That's what Mr. Olsen said. Each night in bed, as she shivered herself to sleep, she agreed.

Start of October and the first snows came. Not the heavy stuff. Inches, not feet. And yet, Adelaide's breathing quickened as she watched it coming down from the doorway of her cabin. She'd read of snow, but never watched it fall.

One good thing came of the snow: she no longer had to march miles to Eagle Creek for fresh water. Instead she could trek to the nearest coulee, where even the "light" snow had accumulated six inches, scoop her buckets full, and return home. She dumped the snow into the water barrels on the side of her shack, where they would soon melt. To keep insects out of the barrels, she covered each tight with a burlap sack. The side of her cabin looked like it was lined with conga drums.

Then, one afternoon, she heard a horse snort and two voices, quite faint, outside her home.

She'd been inside making a plan for the crops she'd plant when the land thawed. Adding up the cost of a plow and harrow, a horse. Figuring out if she could afford to hire a man to break the land first so she could come right behind him and do the planting. Then the horse's snort, and those faint voices, but Adelaide hardly paid it any attention at first. Out here the wind sounded like voices, sometimes a whisper, other times a shout. As if nature was always engaged in a conversation, one she could eavesdrop on but never join. More than once, she swore she heard her mother calling to her as she tried to fall asleep.

But then someone knocked on the cabin door.

The wind had never done that.

And then a face appeared in the window. A little white boy. Small and curious and staring right at Adelaide while she sat in the great chair.

"Don't peek in windows."

This wasn't the child, but a grown woman's voice.

Adelaide felt such shock—a boy's face? a woman's voice?—that she'd gone to mush right there in her seat. Had she reached a delusional phase already? After only five weeks?

"But I see her. She's in a chair. Just sitting there looking all googly."

"Sam Price! You don't see anyone until they greet you."

Adelaide stood.

The book in her lap—a seed catalog—fell to the floor.

The boy in the window yipped and ran away.

"She got up, Momma!"

"Maybe she's going to shut the curtains, since she's got a peeper."

Adelaide walked to the door, but stopped when her hand touched the handle.

"One moment!" she shouted.

"Of course," the woman on the other side said.

Adelaide went to the steamer trunk. She stooped close.

"Keep quiet," she whispered.

Then she rose and opened the door.

GRACE AND SAM PRICE.

Neighbors.

Wow.

Adelaide apologized for keeping them out so long, then offered to make Grace some tea. Grace stood by the front door and surveyed the cabin.

"You should have a rug," she said finally.

Adelaide continued toward the stove, but stumbled slightly. The woman hadn't even entered the cabin and she'd already judged her home? What the hell? Maybe the woman felt annoyed for being kept outside for so long. Adelaide slipped some brown coal into the stove and set the teakettle on.

"Can we go in now, Momma?"

"You're missing a word."

"Please can we go in now, Momma?"

Grace and Sam Price stepped inside; Grace shut the door behind them.

Neighbors.

In her home.

Wow.

"We can give you some wood," Grace said, spying the last of the brown coal sitting in a bucket by the stove. "Before winter we get a team of horses and drive over to the Badlands, get pitch pine roots and stumps. Not the best fire for a stove, but better than that stuff."

Was that another criticism?

Adelaide offered a noncommittal nod.

Sam, nine years old and skinny and red faced, stayed by his mother's side but scanned the shack keenly. While his mother spoke, he looked up at her like a small dog begging its master to set it loose.

"Very good of you to offer some wood, Mrs. Price," Adelaide said as she got the tea bags from a tin. "I was hoping to survive this winter."

Grace clucked at this and Adelaide turned to her. Both were still. Sam looked at each woman. He was too young to understand that Grace and Adelaide were appraising one another. Adelaide, pointedly, had yet to offer Grace a seat.

"Come with anyone?" Grace asked. "This is a lonely place on your own."

Sam scanned the cabin, his eyes landing on one thing, then another.

"And your husband?" Adelaide asked. "He's at your home?"

The teakettle's whistle began, but Adelaide made no move to pick it up yet.

"Me and Sam are east of here," Grace said. "Two of us is more than enough."

Sam locked eyes on the wicker rocker and spoke absently. "Momma don't got any friends."

"Sam Price," Grace said firmly.

Adelaide watched the woman more closely. Grace's hands were clasped in front of her in a way that Adelaide first took as judgmental but now it read as something else. Nervousness. Even desperation.

Adelaide looked at Sam Price and tilted her head. "You want to sit in the rocker? It's all right with me, if it's all right with your mother."

Grace looked up from her son and held Adelaide's gaze. Grace Price stood a foot shorter than Adelaide, barely five feet, and rangy in the same way as her son. Grace stopped clutching her hands together and let them drop to her sides. She waved toward the rocker.

"If Mrs. Henry gave you permission, then I guess there's something you want to say."

Sam nodded and stomped toward the rocker, shouting, "Thank you!"

The kid plopped into the chair and commenced to kicking his legs out, rocking hard right away. The kettle whined louder than the winds outside and this reminded Adelaide to take it off the stove. She lifted it and the whistle turned into a whimper.

"If he's in the rocker, you can take the great chair," Adelaide offered.

"And where will you sit?" Grace asked, looking around again.

Adelaide pointed to another corner. "My bed is right there. I'll shout."

"how did you know I was here, Mrs. Price?" Adelaide asked.

"Sam and me saw the light in your cabin."

"But you said you're nine miles from here."

"At night even candlelight seems bright as a star."

"Well, why couldn't I see yours?" Adelaide asked.

"We close up our windows at night. That's the sensible thing to do. A strong wind can shatter glass easy. You ought to think about preparing shutters for your place."

Adelaide frowned at Grace Price, but this time Grace seemed to hear herself, her tone. She paused, then added, "I can help you put them together, Mrs. Henry."

Here's an interesting moment in any friendship. That time when one person has revealed something essential about themselves and the other must decide if they can accept it. If they became close, would Grace suddenly stop undercutting and criticizing Adelaide's choices? No. Be plain about it, she would not.

But if Adelaide turned Grace Price away, then Grace wouldn't be the only one who had no friends. Adelaide decided she would accept this aspect of Grace. The advisor. Full of suggestions, even when no one asked for them. Hardly the worst trait in a potential friend.

A friend.

Adelaide realized how much she wanted one.

Also, Grace was the only candidate within fifteen miles. So there it was.

While Grace and Adelaide talked, Sam found his way into everything. He creaked in the rocker, going faster and faster, until he nearly fell backward. When Grace hissed his name, Sam came out of the rocker like he'd been sitting on a spring.

Then he perused Adelaide's library, picking up each of the books and leafing through the pages at such speed that it should've surprised no one when he tore a page right out of *The Secret Garden*. Grace barked his name and pulled the book from his hands, then apologized to Adelaide a dozen times.

Adelaide said it was fine.

Though it wasn't.

Sam asked for a spoon next and when Adelaide gave it to him he went to each cooking pan hanging in the corner and smacked all the ones he could reach. Grace had to shout his name five times before Sam heard her. She asked what he thought he was doing and he stared back.

"Bashing," he said.

Wasn't it obvious?

The Prices had been in her cabin for less than an hour and Adelaide felt exhausted.

Grace put out her hand. "Give that to me."

Sam dropped the spoon in his mother's palm, spun to another corner of the cabin. He slapped one hand down on the steamer trunk.

"That's big," Sam said.

Remember when she'd put her hands on Mrs. Mudge? Adelaide did. Which is about the only way she stopped herself from doing the same thing to this child just now. Adelaide caught herself and draped one hand over the trunk, a barrier to the boy. Maybe her face betrayed a more aggressive emotion, though, because Grace reached out and pulled her son backward, until he stood by her side. Grace watched the trunk for a moment, then adjusted her gaze.

"I see your seed catalog," Grace said. "May I make a suggestion, Mrs. Henry? Plant some sugar beets in your first season. They're tough. They'll come up even when everything else fails."

Adelaide nodded but hardly heard. Sam hadn't stopped staring at the trunk. The forbidden thing.

Adelaide knocked on the steamer trunk. "Brought this with me from California."

He pointed at the trunk. "I think it's making a sound," he said.

"That's the wind," Grace said.

"Yes," Adelaide agreed. "It's never quiet."

These two adults could say whatever they wanted; Sam Price did not look convinced. Sam leaned his body against his mother. He pressed his cheek to the side of her neck, taking comfort in the feeling of skin on skin. Adelaide, meanwhile, pressed her hand down against the cold wooden trunk and felt a flicker of envy. Then Sam leaned close to his mother's ear and whispered.

From the folds of Grace's dress—there must have been a pocket in there—she revealed a stack of folded paper. Sam tugged it from her fingers and went on his knees on the floor.

He peeked back at Adelaide to be sure she watched him, then he unfolded each sheet; cutouts from the local newspaper, the *Bear Paw Mountaineer.*

The paper sometimes ran oversized pictures on page one, and Sam Price loved collecting them: a photo from the Panama Pacific International Exposition, national news in February; a clipping showing a map of Europe with a caption reading "The Russian victory over Austria in the Carpathians."

Sam sifted through the papers until he found another.

"The fighting in Europe," he read aloud. "No dashing cavalry charges like the Light Brigade."

"That's fine, Sam," Grace told him.

A war on the other side of the world and the only one studying it here was nine years old. Now he read quieter, to himself. It was like he wanted to prove he had something more interesting than Adelaide's dumb old trunk anyway.

Grace looked to Adelaide. "I'm a teacher, but this is my only regular student."

"Aren't there any children in Big Sandy?" Adelaide asked.

"Yes," Grace answered. "There are."

Sam turned from his place on the floor, looking up at Adelaide. "They won't send their kids to school with me. Think I'm proof Momma is a bad teacher."

Adelaide shook her head, about to tell the child that couldn't be it even though she sat there utterly exhausted by her hour around the boy. Nevertheless, a child says something like that and you soothe them, dismiss such talk. At least that's what Adelaide thought she should do, but then she looked to Grace.

"He's not lying," she said. "Meanwhile, my Sam can read the newspaper from start to finish and most of their children, same age as Sam, can't count past their fingers and toes."

"I get it," Adelaide said. "Queer folk. That's what they call you."

Grace considered this a moment, then laughed. "Probably!"

Eventually, Adelaide saw the pair to the door and agreed to Grace's offer of company again soon. Before they left, Grace went to her horse and brought out canned corn and a small bag of potatoes.

"I was waiting to decide if I liked you," Grace said.

The woman might as well have given Adelaide gold. The idea of dining on a roasted potato made Adelaide feel flush.

Grace climbed onto her horse. She pulled Sam up.

"Goodbye, Mrs. Price. Goodbye, Sam."

Adelaide waved as they rode off, filling the doorway, but Sam stared past her shoulder, eyes for the steamer trunk alone.

16

FOUR DAYS LATER, A SUNDAY, ADELAIDE HEARD THE SNORT OF a horse. She'd been working in the wicker rocker, stitching holes that had developed in her gloves. In the days since Grace and Sam's first visit, she'd already eaten half the potatoes and all the canned corn. Maybe they'd brought more this time. Or perhaps something even more succulent. Some rabbit or beef. Also Grace had promised to bring her wood. Burning brown coal inside the cabin had already made Adelaide develop a cough.

All this took seconds to consider and Adelaide felt her heart rate rising and her face going flush and all at once she had to pinch her thigh to bring her back to herself.

Had she come out here to live off a woman raising her child alone?

Her mother would be particularly appalled to imagine her daughter living off the charity of someone else. And a white woman? Might as well go beg a man for assistance next. Eleanor Henry's child playing the helpless role?

No, thank you.

Adelaide Henry rose from the wicker chair and went to the stove, fed it brown coal, and began a fire as she heard the horse's snort outside. So when the knock came at the door, she felt ready to welcome her guests, her new friend. She would offer hospitality and expect nothing in return. That is how she'd been raised. At the very least, she'd offer some labor of her own to pay back the gifts Grace had already given. That's how a Henry acts.

But when she opened the door, two men were standing there. White men.

Cowboys.

Adelaide felt so surprised she slammed the door shut.

"Ma'am?" one of them said, softly, as if speaking to a skittish horse.

Inside the cabin she scanned the kitchen, trying to decide if she should pick up something, a knife or a skillet. Greet them armed.

"Did we scare you, ma'am?" the same man said. "That was not our intent."

He sounded sincere. Adelaide decided to believe him. At least until he did something that would suggest otherwise. But, she decided, she would not say sorry for her reaction, slamming the door on them. She found this difficult and had to keep her face completely still so that home training wouldn't force the words out.

The two cowboys. They were nearly the same man. Each one thin as fence wire, their cheeks and foreheads a brownish red from years of work outdoors. Their fingertips were stained brown. Both wore denim overalls and boots. The cuffs of the overalls were threadbare, the soles of the boots worn thin. The younger man had a clean face; the one behind him—two decades older—wore a beard. When she opened the door again, they removed their hats. The younger man smiled and his teeth were small, stained. The one behind him nodded his greeting. Both men stood shorter than Adelaide.

"I thought you were my friend, Mrs. Price," Adelaide said. "I'm . . ."

She caught herself and pursed her lips.

"My name is Matthew Kirby. This is my uncle, Finn. We know Mrs. Price," said the younger man. "That's how we heard about you."

Against her will, Adelaide Henry blushed.

"You make me sound like big news."

The older man gave a short laugh. "Ma'am, you are this month's headline."

The teakettle blew on the stove and Adelaide turned to it.

"You were sitting down for tea," said the younger man.

"One moment," she said, gesturing for them to remain at the

doorway. They had not been invited in yet and they didn't presume to enter.

Adelaide stepped inside to get the kettle off the stove. She shut the door because her bed was right there, unmade, and she didn't want them to see it. She set the kettle on a stove plate to cool, quickly pulled the sheets up on her bed, and came back to the door. When she opened it, the bearded man was already walking around the side of the cabin toward the horses.

"You're leaving?" Adelaide asked the younger man. Did she sound disappointed?

Matthew said, "We came to see if you were free."

The bearded man rounded the cabin leading three horses. All of them saddled.

"We hoped . . ." Matthew paused. "*I* hoped you'd come out for a ride."

Adelaide scanned the pair one more time, then looked back into the empty cabin.

"I suppose I'm free," she said.

Matthew Kirby—whose birth name was Matteus, though he'd changed it for a *good* American name—took her out for a wonderful afternoon. Matthew's uncle, Finn, rode a few lengths behind them the whole time. She'd thought they were cowboys but the men worked on threshing crews. Matthew's uncle operated the straw-burning steam engine, and Matthew worked as a separator man.

Adelaide shared the story of her life as a farmer in the Lucerne Valley, some of her life at least. She spoke proudly of the Santa Rosa plums and the forward thinking of her father to grow them. But, for obvious reasons, she kept the last days of the Henry family a mystery. And to her pleasant surprise Matthew never prodded for more. As they rode, Adelaide realized Grace had been much the same. They didn't ask what brought her to the territory. Maybe she wasn't the only one outrunning a past.

Other men like Matthew and Finn visited Adelaide. Men who

worked on threshing crews, and actual cowboys, too—the rise of ranching had already signaled the cowboy's decline, but when they were here in force, nearly half of them were Black men. Not as many of them left in the territory now, Adelaide lamented.

Sheepherders came through, too, men who often spent months on the plains with only one partner and a flock of sheep. Black men and white men, a few brown men who spoke Spanish, not much English. They all came calling once word spread about the new "lone woman" on the land.

Adelaide came to Montana to hide away, but her anonymity was already over. Her name traveled as far as Helena and Butte. Men gossip so much. News of her arrival might as well have gone out over the wire. The visitors made themselves useful, though. Helping bring supplies that she might need. She repaid them with money and, sometimes, a drink or a meal.

Adelaide didn't mind their visits, most of the time. The men asked her out on rides, bringing a saddled horse for her as she didn't have one of her own yet. They might take her to a ranch where they lived and worked and she'd spend the whole evening eating dinner, making conversation. They were all so profoundly lonely. To her surprise, she realized she was, too.

And yet, despite the sense of camaraderie, the warmth, a woman on her own, a Black woman out here in Montana, far from the Black community she'd known in Lucerne Valley, must remain vigilant for her own sense of safety. In truth, she'd never been around so many white people. So far, the experience hadn't been bad, far from it in fact—generally—but she still felt like she was visiting another nation, one where she didn't always know its customs and whose language seemed close to her own but not exactly the same. At times she remembered that conversation with Mr. Olsen, when he'd mentioned two names—Bertie Brown and Annie Morgan—and she would say their names to herself as if they'd been old friends. She missed Black people—Black women in particular.

Nevertheless, the company of all those men meant Adelaide no longer spent every evening locked up inside her cabin, reading the books she'd read many times before, listening to the wind howling outside the shack and the howling, growing louder each night, from the trunk.

17

SHE ENJOYED THE COMPANY OF MANY MEN WHO VISITED, BUT Matthew was the only one she looked forward to seeing. In late October he invited her to a dance. A half day's ride away. She agreed, happily. Even better, Finn invited Grace and Sam. It felt, in a way, like a family outing. Matthew and Finn borrowed two extra horses for Adelaide, Grace, and Sam to ride on. Grace's horse had been a bit lethargic and she worried about making the long trip.

They all wore their rough clothes for the ride out to the party. Adelaide and Grace kept their dresses for the dance in bags on the backs of their horses. At a certain point it began to rain and the men stopped to put on slickers. The women had theirs, and Sam tucked close under his mother's. The rain slowed them down. In warmer months dances were held right outside, under the stars, but Matthew assured Adelaide tonight's dance would not be outdoors.

As they approached the ranch where the dance was being held, Adelaide came closest to seeing something like Mattie T. Cramer had described. A corral sat on the property, nine horses already inside and room for half a dozen more. They had a large barn and a two-story home, as well as a granary, where, it turned out, the dance would be. She would learn, at some point in the night, the husband and wife had each filed for land, side by side, and now controlled 640 acres. Seeing their success made her hope she, too, might prosper, and she sat straighter behind Matthew.

As they rode closer, Matthew joked that he could file for a plot alongside Adelaide's and they could amass a claim that was just as impressive. Adelaide laughed along but sensed Matthew wasn't kidding. The idea made her nervous, but she also leaned into his back slightly, pressing her chest to him. Nice to be thought of in this way. As a person with whom another person could make a future.

After clearing out the granary, the owners of the ranch had spread cornmeal across the granary floor, and by the time Adelaide, Grace, and the boys arrived, people were dancing. The cornmeal made the granary's floor smoother for shuffling one's feet. Musicians had been brought in to play. A woman on the piano and her husband on the fiddle; a guitarist had come down from the mountains for the night, and there were rumors a man was on his way with a horn. Adelaide and Grace changed in the main house and returned to dance with their dates. Sam ran off to bop around with other kids who'd been brought along by their parents.

This dance would be an overnight. This far from home there was nothing to guide you across the land once it got dark. You could ride all night thinking you were almost home and when the sun rose find yourself in Alberta, Canada. When the kids got tired, they'd sleep in the main house, girls on the second floor, boys on the first.

Adelaide shared many dances with Matthew, but sometimes she and Grace traded and Adelaide enjoyed herself with Matthew's soft-spoken uncle. She always addressed him as Mr. Kirby. He, in turn, only asked questions about "Mrs. Price."

But most of Adelaide's time was spent alongside Grace. No one could dance for that many hours. Every little while the men would go off to yap with other men. San Pura cigars were popular with the gentlemen, as they were rolled in Havre and sold in every town.

While the men puffed, the women made conversation. The Montana Senate had recently been considering making Prohibition the law of the state. As if to signal their horror at such an idea, many of the party's guests brought liquor. A whole case of Havre Special Brew cost $4.25, making it the beer of choice. Heartier drinkers enjoyed Monogram rye, but at $4.50 per bottle few at the dance could afford it.

This is all to say that by midnight these people were having a damn good time.

Adelaide drank alongside the other partygoers, but made sure to tip back just a little less than most. She remained the only Negro in attendance and this felt like when she'd gone off to the ranches after rides with men, sometimes sitting at a fire with half a dozen ranch hands or more. They were welcoming and warm, but a part of her remained wary and this was only common sense. The same held true at this party. She was with them, but not of them. Best to always remain a bit more aware.

For instance, on six different occasions Adelaide was mistaken for Bertie Brown, the only other Negro woman currently living in the area. One woman simply wouldn't believe Adelaide wasn't Bertie and turned belligerent when Adelaide wouldn't agree. Bertie had gained local fame for Bertie's Brew—the best homebrew in the state—and the drunk woman was in the mood for some. She thought Adelaide was simply holding out, trying to haggle for a higher price.

Grace became mortified when things turned tense. The woman threw money at Adelaide's chest, then flopped down on her ass. Two other women dragged the drunk to a corner and left her to sleep it off. Grace led Adelaide away and, quite quickly, some other guests snatched up the cash lying on the floor.

Grace brought Adelaide around to meet other women, looking for the ones who didn't seem too sauced. These were her closest neighbors, some of them "lone women," too, if only on paper. Many had come with someone, either siblings or parents; sometimes two women homesteaded together. Most expressed surprise, even awe, that Adelaide had *truly* come to Montana alone.

But she hadn't.

There wasn't a soul here she could tell the truth, though, not even Grace.

It was in this way—with Grace leading Adelaide around like a protective older sister—that Adelaide came to shake hands with a very pale, sharp-angled woman, holding a beer in one hand and facing away from the party, looking out toward the moon and the horse corral that sat beneath it. Grace touched the woman's shoulder and she turned toward them and Adelaide immediately lost her breath.

"Mrs. Mudge?"

The woman, who hadn't even been looking at Adelaide at first, tensed for an instant. You wouldn't be blamed if you missed it. Everyone besides Adelaide certainly did.

Mrs. Mudge.

She looked away from Grace and turned to Adelaide, her face suddenly hard as forged steel.

"No, Mrs. Henry," Grace corrected. "This is Rose Morrison."

The woman offered a tight smile. "That's right. Rose Morrison."

"She's even newer to the territory than you," Grace said. "Just got to Montana this week."

Why do this? Why pretend? Did it matter? Adelaide had come out here to keep her secrets, so maybe the Mudges had, too. Adelaide told herself to share a pleasant farewell and turn away. Say no more.

Adelaide nodded. "Well then, welcome to Montana."

"Aren't you kind," said Mrs. Morrison.

But Adelaide couldn't stop herself. The way Mrs. Mudge had vanished made Adelaide think *she* had been responsible for their disappearance. And Mr. Olsen had treated her like a thief when she'd climbed into his wagon. Meanwhile this woman just changes her name and thinks nothing of the aftereffects? And now Adelaide should grin and pretend? She felt herself trembling, either with shock or rage or both.

Then she said it.

"Did you bring your boys?"

Grace squeezed Adelaide's elbow. "Mrs. Morrison is a *widow*. She and her husband never had children."

Adelaide laughed. Actually laughed.

Grace let Adelaide's arm go and her mouth gaped in shock. There were other women nearby and they turned to watch as well. How loudly had Adelaide laughed? Adelaide realized how insane she must look. How monstrous. The Negro laughing at the poor white woman whose husband had died and left her alone.

Mrs. Mudge watched Adelaide in silence.

"I'm so sorry," Adelaide said, regaining self-control. "I must have been thinking of someone else entirely."

This calmed Grace, made her perceive the laughter as embarrassment rather than cruelty. Mrs. Morrison nodded and said, "That's quite all right."

"I mean, really," Adelaide said. "I must have been *blind*."

A long, slow second passed between them.

The silence seemed to poison the air.

The other women stepped back, sensing something bad about to pop off.

Then Mrs. Mudge, or Morrison, or whatever the hell else she might call herself, turned on her heels and marched out of the granary.

She disappeared into the night.

"Mrs. Henry!" Grace hissed. "What's come over you?"

Adelaide looked at Grace. Her friend. With whom there would always be a divide. Better to give her the easy answer, the lie.

"I drank too much," Adelaide said. "You should just ignore me."

18

ADELAIDE, LIKE ALL THE OTHER WOMEN WHO STAYED OVER, WAS invited to sleep in the main house. The bedrooms filled with children and their mothers, so Adelaide was left to sleep in a chair in the living room on the ground floor. There were two other chairs here. Grace slept in one. Sam chose not to sleep with the boys in the nearby bedroom, but out here by his mother. Maybe it was true that he didn't get along well with other kids. Funny how this only made Adelaide feel more tender toward the child. Men bedded down out on the granary floor.

Difficult to claim Adelaide enjoyed any rest. Instead, she kept getting up to wander the main house, scanning for Mrs. Mudge. Why did this woman's lie bother her? A guilty soul is always troubled by its reflection.

Eventually Adelaide had to stay in her seat, though, no matter how agitated. A Black woman wandering a white person's home in the night risks being treated like a servant or a thief. Adelaide eventually shut her eyes, but it hardly counted as rest.

In the morning Matthew Kirby came inside and woke her up. He leaned over her, looking like he could use a bath. Smelling that way, too. She reached out and touched his face and he seemed to glow under the tenderness. The night before, while they were dancing, he'd told her he was all of twenty-three.

She looked for Grace, but Grace and Sam had already risen. When Matthew helped her up, led her out of the main house, she felt relieved he hadn't tried to kiss her last night. Sweet as he was, she'd decided—when, she couldn't be sure—they were never going to become a couple.

Was it his age? Partly. But even more she had resigned herself to a certain life, and already her closeness with Grace and Sam and Finn and Matthew had expanded her heart farther than she'd imagined it could grow. She just couldn't imagine giving any more of herself. That wasn't why she'd come here. She had a burden that was hers to shoulder.

And as the last of the Henry family, she had to carry it alone.

Now Matthew led her into the morning light, past the granary, which had already been swept clean, equipment hauled back inside. Outside the corral, Grace and Sam were on a horse and Finn, still half asleep, held it by the reins.

"How did Sam sleep?" Adelaide asked Grace.

But Grace didn't look at her. Instead, she tapped her boy's arm and said, "Answer Mrs. Henry."

Sam, who had been busy counting clouds, looked to Adelaide, nodded, and said, "Good." Then he returned to scanning the skies.

"And you, Mrs. Price?" Adelaide asked Grace.

Grace nodded, nothing more. She spoke to Finn instead.

"Long trip. Should we begin, Mr. Kirby?"

Finn waved one hand in the air and didn't stir at all. How late had he stayed up? How much Special Brew had he hit? It seemed a lucky thing Finn could walk straight at all.

Adelaide watched them move on. She felt stung by Grace's coldness, and confused by it. Matthew brought Adelaide to another horse and helped her up. He pulled the reins of the horse and led it forward. Adelaide watched Grace, waiting for her to look back so they might talk, but Grace only stared into the horizon.

They'd gone a quarter mile before Adelaide realized Matthew and Finn weren't leading them to the other two horses.

"We rode here on four horses," she said. "Why are we only returning on two?"

"Horses gone missing," said Matthew.

The words came out weary and she realized he and his uncle must've been up looking for the other horses for hours already. She remembered the bone-deep exhaustion on Mr. Olsen's face the morning after pulling the wagon out of the coulee. She hadn't known him well enough to offer much kindness, but she knew Matthew better. She felt her tenderness like a shawl she wanted to drape across his shoulders.

"Well, you're not going to walk all the way back, are you?"

"Weren't sure how you'd feel about riding with me."

"I don't want to see you drop dead from exhaustion, Mr. Kirby."

He stopped and called over to his uncle, who had a few words with Grace.

Grace spoke loudly, almost exasperated. "Why didn't you just say so, Mr. Kirby!"

The men climbed up and got the horses trotting. With so much weight on the animals, they took the journey slow.

"What happened?" Adelaide asked. "To your horses."

Matthew grunted as they rode. He remained quiet for another quarter mile.

"Four horses gone missing this morning," Matthew said. "Two of ours and two from the folks that own this place."

"Stolen?"

"That's right," Matthew said. "By kids."

"Kids?" Adelaide asked.

"Four boys. Seen riding off on them before the sun came up."

Adelaide had her hand around Matthew's middle. She squeezed so tightly he coughed with surprise.

Four boys.

19

ON THE RIDE BACK ADELAIDE TOLD MATTHEW ABOUT MRS.
Mudge and her boys. He had a hard time believing it. First that Mrs.
Morrison was really Mrs. Mudge but also that four blind boys could
steal four horses.

Though he wasn't convinced, Adelaide's story still left him twitchy
and protective. As they approached Grace's homestead, Finn waved
them off. Adelaide shouted her goodbye, but only Finn and Sam returned it. Grace didn't even look back.

Along the ride to her cabin it occurred to Adelaide that she was the
only person, besides Mr. Olsen, who could testify that Mrs. Mudge
had four boys, identify their faces in a court of law. If the Mudges stole
horses, what else might they do? The ride to Adelaide's had taken
much of the day and very soon it would be that fathomless Montana
night. And that family would be out there, somewhere.

When Adelaide and Matthew reached her home, he insisted on
standing at the threshold of her cabin and inspecting the interior. Adelaide didn't argue.

Then she invited him in.

He set his rifle upright in the parlor.

Adelaide offered him tea, but he didn't say yes or no. Instead, he
looked out one window. "I can make it to the ranch if I leave right
now," he said.

She realized, in that moment, that he wanted to stay. A second after
that she understood that despite all she'd been thinking only hours

ago, she wanted him to stay as well. She wasn't in love, but affection and caution would do well enough out here on the plains.

Wasn't company a fine reason to keep a man around? Even just for tonight? She reminded herself how long it had been since she'd been held. They'd been an isolated family, distrustful of outsiders, but she wasn't a virgin. Adelaide had known intimacy before. No need to go into detail except to say that she missed it.

"Go get your things," she said. "I'll make us something to eat."

Matthew tried not to smile but couldn't help himself. His chest rose and fell with enthusiasm. He was only twenty-three, and just then he seemed even younger.

"You're sure?" he asked.

"Don't make a woman offer twice."

20

MATTHEW SECURED HIS HORSE WHILE ADELAIDE WENT DOWN to the root cellar for the last of her beans and two of the eggs Grace had given her the week before. Adelaide felt more ashamed of surviving on Grace's charity than she did about the young man sitting in her cabin that evening. About the only thing left in the cellar when she was done was that box of old photos the Mudges left behind. With a gasp she realized she might be able to find pictures of them, turn them in to the sheriff in Big Sandy so they'd have an easier time tracking the horse thieves.

She brought the box inside, along with the food, but didn't open it now. She thought only of Matthew. And herself. She made dinner for two.

"What will you do first, Mrs. Henry?" Matthew asked.

It didn't sound like a question, more like a quiz. To Matthew, Adelaide remained a newcomer, a tenderfoot, a pilgrim. Matthew's tone played like Grace's when she'd first visited the cabin with Sam. He'd probably asked what she planned to do only so he could overwhelm her with advice about what she *should* do. But Adelaide had been thinking about all this quite seriously.

"I'm not required to plow up a whole forty acres when I plant for my first year, so I'm going to have just enough land broken for a garden. That way I'm not setting myself up for the whole thing to fail in year one. Especially if there isn't much rain."

"You'll hire a man to break the land?" Matthew asked, as if insulted.

"I would pay a man to do it," she said. "Even if I knew him very well."

Matthew blushed and looked down at his plate, took a bite of egg.

"I've got a few vegetable seeds I'll order but I'll plant sugar beets in half the garden."

Matthew raised his eyebrows. "They'll grow even if there's drought. That's a smart choice, Mrs. Henry."

Now, that was the tone she wanted to hear. Respect. So what if Grace had been the one to pass on this suggestion? It was her plan now.

"You'll call me Adelaide if you're here this late."

Then she set down her utensils and removed the wrap she'd been wearing over her hair during the ride.

Matthew set down his fork.

"Adelaide," he said.

They were awkward together. She stood taller than him, and heavier as well. But though Matthew was small and slim, the man was strong. He climbed over her with a playful grin and when they wrestled each other neither of them held back. He touched her arms and found the small scars that ran along both forearms. More than a dozen little divots in the flesh of each one. He looked at her to ask the question—*where did you get these?*—but was smart enough to read the expression in her half-closed eyes. This wasn't the time for telling histories. This wasn't the time for words.

When she wrapped her legs around his waist, he seemed to lift her whole body so he could enter her. The Montana winds were no calmer than any night before, but for the first time Adelaide didn't hear them.

21

WHEN ADELAIDE FINALLY WOKE UP, MATTHEW KIRBY HAD LOST a lot of blood.

She didn't hear him scream because his mouth was covered, the howls muffled. It was almost as if the thumping of his frenzied heart had shaken her awake, and for a moment she wasn't sure where she was—in Montana or back in California. The horror had a familiarity that reminded her of home.

Adelaide opened her eyes. She wore nothing and the covers were still drawn up around her. This was the only aspect of the cabin that seemed safe and sane anymore. The rest of the place had gone madhouse.

The great chair lay on its side and the top half of the wicker rocker was shredded, serrated, as if it had been bitten off. The books in the parlor were little more than shreds of paper scattered on the furniture like ash. The pans on the walls had all come down. Matthew's blood was spread on the floor and across the walls and windows.

The steamer trunk sat open and empty.

How had Adelaide slept through all this? When had the world gone so wrong?

Outside it was still nighttime. Dawn seemed impossibly far off. She threw off the covers and shivered. She could hear the Montana wind again; it howled as it crept up the side of her cabin and looped under the roof, then crashed down to chill the room.

And there, in the corner where the great chair had once sat upright, she saw it, out of the steamer trunk, its back to her, the mighty body pressed against the cabin wall.

Great folds of leathery skin hung from the bottom of its arms.

It was out.

And just below those folds was a pair of bare feet.

Matthew Kirby's feet.

Listlessly kicking.

Not the sign of someone fighting, but someone fading.

This thing, Adelaide Henry's burden, stooped over the man, consuming him.

Adelaide felt, very quickly, the utter exhaustion of her life; almost all of her thirty-one years had been spent like this. Catching up, cleaning up, covering up. If she couldn't save her own mother and father, what did it matter if she let a man she hardly knew die?

But this was only a moment of weariness. She wouldn't abandon Matthew.

Now she leapt on the body, the being. Some would call it a *creature*. But all her life Adelaide and her family had called it something else: their curse.

Its skin wasn't really skin, but thousands and thousands of tiny gray scales, linked so tightly they became a natural armor. Impervious to blades and bullets, a fact her father and mother had tested once, and only once. The scales felt like sandpaper to the touch, rougher, so even grappling with it could make a person, nearly any person, bleed.

Except Adelaide.

Ever since she was a child, Adelaide could grip the creature's scales and come away unscathed. Even their mother hadn't been so lucky. Breastfeeding had been a short-lived experiment. Adelaide could grip that skin, and was sturdy enough to yoke the creature. Of all the living things in the world, Adelaide was the only one who could restrain it. Their father once said that nature had designed Adelaide for this very purpose. Why else would a girl as strong as her be born into this family, if she wasn't meant to yoke the thing they'd been punished with?

Adelaide Henry had been born with a purpose. Her parents believed this, and told her so nearly every day.

Now Adelaide went after the creature as a veteran rodeo rider might approach a bull. Except Adelaide didn't need the aid of a flank strap to make the thing buck and jump. Adelaide squeezed its throat with one arm and pulled backward with all her weight. She had the mass to peel the creature away from Matthew Kirby and to twist its massive head.

The legs were short and thin, so it buckled when Adelaide pressed all her body weight down. But with the head turned, now there were the teeth to contend with. Always the teeth were the hardest part.

When Adelaide was young there had been so many times like this, when Adelaide let her arm stray too high, too close to this thing's maw. Those dimpled scars running between Adelaide's elbow and wrist were the proof of all her practice.

With the creature turned away from Matthew, Adelaide climbed higher onto its back. It was like scaling a pterodactyl. The thing crashed forward, onto its softer belly, cracking some of the floorboards beneath them.

Now the head was flush against the ground, and this was the trick Adelaide had learned long ago. If the lower jaw was pressed to the ground and one hundred eighty-five pounds of Adelaide Henry lay against the back of the head, well, that head wasn't coming up. She'd learned this trick after watching alligator wrestlers in a traveling show.

The creature sputtered and snorted but Adelaide held it down. She breathed heavily, but maintained the hold.

Adelaide looked back to Matthew.

Hard to tell, in the darkness, if he'd lost any limbs. She heard him choking and coughing, so he still had a head attached. Better than how she'd found her father. She'd had to retrieve the head and arrange it on the pillow so the silhouette made it seem like the man had been intact.

"Can you hear me?" she asked Matthew between breaths.

More coughing. Was he nodding or having a spasm? She couldn't wait to find out. She leaned close to his ear.

"How did it get out?" she asked. "Did it break the lock?"

The thing hissed now and belched and through its clenched teeth brought up a spray of blood that soaked the floor.

Matthew's blood of course.

Adelaide had got the creature into the steamer trunk back at the farmhouse. If she'd done it then, she could do it again now. She wrestled it around, pushing it toward the trunk while keeping one hand against the back of the head so the jaws wouldn't lift from the floor and snap at her.

And now, seeing the trunk, the thing gave a choked howl. Monstrous or not, nothing loves confinement. Its nostrils flared, inhaling the scent of Matthew's slaughter. It whined as if begging Adelaide to let it take just one more bite. But Adelaide kept pushing it forward.

Behind her, Matthew Kirby fell forward at the waist like an infant trying, and failing, to sit upright. Adelaide couldn't look back at him right then; she and the creature were at the trunk and this was the trickiest part. Adelaide reached for one of its arms and pulled it backward until the thing shivered.

And now Adelaide sang to it.

"*Your mother wants you to sleep. Your father wants you to sleep.*"

The vigor seeped out of its body. Music, savage beast, an old story.

"*Now it's time to sleep, to sleep. Now it's time to sleep.*"

The creature climbed inside. Adelaide closed the lid, but secrets, once revealed, are no longer secrets, no matter how tightly you try to seal them away. It had got out; how much longer until it tried again?

22

ADELAIDE FOUND THE PADLOCK ON THE GROUND, HELD IT UP to inspect. Not broken open.

It had been unlocked.

Her key no longer hung on the nail by the stove.

It was on the ground, here by the trunk.

"You opened this," Adelaide said softly.

When she finally looked back, Matthew was propped against the overturned great chair. He held his rifle at his waist. The barrel aimed at her.

"Move aside," Matthew said, though his voice came out weak. "Move aside and I'll kill it."

Adelaide slipped the padlock back into its slot. Inside the trunk the creature breathed slowly, already returned to a kind of hibernation.

"You opened this," Adelaide repeated.

"Only thing in here that's all locked up," he said.

The rifle barrel quivered with the weight. He held the rifle in his left arm but he was right-handed. His right arm lay tucked tight against his side, the sleeve of his shirt sagged loosely up by the shoulder. But then she realized he was just as naked as her and the sagging fabric was actually his skin.

"I just wanted to see what was inside," he told her.

"While I was asleep?"

He shook his head stiffly. "Call me a thief but you've got a devil in your home."

Adelaide watched him a moment. Already he seemed a bit stronger than he had been. Not recovered, nowhere near it, but maybe he wouldn't die. Instead, he would only disappoint.

Adelaide wasn't even angry with him. Not truly. Every man and woman out here, every child and every beast, was well acquainted with desperation. Mr. Olsen had been right. *This land is trying to kill every single one of us, let me tell you.*

Matthew had thought to pilfer her treasure but found only her curse.

"You're bleeding," she said. "Let me help you."

The rifle dipped down, as if it was nodding off, but rose once more.

"Will it get out again?" he asked.

"Not if you don't steal my key again."

Adelaide brought down a lamp near the stove and lit it. She scanned his right arm, his head and back. "I've seen it do worse," Adelaide said.

She dressed his wounds, using napkins and a tablecloth, and set him on her bed to sleep the last of the night away. His eyes fluttered shut.

As she cleaned the cabin, she felt strangely relieved. She didn't know what Matthew would do with what he'd seen tonight. Spread the news around his camp? Wrangle up his uncle and a few other boys, then come back to try and kill the creature? If she'd been younger, more naïve, she might have hoped for such a thing. For the cavalry, for rescue. But she wasn't a child. Matthew would have to bring a lot of men if he hoped to hurt the creature. She doubted there were enough in all of Montana. That's the whole point of a curse, isn't it? You are doomed to live with it.

While he lay in the bed, eyelids half closed and his eyes swimming, Adelaide spoke to him.

"It arrived on our doorstep the same day, the same minute, my mother gave birth to me. She received her blessing and her curse in an instant. Was it left there? Did it bubble up from the depths of hell? No one could say. My father had been in the fields working while my mother was in labor. It was the midwife who found it.

"At first she took it for an animal. Maybe a mountain lion's cub, or a rattlesnake, but when she picked it up it bit off the top of her thumb and she threw it down in our home and she fled, never returned. But folks began telling tales. *Queer folk,* that's what they said about the Henrys."

Adelaide shivered, not from the cold but from the confession. Why didn't her parents get rid of it? Stomp it to death there on the threshold of their home? She'd asked them this question when she was young, but their answers always seemed to skirt the truth. By the time Adelaide had been old enough to understand anything, her parents had already become resigned to life with their burden and couldn't imagine it any other way, so they chose privacy instead. Her parents barricaded themselves from the rest of the world and thus they trapped her inside the family's secret, too. *Shut your mouth; don't share our shame.* This might have been the Henry family's motto.

Sure, the other families in Lucerne Valley might have whispered about them, but all they truly knew was that Glenville and Eleanor ran a profitable farm, that their daughter worked the land and rarely played with other children, and when they came to church on Sundays the Henrys always sat in the back pew, last to arrive and first to leave. They did bring plums to share with the congregation after service, and that's the only thing that kept them in good standing.

Even though Matthew had fallen into the deep sleep of damaged health, Adelaide felt good speaking her family history out loud. Just letting the words escape her lips made her feel close to crying. This story had spent three decades chewing up her insides.

"But the question I used to ask my mother and father most of all was, Why us? What did they do to bring this curse down upon them?"

She watched Matthew as if he might, right now, whisper the answer, but of course he could barely breathe. She patted Matthew's face with a cloth.

"Or was it my fault?" she whispered.

23

MATTHEW KIRBY RECUPERATED IN HER CABIN. DAYS WENT BY
when he hardly opened his eyes. Muttering in the language he was
born into, not the one he learned on these shores.

"*Yks kalja,*" he whispered more than once.

She didn't have any idea what he was saying, but she hoped it was
something nice. She said it to Matthew's horse when she went out to
feed it; maybe it was a phrase the animal would recognize and find
soothing.

More than once Adelaide thought of killing him. She held no mal-
ice toward him, this was just instinct that came from three decades of
keeping a secret. Her parents made her feel like the world would end
if anyone else found out. And now this man knew. So she considered
killing him. His rifle right there in a corner. Uncle Finn would've
dropped Grace and Sam home days ago and gone back to their camp.
If he appeared at her door, asked after Matthew, it would be easy to say
he rode off hoping to reach home before nightfall and never made it.
These plains could erase a rider. She considered it, but made a con-
scious decision not to kill him. It felt like an act of defiance. She could
hear her parents telling her this choice would be her great mistake.

While Matthew rested in a state somewhere between sleep and
death, she dragged the trunk out of the cabin and down into the root
cellar. Farm life had made her strong; a few months of homesteading—
all alone—made her even more powerful.

Not a sound came from inside the trunk the whole time. The dead weight of the trunk was proof the creature still lay curled within. With it locked away inside the root cellar, Adelaide could almost imagine it had never been there; in the cabin, in her life. If not for Matthew's blood, dried along the floorboards, she might've forgotten everything.

She cleaned the cabin the best she could. The rocker had been obliterated, so she swept its pieces up. She gathered up the loose pages from her novels; they were only kindling now. She slept in the great chair while Matthew lay in her bed. She wore the key to the lock around her neck again. She would never sleep without it.

On the fifth night she found the box of photos she'd brought in from the root cellar. Tomorrow she'd take Matthew's horse and ride into Big Sandy, turn any photos of Mrs. Mudge and her boys over to the local sheriff. But the box held quite a surprise. Full of pictures, but not one of them with Mrs. Mudge, or her four sons. No one who even resembled the Mudges much.

Family photos. But whose?

After four more days Matthew Kirby recovered enough to sit up and sup. They hardly spoke. He scanned the cabin: no more wicker chair in the corner, the floor slats still cracked where Adelaide had wrestled the creature down. The trunk had disappeared. This seemed to relieve him. He said he'd heard her but the things she said made no sense.

"Not a mountain lion," he said. "Not a rattlesnake."

He watched her and she turned stiff, her courage faltered.

"Are you sure?" she asked him. "I found you all torn up. Outside."

Matthew Kirby looked angry at her lie, but then bewildered by it. Could it be that he'd imagined everything? It didn't help that he still looked so groggy, not many paces from the threshold of death. Confused, he tried to recall what happened. Could it be that he had imagined . . . ?

He looked back at her and she hid behind a mask of indifference, even as she felt her stomach tighten up.

"Then what happened to me?" he whispered. "You tell me."

Adelaide crossed her arms. "This land is trying to kill every single one of us," she said.

Matthew lay back down and pulled the blanket over himself and turned his face toward the cabin wall, and the days of their tenderness were finished.

When he finally felt fit enough to mount his horse, she helped him stow his rifle and gear; she filled a leather sack with water from her barrels. Before she walked him outside, she opened his hand and gave him twenty dollars. She hadn't earned a dime yet and now she gave Matthew most of what she had left in the world. Not even eight dollars left to her name.

He looked at the loot, then back to her.

Did she have to tell him she was buying his silence? No. She'd thought he might refuse the money, out of pride or perhaps some lingering affection.

But he slipped the money in his boot and, with her help, climbed up into the saddle.

Matthew Kirby slumped in the saddle and she wondered if he'd make it back to Finn. If he fell off, that would be the end of him. And it wouldn't be her fault. Not like if she'd shot him and buried him out here.

Did she want that to happen? No.

Yes.

Both.

That's the truth of it.

She watched him ride off. If he fell while she could see him, she decided she would go help. But after that? After that it was between Matthew and the land.

She hoped she would never see him again. But she would.

Twice more.

24

ALONE AGAIN, ADELAIDE PUSHED MATTHEW OUT OF HER MIND
and occupied herself with the business of survival. She put on her boots
and heavy coat and brought two buckets to the nearest coulee and filled
them both with snow. They still hadn't hit the true Montana winter.
The fact that she could march to the coulee and back on foot was proof.

Once back with the snow, she took stock of her brown coal. The
supply was nearly exhausted and burning it continued to have an ill
effect. Unlike wood, the smoke from the brown coal backed up into
the cabin and stung her eyes, made her cough, if she burned too much
of it for too long. When the heavier snows hit, she'd be stuck in this
cabin even more, and the idea of living on brown coal alone made her
choke. Grace had shared some wood with her, but that had run out
weeks ago. She needed more.

Adelaide washed the bedsheets that had collected Matthew's blood
while he slept. The napkins and tablecloth she'd used on his wounds
were never going to be clean again. Between the washing and collecting
snow, the day was done. In the night she felt a new cold, ten degrees
chillier at least. Adelaide wondered if the creature could feel the chill.

In the depth of the harsh night, Adelaide opened the cabin door
and stumbled the fifteen paces to the root cellar. The cold, already terrible inside the cabin, felt as if it was flaying her skin out here. She was
winded by the cold; it made her gulp and gasp.

She opened the root cellar door, descended the six earthen steps
and squatted there, catching her breath. At least down here she was

out of the wind's direct path. She held her face, it hurt so much from the chill. And now she listened for something, anything, but who could hear over the howling night?

Adelaide leaned close to the trunk. She breathed and focused. Would it die? *Could* it die? What if the Montana cold did what she and her parents never could?

She raised a hand and knocked against the side of the trunk three times.

She breathed and focused.

No sound at first, but then the trunk thumped.

The wood creaked.

Then she heard a single deep grunt, like a lion irritated at having been woken up.

Adelaide fell back on her ass, as if she'd been pushed. *Ah, well.*

Still strong. Still alive.

Adelaide rose and climbed out of the root cellar, slammed the door shut. Back in the cabin, she wrapped herself in three layers of clothing and the bedsheets and still hardly slept for all her shivering. She burned the last of her brown coal but then spent hours coughing on the acrid smoke. By dawn she knew she wouldn't survive another night without wood heat. And would that be so bad? Shiver in bed until she shuffled off. Sleep. Rest. Relief.

But what if she froze to death, then someone came along, found the trunk in the root cellar, and opened it? And who would that someone be? The people most likely to check on her were Grace and Sam. Imagine what that monster would do to the two of them.

Grace had been stiff with her when they left the dance, but she didn't want any harm to come to her only friend. And Sam. Forget what anyone else in town felt, she liked that boy immensely. She would never be responsible for any harm coming to him. She needed to get wood for her own survival, and for theirs. Before dawn, Adelaide resolved to reach Grace's claim. Miles away, and she'd have to do it on foot.

When the sun rose, she set out.

25

DIDN'T TAKE LONG FOR ADELAIDE TO REGRET THIS DECISION. After twenty minutes Adelaide felt as if she might have to crawl the whole way. The wind wouldn't let her keep balanced. She at first felt the buffeting as malevolence, the wind as a force bent on killing her, but after half an hour she saw the folly of such thinking. This land overpowered people, but it hadn't come to them, they had come to it. It wasn't trying to kill them; it didn't even notice them.

Adelaide stopped to adjust her wool scarf, pull it tighter across her mouth and nose, but it made no difference. She wore gloves. Boots. Two layers of clothing and then her great coat but she might as well be skipping around in her slip, that's how chilled she felt.

After another hour—or had it only been ten more minutes?—it seemed like she'd hardly left her cabin behind. So tough to judge scale and distance out here. Did she have two more miles to go or five? Five hundred, it felt like. She'd brought water and pilot bread on this walk, what her father would've dismissed as "dog biscuits." She crouched down to eat and drink, hunched over like a caveman.

By the second hour she felt nearly delirious. The cold turned her forehead and the bridge of her nose raw. She couldn't feel her nose or lips, even with the scarf for protection. She should've invested in a horse as soon as she'd arrived, but she'd become used to having people come to her—Grace and Matthew and the other men who visited. And each day there were fifteen things to do right there on the property. All excuses. All ways she proved herself unable to live on her own, to become a grown woman.

"You surprised me."

That was Eleanor Henry speaking. She walked beside Adelaide, calm as could be.

But Adelaide's mother wore only her nightgown, and the flesh across her chest and neck had been slashed to ribbons, the muscles underneath raw and nearly purple. Because her throat had been torn open, her voice didn't sound quite the same. A faint, gasping aspect to it. The woman walked on bare feet.

Adelaide didn't startle at the haint beside her. She'd felt this woman walking beside her since the moment she'd fled the farm.

"I told you to stay out the barn," Eleanor said.

"I tried to stay away," Adelaide whispered. "But I heard you ..."

"Screaming," Eleanor finished.

Adelaide nodded. "After I heard you and Daddy both screaming, I tried to stop it."

Eleanor laughed, but the sound had no warmth in it. It nearly sounded like howling when it played through the holes in her flesh.

"Is that what happened?" Eleanor asked.

Adelaide didn't answer her mother and her mother's dead eyes never left Adelaide's face.

"Maybe you didn't want to stop it," Eleanor hissed. "Not until we were dead."

The words hit her harder than the wind. She stooped forward, bracing herself against the hurt.

"You and the demon," Eleanor said. "The best thing and the worst thing, both came to us the same morning. You ever wondered why?"

Of course she had. Nearly every day since she'd been old enough to understand the symmetry.

"Why that day?" Adelaide asked her mother, just to talk about something else. "Why'd you two go into the barn with the shotgun that day?"

Eleanor slowed her pace until she came to a stop, but Adelaide kept going.

"We got tired of keeping secrets," Eleanor called after her. "You feeling tired yet?"

She looked back to answer her mother, but her mother was gone.

When she turned around again, she slammed face-first into the side of Grace's cabin.

26

THERE WERE TWO SMALL CABINS, SIDE BY SIDE, BOTH TEN FEET by ten feet. An outhouse with two stalls right behind that. Compared to Adelaide's cabin this spread seemed palatial. Grace had done her three years on the claim and proved up in 1913. Nearby, Adelaide saw a horse shed with a corral, but no horses.

By now Adelaide had developed a limp in her right leg because of all the walking. Her foot hurt badly and she felt nothing but a constant burning on her cheeks and forehead. Burning was better than numbness. If those parts still flared, that meant the nerves remained alive.

Adelaide had finished her water and pilot bread already. She'd hoped to find Grace and Sam sitting down for lunch. Maybe they'd even have meat. She hadn't eaten any since arriving in Montana. But now, with the horse gone, she feared Grace might be off running errands with Sam. Off in Big Sandy, or even—imagine the irony—pulling up to Adelaide's place right now.

If that turned out to be the case, she would simply have to slip into one of these cabins and collapse. She could always apologize later when Grace returned and roused her. Adelaide tried the first cabin door and found it unlocked.

Turned out Grace was at home.

Curled up on the floor.

Her dress stained with blood.

"Mrs. Price!" Adelaide shouted as she stumbled in.

Grace Price had fallen into a kind of trance, breathing fast and faint. Adelaide's voice didn't even seem to register. It was only once Adelaide got down on her knees and touched the top of Grace's head that the sharp breaths ceased. The eyes fluttered but finally focused. She looked up at Adelaide.

Her face had gone pale with loss of blood, whiter than the lace curtains on the windows. Seeing the blood spread across the clothes and on the wood slats brought Matthew Kirby's ravaged body to mind. Had the creature broken free somehow? Climbed out of the trunk, slithered from the root cellar, and beat her here?

"Sam," Grace whispered. "Find Sam for me."

Now her heart turned colder than her extremities. If it had hurt the boy, what would Adelaide do?

She looked around the cabin. Though the space was a little tighter than her own, the general layout proved similar. Except Grace had an oven, not just a stove. The oven had been tipped over. Pots and pans tossed everywhere. There were two beds, one for a child and one for an adult, both flipped over. Two of the cabin's windows were shattered, fragments of glass sprinkled inside the cabin.

"It broke in?" Adelaide asked, nearly breathless.

"Get Sam!" Grace shouted. "They threw him in the cellar."

Grace had her right hand pulled tightly against her belly. Her blouse had soaked up so much blood. Grace returned to the short, sharp breathing, back to that meditative state.

Adelaide scrambled out of the cabin, stumbled to the root cellar. When she opened the door, she saw a pair of small feet at the bottom of the short stairway, the rest lost in shadows.

"Sam!" Adelaide called. She leapt down the steps so quick she nearly fell on top of him.

His bare feet were nearly blue, but they trembled at the sound of her voice. Signs of life. From the darkness came his cry, shrill and terrified, something closer to an infant's shrieking.

"It's Mrs. Henry," she said as she grabbed him up. "It's Adelaide."

His hands were tied behind his back and a pillowcase had been pulled over his head. He'd thrown up inside it and it stuck to his skin when Adelaide peeled it off. She wiped at his face with the sleeve of her coat. She pulled him close and tucked him into a ball, hoping to protect every exposed part of him.

"Oh, Sam," Adelaide whispered as she rubbed her arms up and down his body. "I'm sorry, I'm sorry."

And only now did she hear what Grace had said.

They threw him in the cellar.

They.

After a moment, who knows how many, Sam's eyes focused on Adelaide.

He reached up and placed one cold hand against her cheek. She closed one hand around his. Trust flowed between them like a current.

She kissed the top of his head. Finally, he spoke.

"The youngest boy took my shoes," Sam told her. "He said he likes souvenirs."

27

"MUDGES."

Grace said the name as if it were a poison she was trying to spit out.

Nighttime now. When Adelaide brought Sam back into the cabin, Grace wept with relief to see him. The sight of her child gave her strength. She couldn't very well lie there and let her son witness her weakness. To protect him she composed herself. She let Adelaide help her up and dress her wound.

"Shot me right in my hand," Grace said.

Grace's limp right hand lay in Adelaide's lap. The loss of blood had been bad. The hand was bloated where the bullet had entered. Adelaide didn't risk testing to see if any bones had been broken. She found a pillowcase and wrapped the palm tightly. Matthew's wounds had been much worse and he survived. She almost said this to Grace, but caught herself. Sam sat next to his mother but couldn't watch. His face was pressed against Grace's left shoulder.

"Gotta get into Big Sandy," Grace said, more to herself than Adelaide. As if already planning out her next day's to-do list, a mother's instinct, no matter the difficulty; if she didn't make a plan, then the work would never get done.

"Emma Gallagher is working over at Worstell's hospital now," Grace said. "Trust her to set this more than that doctor. But how to get there, that's the hard part."

"Why would they shoot you in the hand of all places?" Adelaide asked after she'd finished wrapping.

"He aimed for my head," Grace said. "But the shooter was only twelve."

Was it wrong to feel relief? A boy of twelve and not the monster she'd brought with her from California. Better to have a human cause for this horror. Something that could be understood by all, explained easily, brought to justice.

"I'm surprised a blind boy could hit you at all," Adelaide said.

Sam pulled away from his mother. "Those boys can't see?"

"They found my horse sure enough," Grace said. "Mrs. Morrison came knocking at my door like she was just over for a visit. I saw that woman's face, so of course I let her in. Meanwhile her children were in the corral."

"I'm the one who saw them out there," Sam said. "I told Momma."

"That's when Mrs. Morrison—" Grace stopped herself, looked at Adelaide. "That's when *Mrs. Mudge* pulled her revolver."

Adelaide set the wounded hand in Grace's lap. She lifted the oven back onto its legs, gathered the scattered pans. She set the beds upright. She'd walked nine miles for help and it turned out she was the cavalry.

Sam moved slowly to a corner where a shelf had been hung. He pulled down the small stack of newspaper cutouts, then returned to his now upright bed. He lay on his stomach and stared at them, seemed to wish he was anywhere but here. Even the maps of the war in Europe likely gave off a romantic glow compared to what he and his mother had just survived.

"I owe you an apology, Mrs. Henry."

Adelaide looked back at her, a distance of only feet, and stopped collecting fallen things.

"I felt cross with you after the dance." Grace lowered her head, her eyes fluttered. "I felt embarrassed because I thought you had been so rude . . ."

"To Mrs. Mudge."

"Yes."

"The one who stole your horse and nearly killed you and Sam."

Grace looked up at Adelaide. "Yes, Mrs. Henry. That same one."

Adelaide nodded. "Well, from now on, who are you going to trust?"

Grace smiled. "You, Mrs. Henry. I'm going to trust you."

28

ADELAIDE WOULD STAY OVERNIGHT. GRACE AND SAM GATHERED together in the adult bed and Adelaide did her best on Sam's smaller frame. Before shutting her eyes, Grace instructed Adelaide to light a candle and leave it in the western-facing window; said she shouldn't close the shutters. The flame must burn through the night.

With the shutter open, the window shook but it didn't shatter; the light flickered on the sill. It went out twice and Adelaide lit it again both times. She checked on Grace and Sam. Neither looked good, pale and frail. Hardly much warmth in the cabin, but she felt as if she brought the candle with her into her dreams. It burned there and kept her mind from freezing with despair.

In the morning she cooked for them, cleaned up. Sam worked as her helper, but also her informant when they stepped out of the home. There were two cabins on this property, so who occupied the other one?

"Mr. Price," Sam said as they were in the root cellar, gathering food for breakfast.

"Your father?" she asked.

"Well, I never knew him," Sam said as he took down two Atlas jars of preserves.

"And where is he now?" Adelaide asked.

"Behind the corral," Sam said, then scurried up the stairs and returned to his mother.

Adelaide returned to the cabin with the last of Grace's eggs. She peeked back at the corral, but then more pressing concerns arose. With the horse stolen, Adelaide would have to walk all the way to Big Sandy. Maybe she could get the nurse, Emma Gallagher, to ride out.

Adelaide tried to make this plan sound reasonable in her head because she knew it to be anything but. Grace's claim lay closer to town than Adelaide's, but that still meant a march of six or seven miles. And the temperature seemed colder already than it had been only a day ago. But what else could she do? Grace sure wouldn't make it that far on foot. And what about Sam?

But before she'd finished cooking breakfast, they heard a horse's approach.

"Where's your rifle?" Adelaide asked.

"Mudges took the rifle," Grace said. "Sam, tuck under my bed."

Grace watched Sam until he'd disappeared below the bedframe. She pulled the bed curtain down to hide the child.

Adelaide picked up the skillet and dumped the half-finished eggs into a bowl. At least if she hit someone with it, the surface would be hot as well as hard. The horse approached, the rider slowly circling the cabin.

A woman's voice: "I saw your candle, Mrs. Price. Burning through the night."

Grace visibly relaxed, like watching ice melt quickly.

She shouted, "I think you only came because you smelled breakfast cooking!"

Grace rose from the bed and Sam wriggled out from beneath like a larva. Grace opened the cabin door, but Adelaide didn't set the skillet down just yet. Sharing the same sex didn't guarantee they were allies; Mrs. Mudge was a woman after all.

The rider put up her horse in the corral.

When she appeared in the doorway, Adelaide recognized her, even though they'd never met. A Black woman. If Annie Morgan was dead, then this was the famous Bertie Brown, the only other Black woman in all of Chouteau County.

Bertie eyed Adelaide, looking her up and down.

"You must be Mrs. Henry."

BERTIE BROWN STOOD SMALLER than Adelaide, but nearly everyone did.

She might've been Eleanor Henry's age, perhaps even older, but somehow she looked younger than Adelaide. It wasn't her face so much as her carriage. She entered the cabin and Adelaide nearly crossed the room and hugged her. Months without seeing another Black woman when, in her previous life in California, she'd seen herself reflected back every single day. Her mother, their neighbors, even the congregants of their church. All Black. And then nothing. Until now. Until Bertie Brown.

Bertie, it must be said, seemed less sentimental about the moment. In fact, she offered Adelaide only the quickest of greetings before she got to Grace on the bed. To be fair, she'd never met Adelaide and her friend had been shot and left for dead.

"How bad's the pain, Mrs. Price?" Bertie asked.

Grace looked to Sam, then back to Bertie. "Substantial."

Bertie left the cabin and returned with two sacks; from one she revealed eight fresh eggs, raw chicken patties, and a mince pie. She pulled a large, opaque glass bottle from the other. Bertie's Brew.

Bertie uncorked the bottle, took down a cup, and poured a drink the color of muddy water. Grace brought it to her lips and sank the whole thing.

Grace sighed. "Bless you, Mrs. Brown."

"You take one more pull," Bertie said to Grace. "Then I ride you into Big Sandy."

"And what am I going to do?" Adelaide asked, feeling like a whiny child as soon as she said it.

Bertie turned to Adelaide and took her hand. Adelaide looked down at their two hands clasped and melted at the sight. She might as well be holding her mother's fingers in her own.

"You're going to keep an eye on Sam," Bertie said firmly.

Grace rose to her feet and kissed her son, told him to mind Adelaide's rules. While Grace dressed, Bertie leaned close to Adelaide's ear and whispered.

"And when I get back, we'll do something about your hair."

Adelaide pulled away, nearly as horrified as when she'd found Grace on the floor.

She brought one hand to her hairline. "That bad?"

Bertie Brown raised both eyebrows. "Don't fuss," she said. "I've got you."

She touched one hand to Adelaide's cheek and Adelaide felt the warmth.

Then she and Grace were gone, headed for Big Sandy.

Sam had chores for the day, but before that he was expected to do his reading and writing. To practice penmanship, Grace had him copy Bible verses; by now he'd reached Obadiah. Would Adelaide help him through it? She agreed but, in truth, she'd never much listened in church. You weren't supposed to say that. Or maybe that would be one more sign she didn't fit in properly with the community. During all her years of attending church, she'd sat there wishing she was anywhere else. What was the point of the place if they couldn't tell the truth of what they were enduring back on the farm? And she always had the strong sense most of the other congregants hadn't come to church to tell their truths either. It had been a place to perform. Little more. Sam had to explain what this book of the Bible even meant.

Obadiah. The shortest book of the Hebrew Bible. A book of furious judgment, damning the neighboring nation of Edom for its mistreatment of the Israelites. The Edomites would fall because of their pride and cruelty.

Sam read aloud as he copied the verses.

"Who are the Edomites?" Sam asked. "Are they still around?"

"Damn if I know," Adelaide said, back at the oven.

Sam laughed in shock and Adelaide realized she'd cursed in front of the child.

"Don't tell your momma."

Sam looked back down at the composition notebook. "I can keep a secret."

29

TWO DAYS LATER ADELAIDE HENRY RODE TO HER CABIN ON A gelding.

Her gelding.

Purchased in her name through a loan secured with the help of Bertie Brown. Bertie reminded Adelaide to ride into Big Sandy and find Hugh Schrammeck's office so he might know her face and have her signature on the paperwork for the loan. If Adelaide did not do this, then Mr. Schrammeck would place the horse's cost on Bertie's books. And if that happened, Bertie would come looking for Adelaide.

We clear?

Yes indeed.

Bertie gave Adelaide a small sack of food, then rode Sam into town so he could be with his mother during the recovery. And just like that, Adelaide stood alone on Grace Price's claim.

The horse remained in the corral and Adelaide took the moment to wander with her curiosity. She walked to the second cabin and peeked into its single window. What did she expect to see?

Not two benches, set in rows. An easel propped against one wall. A small desk beside the easel. A school. That's what it was. Grace Price's school. It looked so organized, so professional. What could it be about Sam that would make other parents keep their children away? Or could Grace be the reason somehow? Adelaide couldn't imagine what the answer could be because now she cherished mother and child so dearly.

The sun, already rising in the sky, turned the window of the second cabin into a mirror. Adelaide saw less and less of the schoolroom and more and more of her own face.

And a man standing behind her.

She turned with a start, her hands already rising to tear and thrash at whoever had crept so close. But no one was there. There was Adelaide, her new horse, and the wind. Nothing else.

ADELAIDE AND HER HORSE took a little time to get to know each other, about a mile or three. It didn't take long to figure out why Bertie Brown was able to secure a loan for this one, even with Adelaide absent. The sway to his back made the saddle fit loosely; the prominence of his withers; and nobody was getting this horse to do more than trot. But bless this old beast anyway. The walk that took her half a day, the one that nearly killed her, now took less than an hour on the return. That was even with the sack of food Bertie gave her, and the wood she'd bundled from Grace's stockpile. Good to have a horse. By the time she reached her cabin, she'd decided on a name for him. Obadiah.

"Here we are," she said as they reached her claim. "This is your home now, Obadiah."

But as she neared the cabin she saw something had gone wrong.

The door to the root cellar, it was gone. Nearly torn off the hinges. But it hadn't been kicked in. Something had broken out.

She dismounted Obadiah. Her father had been quite fine at ground-tying a horse, but Adelaide didn't have the time to train Obadiah now. She led him toward the root cellar, came close enough that she could see, for sure, that the trunk lay empty. The trunk had splintered where the lock once held, and the lid was flipped so far back it was a surprise the hinges still held at all.

One of the doorway beams had been yanked out so far it formed a shape close to a Y, and without any better option, she tied Obadiah off right there. She gave the horse a calming touch and then she moved on. As soon as she took two steps, Obadiah stepped forward, too, trying to keep close to her. She put up her hand and urged him back but returned to his side and offered another calming touch to his neck. When she walked away the second time, the old horse didn't try to follow.

Now she traced the path from the root cellar; the dirt had been smoothed flat, as if a snake had dragged itself forward. She followed it all the way to the cabin. That door had been damaged, too, but it was much weaker than the one in the root cellar. A little weight had been applied and it simply fell in. It lay there, flat as a coffin lid.

She walked inside the cabin and found the place not exactly as she'd left it three days ago. The bed had been pushed away from the wall and lay at an angle. The iron stove and all the pots littered the floor. The great chair had been flipped over.

And then she heard it: a soft panting sound filled the space.

"You got out," Adelaide said.

From the looks of that trunk, there would be no more going back in.

The panting continued and Adelaide located it coming from the bed. The frame lay tilted at such an angle that it formed a crawl space, a makeshift nook where the creature might tuck itself without being closed in on all sides, as it was in the trunk.

Her instinct, immediate and nearly overwhelming, was to run. This beast had torn her mother and father apart, why wouldn't it do the same to her? Maybe it would. Maybe that would be welcome.

She moved to the stove and grabbed the sharpest of her blades, a boning knife.

Adelaide sat on the floor, cross-legged. She peered into the darkness of that space until its head—*its face*—became clearer. Its eyes were large and yellow in the dark. It watched her just as cautiously as she watched it.

"If I cut my throat right now," Adelaide said, "would you drop down dead? You showed up when I was born. Maybe it takes me dying to kill you, too."

The panting continued but the pace didn't change. Had it understood her?

She brought the tip of the blade to her neck and pressed it there.

The panting picked up its pace. The sound of anxiousness or worry. Or anger.

She lowered the blade and the panting slowed again.

"All these years, I wish you could tell me the nature of this curse, demon. Is it to make us reviled by our neighbors? Cast out from society? Even if you told me that, told me anything, I could endure it better. But maybe that's the whole point of your evil. No answers. No explanations. The silence is the worst part of this suffering."

Adelaide looked out the open doorway. Obadiah hadn't fled yet. He watched her intently from the place where he'd been tied. She waved to the horse, surprised by how comforted she felt to see the old boy there. Nice to have something in her life besides the monster.

She looked to the shadows where the demon still crouched.

"If Daddy's shotgun couldn't stop you, I doubt this knife will give you more than a tickle."

Adelaide rose from the floor and returned the boning knife to its place by the stove.

"I'm going to clean up this mess you made," she said. "If you are planning to attack me like you did Mr. Kirby, I promise I will put up a better fight."

Adelaide went about her business. First, and most important, fix that front door. She lifted it and set it upright. The door had leather hinges. Three straps: one at the top, another at the center, and a third down below. The hardest trouble was balancing the door while tying off the leather. Yet one more reason Adelaide blessed her size. Once the door had been put in place, the chill winds were shut out, at least as much as they could ever be out here.

Next, she righted the stove and gathered up the pans. She lifted the great chair. But when she went to fix the bed, the panting changed. It slowed and the register dropped. Becoming something more like a growl. You might think it was a mountain lion hiding under there, set to pounce.

"Fine," she muttered. "That's just fine."

Adelaide ran out into the cold and fed Obadiah a handful of prairie turnips, just one of the gifts in Bertie's bag. She touched the animal gently as she fed it, then secured the tie before going back inside.

She fed the wood into her stove and started the fire.

She sat in the great chair.

Adelaide Henry had never been the type for prayer. Her parents had lost the spirit before Adelaide was old enough to read. At times, in church, as they'd watched others prosper they only felt farther outside the protection of the Lord. And who could they tell? Eleanor tried the pastor, and do you know what he'd done? He recommended she join him in prayer. At his home. Alone. Eleanor never told Glenville about that part—last thing the Henrys needed was for Glenville to murder the local pastor—but when Adelaide became a young woman, Eleanor warned her daughter to keep a far distance from the pastor, that's for sure.

"Did you think I'd fled?" Adelaide asked. "Were you scared? Is that why you broke out and tore my place up?"

She listened for some response, but all she heard was the snap of the wood combusting in the stove.

"Or were you jealous, angry I wasn't shackled to you for one damn moment in my life?"

No answer came, of course. Only sleep arrived, all at once.

Adelaide didn't open her eyes again for half a day.

30

IN HER DREAM SHE SAW NOTHING, BUT HEARD HER FATHER'S voice.

My father, as you know, was a sort of gentleman farmer in–shire; and I, by his express desire, succeeded him in the same quiet occupation, not very willingly . . .

It was as though he read to her from the other side of the veil, still comforting her like the good father he'd always been.

. . . for ambition urged me to higher aims, and self-conceit assured me that, in disregarding its voice, I was burying my talent in the earth, and hiding my light under a bushel.

She listened to him and felt soothed. She understood, within the dream, that it was a dream, and prayed that it wouldn't end. Glenville Henry could read the book in its entirety and then start all over again and she would remain blissful in his company.

All she needed was her mother's touch on her scalp, Eleanor's knees on either side of her shoulders, a pressure as calming as the close quarters of the womb.

I would not send a poor girl into the world unarmed against her foes, and ignorant of the snares that beset her path; nor would I watch and guard her, till, deprived of self-respect and self-reliance, she lost the power or the will to watch and guard herself.

"Looks empty."

Adelaide's eyes opened like a snap. That was not her father.

Back in Montana. Back in her cabin.

Nearly nighttime. The evening sun going down.

Her in the great chair; the panting still playing from the overturned bed.

A child's voice. A boy.

Sam?

Another voice. A woman. "Then why is there a horse tied up out here?"

That wasn't Grace. Not Bertie.

She sat up and spied the bed. The panting underneath picked up pace.

Adelaide leaned forward in her chair, going as low as she could, creeping to one of the windows that seemed farthest from the voices.

From here she saw the boy. Twelve or thirteen, though he might be mistaken for younger. Thin as wire and small for his age. He'd gone up on his toes, peeking into one of the other windows. If not for the curtains, he would've seen everything inside.

"I don't see her."

Joab.

The name returned to her, as clearly as his story of pushing a child down a well for teasing him. The youngest of the Mudge boys. The woman's voice would have to belong to their mother.

A loud knock at the front door, followed by Mrs. Mudge's voice.

"Mrs. Henry? Mrs. Henry. Open your door."

A sound—a snort—came from under the mattress. The creature was waking up. Which monsters were worse? The one in here or the family out there?

"Should I call you Mudge or Morrison?" Adelaide asked.

"You know my name," Mrs. Mudge said coolly. "Let me show you my pistol."

Adelaide stopped crouching. Rose to her full height.

"I see her!" shouted Joab. He stood at the second window. "She's got the stove we took from the old people in Oregon. Was that in Oregon?"

Mrs. Mudge said, "Doesn't matter, we'll be taking it all back."

Mrs. Mudge clapped at the wall of the cabin with the butt of her pistol.

"We're tired of hiding up in the mountains. Rocky Point gets so cold. We wake up with our hair frosting over. I can't have that for my boys. You understand."

The bed shifted now and the demon reached a single paw out from its shelter. The claws dug into the floorboards.

"I think she's got a dog," Joab said, up on his toes now. "I want it."

"What happened to the blindfolds?" Adelaide shouted.

"Tell me what you remember about my boys. Height? Hair color? Accents? Or just a couple of handkerchiefs over their eyes?"

Mrs. Mudge laughed with satisfaction.

Now a new sound. Rain splashing the cabin walls.

Not rain.

The Mudge boys were peeing on Adelaide's home.

Adelaide moved toward the stove, where her rifle stood upright in a corner. As she reached for it, the demon crawled out from beneath the bed in its entirety.

She'd forgotten. Somehow Adelaide always forgot the size of it, clear in the last gasps of sunlight coming through the windows. The gray scales of its skin, the *reality* of such a thing in this world, she always forgot until she faced it once more. Maybe this was how climbers felt when they scaled a formidable mountain. Every summit is singular; every sighting of this beast might as well be the first time.

"You boys will clean those walls when we take this place over, you hear?"

All four boys shouted back as one. "Yes, ma'am!"

"Now listen," Mrs. Mudge said to Adelaide. "I got a little turned around and ended up at your neighbor's place. It might make you feel better to know you'll be joining them in the Realm Eternal."

"They survived," Adelaide said, the rifle in hand now.

"Momma," one of the boys whispered. "Is she telling the truth?"

"Of course not," Mrs. Mudge said. "She's just stalling for time."

Five guns against one. She presumed they were all armed. It was true she really was stalling for time. Already the sun had finished its journey, disappearing behind the horizon, and the darkness of night-time fell across the cabin quick.

Which meant Adelaide heard the demon more than she saw it. The sound of its heavy frame dragging across the floorboards, slithering past her until it reached the front door.

And a moment after that the door was kicked in.

Mrs. Mudge raised her pistol. A silhouette, framed in the doorway.

But then Mrs. Mudge looked down at the ground and she saw the large shape there.

"Oh my," she said.

The demon leapt out and tore off Mrs. Mudge's left arm.

The boys weren't standing there with Mom, so they didn't see what happened but they sure could hear it. Their mother howled as if she'd been shot. Only for them to round the cabin and find something so much worse.

A creature crouched over their mother; a beast guarding its kill.

The youngest boy was the only one to find his voice.

"What in hell," he croaked.

In that instant Adelaide understood them as they truly were. Four boys. Seventeen, sixteen, fifteen, and twelve. Watching blood run from their mother's shoulder like a stream.

Mrs. Mudge panted. Her eyes swam wild in their sockets. Her lips moved, saying only one word, again and again, but there was no volume to it so no one could tell just what it was.

The two youngest couldn't look away from their mother.

The older boys recovered more quickly. And what did they do?

They ran away.

Sprinted to the outhouse, where the Mudges had tied up three horses. The older boys didn't look back once. The two youngest only noticed the eldest brother was fleeing when he was already up on his horse.

"Edward!" they shouted in unison.

Edward didn't answer. Edward rode away.

The second oldest followed after.

The two rode north from the outhouse. One can see a light from miles away in the night, but the boys carried no light. In seconds they'd disappeared into the cavernous gloom of a Montana night. The rumble of their horses' hooves was the only proof they were still out there.

The demon did something new. New to Adelaide.

It barked once. She'd never heard it make such a sound.

Then something else new: It moved from the cabin's threshold into the clear ground between the cabin and the outhouse. It rose onto its legs and spread its arms. The loose skin under there expanded like sails. That unstoppable Montana wind gathered in the loose skin and sent the creature tumbling sideways, like an infant that's still unsure on its legs. Such a strange thing to see that Adelaide, and even the two remaining Mudge boys, looked away from Mrs. Mudge and watched the demon right itself.

It crouched lower this time and spread its arms slowly, letting the wind gather under the loose skin. It stayed upright and then the creature snapped its arms down and it shot up into the sky.

The demon took flight.

Adelaide and the boys went rigid with shock.

That barking sound returned as an echo through the night sky. It came from farther north now. Another bark and then a horse screamed as it was taken down somewhere out there on the darkened plain.

A young man's voice called out once, pleading—*Edward!*—but just as quickly it was silenced.

Soon there were pistol shots, but only two.

The sound of the second horse's gallop snuffed out.

Adelaide came back to herself. She'd been so busy listening to the darkness that she'd stopped seeing what lay in front of her.

Mrs. Mudge.

The body not yet cold, but the soul already gone. Quickly Adelaide crouched and pulled the pistol—a Colt Single Action Army—from the woman's intact hand.

But the last two Mudge boys had run off by now. They'd made it to their last horse and mounted it together. They rode back toward her. They became clearer to her as they approached. She could barely see past an arm's length in the night. The fifteen-year-old held the reins. His younger brother, Joab, sat in front. They stopped directly at Adelaide's door. Adelaide raised the pistol, but the boys only looked at their mother.

The fifteen-year-old's eyes showed bright with rage, but it was the gaze of the twelve-year-old that chilled Adelaide. Joab watched her with a dispassionate eye.

"Mudges never forget," Joab said.

Then he tapped his brother's shoulder and the boys galloped off.

They rode fast, no doubt wary of the demon coming for them as well. But out there, in the dark, it had already hunted. Adelaide tried not to think of which prey the beast was more likely to be eating, the horses or the boys.

It took Adelaide some time to return to common sense. She stood in the doorway aghast at all she'd seen. Unable to understand how quickly bad had gone to much worse. Maybe the boys would go to the law in town. How would she explain a dead woman, a dead *white* woman—one arm torn away—lying here on her doorstep? What was she going to do? No chance of burying a body in the hard soil. She would have to think of something but she realized this wasn't actually the most pressing concern.

Where had *it* gone?

Obadiah remained where he'd been tied up. No doubt the Mudges would have stolen him after they'd disposed of Adelaide's corpse. Instead, he remained. Though now that she slowed her breathing and looked at him, she understood how frightened he seemed. And who could blame him?

Adelaide found another handful of prairie turnips and approached the horse. She stood where he could see her and he watched her warily. She didn't rush in close; instead she held out a turnip, close enough that he could catch the scent. Only then did she come closer, feed him, place a hand on him.

As they stood together she looked at the night sky again, listened for that barking, but now all she heard were the howling winds.

The demon had saved her life. But that seemed almost accidental. Five kills. And now the first deaths outside the family. What would she do with the beast when it returned? she wondered.

She might move again, but the thought made her buckle. She didn't have the energy, or the desire, to settle down somewhere new.

But then another thought occurred. One that made her shiver with a kind of electric thrill. She'd spent her life wondering if she could ever escape her family's curse, but she'd never considered the possibility that *the curse* could be the one to leave.

What if she found a way to hide Mrs. Mudge's body, and those boys—members of a criminal family who'd already done enough to get themselves hung, no matter their age—what if those boys didn't say a damn thing to the law and simply fled Montana to start over somewhere else?

She fed Obadiah another prairie turnip and the horror of the night became the potential for promise by the dawn. The winds were cold but for the moment she couldn't feel them.

What if it didn't come back?

She knew her next thought was a selfish one, but nevertheless, it was the next one that came to her.

What if, for the first time in her life, she was *free*?

TWO

31

JOHN MING, SUCCESSFUL CATTLEMAN, BUILT THE MING OPERA House in Helena in 1880. There had been human beings in Montana before the likes of John Ming, of course, but buildings like the opera house were erected to erase their memory. Majestic and ambitious but also a bit like introducing a non-native plant to a new land. In time it would seem as though the Ming Opera House had always been around and there was no "before" before it. Only a wild and empty land.

Even for Helena, Ming's opera house impressed. Seating for nine hundred, thirty-two sets of scenery, gas lighting throughout the building. A granite foundation, sod basement and dressing rooms beneath the stage. Tiered seating with side-boxes faced with wrought iron. The Ming Opera House thrilled its visitors.

Jack and Jerrine Reed—the wealthiest couple in Big Sandy—were also inspired.

The Big Sandy Opera House couldn't compare to Ming's behemoth, but the Reeds still did their best. Seating for two hundred, six sets of scenery, and gas lighting throughout the building, though it hadn't been installed well; once, a leak had been detected only when members of the audience began passing out. The Reeds made a practice of running the gas for the thirty minutes preceding shows to make sure they'd catch any leaks before the theatergoers arrived.

And yet, the Reeds' opera house—people would simply say they were going to a show at "the Reeds'"—nourished Big Sandy. Mysterious Smith's magic show the year before had been a terrific success. *The*

Missouri Girl came through Big Sandy; few towns this far north could show films. Billy Sunday's sermons were repeated nearly verbatim by two local evangelists who had seen the preacher live. And of course there were local shows. Like tonight. The bell of the opera house had been rung by Mrs. Reed herself. Loud enough to be heard for miles in any direction, reaching all but the most distant of homesteads.

And tonight, Jerrine Reed also hosted the show.

"I want to welcome all you fine ladies, and your children, and those few men I see snuck in as well, on behalf of Big Sandy's local chapter of the Busy Bees. And just a reminder that you are also welcome to attend our weekly meetings, held in our homes. Though if we keep expanding membership, we may have to meet here at the opera house regularly instead!"

Applause for this, less the joke than the implication of growth, of success. And who would know about achievement more than Mrs. Reed, head of the local Busy Bees and the Big Sandy Suffragettes. Recently Mrs. Reed had supported a bill that would allow women to file paperwork and register to vote in their own homes rather than having to go down to the courthouse and do so before a justice. After all, such extra steps weren't demanded of the men.

"I make it a practice to greet every train that arrives in Big Sandy," Mrs. Reed continued. "I am sure I have offered a smile and a kind word to at least half of you here. And to the other half, please don't be offended; if I've missed you in the past, I'll find you in the future."

Jack and Jerrine Reed were both small in figure, but she dominated the big stage. The attention of nearly sixty townspeople on her and she did not demur. She gazed at the audience directly; she walked from one side of the stage to the other, addressing them with warmth and intimacy. She seemed like a woman who had never been told to shrink.

Mrs. Reed wore her bluebird pin again and a black lace ribbon appliqué dress that ran to the floor and hid her feet so it looked like the woman might be gliding from one end of the stage to the next. Adelaide marveled at the sight of her.

Yes, Adelaide had come to the Big Sandy Opera House this evening.

And she wasn't alone.

Sam sat beside her, with Grace on the other side. Adelaide wore a green wool skirt suit, the best piece of clothing she owned, which she'd bought used in town when Grace recovered enough to invite Adelaide out for a night at the opera house. The outfit cost her only fifty cents. When she met Grace and Sam, Grace admired the outfit, and that felt nice. Grace also paid for their tickets, a small thank-you for finding them, saving their lives.

They'd chosen seats in the balcony, if only so they could leave without making a fuss. Grace knew her child well enough to prepare for that moment when Sam's patience ended and it was best to make a quiet retreat.

When they met, when they sat down, when Mrs. Reed first took the stage—there were so many moments when Adelaide almost opened her mouth and told Grace what had happened two weeks ago. *It left and it didn't come back.*

But if she started to talk, where would it end? How much would she have to explain? And, really, wouldn't she just be hoping Grace would absolve her of the guilt she felt dragging at her ankles every time she took a step? So no, Adelaide didn't confess. Instead, she listened to Mrs. Reed, if only to drown out her own thoughts.

Mrs. Reed now came right to the lip of the stage.

"My husband and I have lived in Big Sandy for over a decade now, and let me tell you what I know. Now that we have made it to November, we have separated the wheat from the chaff. The chaff have fled their homesteads, as the law allows during the worst winter months, but they betray themselves as the kind who will not see the difficult job through. You listening to me now in this audience, you are the wheat. I don't mean to insult those who will return to us next spring. Don't tell them I said any of this. I'm only telling you how proud I am to find you here with me tonight.

"When the snows come, we lose more than half the population of this town. And worse, many of them won't return. They'll abandon their claims and all the work they've done to maintain them. But we remain, don't we? We remain."

Adelaide looked down at Sam beside her, reading the caption beneath another photo from the *Mountaineer*. Without meaning to do it, Adelaide reached out and brushed her hand across the top of Sam's head. And without breaking his concentration, he leaned toward her body and rested against her side.

"Well now, ladies," Mrs. Reed continued. "After much advocacy behind the scenes, I am happy to say the *Bear Paw Mountaineer* has begun printing a brand-new column: Montana Women in the Week's News!"

As the audience applauded, Mrs. Reed turned and another member of the Busy Bees walked out and handed her a copy of the newspaper. Mrs. Reed made a big show of snapping the pages until she reached the column.

"'Mrs. Julia Prescott, of Big Timber, clubwoman and general factotum on the *Big Timber Pioneer*, took charge of that paper the past few weeks while the editor and owner, Jerry Williams, was absent on a vacation.'" Mrs. Reed looked up from the paper. "Let's hear what you think of Mrs. Prescott then."

As the audience clapped, Adelaide looked to her right, where she found Grace watching her. What did Grace see? Sam leaning against Adelaide; Adelaide's arm wrapped around the kid's shoulder.

Her immediate instinct was to pull away. How would Eleanor and Glenville have reacted to such a sight? Seeing their child in the embrace of a neighbor? Even in church they'd hardly ever shared that back pew, and if they had, Adelaide was always sat between her parents. A moment like this could never have happened and that was by design. So, instinctively, she lifted her arm from around Sam, but then she noticed, with great surprise, the expression on Grace's face. Grace smiled at the sight, a soft grin.

Adelaide settled her arm back down where it had been.

And she did not think about where *it* had gone.

And she did not think about what *it* might be doing.

And she did not think about—

Meanwhile, down on the stage, Mrs. Reed scanned for another note. The Busy Bees promised to hold evenings like this every week the *Mountaineer* ran the column. The paper liked the idea because it meant they could solicit every household in attendance for a subscription.

"Here's one," Mrs. Reed said. "Though it's not about a Montana woman, I felt you all had to hear it.

"'Petrograd,'" Mrs. Reed began. "'Princess Volonsky, twenty-two, whose husband, father, and brother were killed early in the war, cut her hair, adopted men's clothing, enlisted as a private, and fought on the southern front for several months.'"

Mrs. Reed now sat down, her legs dangling over the side of the stage. If she extended one leg as far as it would go, she could touch the women sitting in the first row.

"'Her sex being discovered, she was sent to Kieff to be discharged, but eluded her guards and returned to the fighting line. Now she has been found wounded in a Karkoff hospital.'"

Mrs. Reed folded the paper and it was the loudest sound in the opera house.

"History is simple," she began. "Men take everything that happened and try to make a story out of it. Which is fine. But when the tale becomes too complicated, they just . . . leave things out. For instance, this brave young woman, Princess Volonsky. I hope I'm pronouncing that correctly.

"This woman. Will we see her recorded as a brave soldier in their war? Or will she risk being forgotten? We can do our part. We can remember her. History is simple, but the past is complicated. I, for one, embrace the complications."

Mrs. Reed closed her eyes.

"Let us all bow our heads and pray for this brave young woman. Everyone, let's do it now."

Adelaide shut her eyes and lowered her head. As did every woman in the opera house. Some of the older children and the few men in attendance did as well.

Adelaide thought on this woman, fighting so fiercely despite all she'd lost. Next to her, Sam shifted, pulled away, so he could now rest against his mother. Adelaide gazed at the mother and child and recognized the pose. The special point of contact between them. She could feel her mother's pointer finger rubbing along her scalp.

"Now then," Mrs. Reed said, eyes open and back to good cheer. She slid backward on the stage a few inches, then turned over and pushed herself back up to her feet. Nothing remotely graceful about the movement and she didn't seem self-conscious about it at all. She rose and waved to the wings of the stage and out walked eleven women, nearly as well dressed as Mrs. Reed. The Busy Bees.

In this context, at this moment, they might as well have been a dozen demigods up onstage. They waved to the audience and joined Mrs. Reed at the edge of the stage. They spread out so each one might be catching the eye of at least one woman in the crowd.

Mrs. Reed said, "We wanted to join together onstage to share some wonderful local news. As of tomorrow, we will be welcoming a new business to this town. Mrs. Metta Sterling and her son Melvin will be operating Big Sandy's first power laundry! We plan to bring all our clothes and linens to her when they need to be washed. We encourage all of you to do the same and support our local friend."

The Busy Bees applauded together and at that moment Mrs. Metta Sterling, seated in the front row, rose and turned to wave at the audience. All applauded even if, more than likely, the majority could not afford the expense of having their laundry done by others. Nevertheless, their cheer was sincere.

Adelaide's gaze left Mrs. Sterling and traveled across the crowd down below. She'd still never met most of these women. She couldn't say which ones lived in town and which lived on claims like she and Grace did. They, too, had taken care with their clothing, though, to a woman, each outfit showed its wear. Only the Busy Bees were pristine.

Their clothes appeared flawless, as did their hats. This didn't make them seem unapproachable or vain—after all, there wasn't too much room between the seats on the floor and the women on the stage; anyone could make that climb.

She might've continued like this—lost in her thoughts—until the show ended, but Adelaide realized that someone was gazing up at her from the orchestra seats. A man she knew.

Finn Kirby.

Not gazing. Glaring. And beside him?

Matthew.

Matthew wasn't looking at her. He sat facing forward, watching the women onstage. She expected the older man to tap his nephew, point up into the balcony, but that didn't happen. Instead, Finn rose from his chair, without breaking his view of Adelaide, and Adelaide suddenly found it hard to breathe. *Was he coming up here?*

"Adelaide!"

She turned to find Grace leaning close, tugging at her sleeve. How long had she been whispering Adelaide's name?

She peeped below again to find Finn skirting past Matthew's knees, Matthew who hardly seemed to be there at all, listless and dazed. Where else could Finn be headed but here? Adelaide felt absolutely sure she did not want to be present when he arrived.

"Sam is hungry," Grace whispered. "And he's run out of patience."

Adelaide stayed quiet a moment, trying to translate the words while working to control her panic. Sam had already disappeared down the aisle, no doubt already descending the steps to the lobby below.

"I'll take him to the Grill Cafe!" Adelaide offered, practically climbing over Grace's lap.

"I'll be right behind you," Grace whispered. "I need to have a word with someone."

As Adelaide scrambled down the aisle and the stairs, Mrs. Reed clapped for the crowd's attention. Adelaide couldn't see her, but the voice carried. The opera house had been built with exquisite acoustics.

"Mr. Reed is always by my side, so you may be wondering where

I've kept my husband tonight. Bless his heart, he's at our home, right next door, counting horses on a ledger sheet. That man's industriousness is matched only by his generosity. Each of you who came tonight will go home with a sack of potatoes. It is our great hope that this will prove useful as the winter snows begin to fall. And always look out for the pilot fire of the opera house, up there in our spire. We keep it burning through every winter night so you will never be lost in the dark. You can always find your way back home, to us.

"Now, before you go, our theater organ has *finally* been installed correctly. And one of our very own Busy Bees, Mrs. Estella Powers, will lead us in song. What will it be? Oh yes. Perfect. 'When You're a Long, Long Way from Home.'"

32

WHEN SHE SPOKE ONSTAGE, MRS. JERRINE REED TOLD THE audience her husband had stayed at home to go over budgets and books. But no. Mr. Jack Reed was *not* at home counting horses.

At this point in the evening, it's fair to say he had trouble simply staying upright in his seat. Luckily, he didn't have to stand. His drinks were brought to him by Bertie Brown. All he had to do was lift the mug to his lips.

"Three eggs," Jack Reed said.

He looked up to be sure Bertie Brown heard him, but who else could she listen to? Tonight, he was her only customer.

Bertie Brown sold the best homebrew in Montana and ran a small business, the Blind Pig. Calling it a bar seemed like a stretch. The Blind Pig was Bertie Brown's home, a single-story log cabin on 320 acres. Bertie had proved up in 1912. The *Bear Paw Mountaineer* ran the notice in the paper, as was required for all claims to be legally recognized.

"Notice for Publication—Department of the Interior U.S. Land Office at Havre, Montana, Sept. 12, 1912. Notice is hereby given that Bertie Brown, Big Sandy, Montana, who on June 17, 1909, made homestead entry number 171891, has filed notice of intention to make Final Commutation Proof to establish claim to the land above described. . . ."

The notice ran longer, but the rest didn't matter much. Only her name, the dates of when she began the process and when it ended. And most of all, the fact that the U.S. Department of the Interior officially recognized this territory as hers. A proud day for any home-steader, but for a Black woman born in the last years of American slavery this feat amounted to a major historic victory. How had Bertie celebrated? By never tending her land again.

She built a still on her property and produced the finest liquor in the state. All of Montana knew Bertie's Brew. Men, and women, rode down from Canada to take a jug home. You can't simply sell your wares to such travelers and then shut the door. Not if you're a good business-woman. You let them in, offer a meal and some company. Then you charge for all three. That's how you build a prosperous business.

A modest place by the standards of Helena or Butte maybe, but thirteen miles northwest of Big Sandy the Blind Pig had no equal: three outhouses behind the cabin; a corral large enough for six horses to shelter. The still sat alone, farthest from the cabin; if there was a fire—or an explosion—the only thing that would be bothered was the dirt and the wolves. And maybe Bertie if the damn thing blew up while she was tending it. But no one makes her own liquor without incurring a bit of risk. Bertie Brown had made this happen, all of it, and if she felt quite proud, then who could blame her?

"Three eggs?" she asked, repeating Mr. Reed's words to him.

They both held a mug of Bertie's Brew and had been drinking to-gether since about seven o'clock, about the same time Mrs. Reed walked onstage back in town and welcomed all the women and chil-dren and even a few men to her show.

"That's what I said she could offer to the audience as they left. Three eggs per household. That's all I approved."

Bertie sipped at her mug. She'd had as much as Mr. Reed. She wasn't the type of hostess to sip water with her guests. Some might call this foolish, bad business, especially risky for a woman alone, but Ber-tie wasn't alone. That's why she could do it.

"And what do you think Mrs. Reed *actually* gave them?"

Mr. Reed leaned back in his chair. He didn't look vexed. He grinned. "A dozen eggs. Per family. That's my guess. Anything more would be madness."

Bertie raised her mug but didn't sip from it. "If I know Mrs. Reed . . ."

Mr. Reed looked toward the ceiling and laughed softly. "Potatoes. Just this morning she had a wagonful delivered."

"And you didn't guess?" Bertie asked, smiling.

"She told me she was preparing for the winter."

"You don't seem the type to be so easily fooled," Bertie told him.

Mr. Reed looked back down at the table. "I can't help it," he said. "She always gets me."

"I don't think you mind it, if it's her."

"No," Mr. Reed agreed. "I suppose every captain needs his North Star."

To this they both raised their mugs and took a gulp.

"Call the Celestial back in, would you?" Mr. Reed said. "My cards are getting cold."

Bertie's hand wobbled and a bit of her brew spilled on the table. Fiona. That's who he was talking about. Fiona Wong. Celestial was a common slur for the Chinese. A citizen of "the Celestial Empire of China," but in the States the citizens of such an august-sounding nation washed laundry, cooked food, cleared land. What a laugh. A common enough slur that it had turned into a nickname. *Call the Celestial back in.*

Bertie set the mug down so she wouldn't spill any of it. Then she turned in her chair and called out, "Will you come back to the table, Mrs. Wong?"

Mr. Reed had sent his driver with word the day before: *I'm coming to drink and play cards. I'd like to play alone.* "Alone" in this case meant no other men at the bar. Mr. Reed liked to come out and play his favorite card game with Bertie and Fiona, a game called Five Hundred. But it was a shameful bit of fun in the eyes of other men out here. A woman's parlor game. Mr. Reed had to pick the times and places where he could play it. In thirty years of marriage, he'd never even told his wife how much he loved the game. Only Bertie and Fiona knew, and it happened nowhere else but the Blind Pig.

In walked Fiona Wong, the youngest of the three in the room. Short and barrel-shaped. She carried three fresh mugs of Bertie's Brew and set them on the table. She took her seat again, glancing quickly at Bertie, shaking her head to say, *Don't make a fuss.*

"Her name is Mrs. Wong," Bertie said, because Bertie *was* the type to make a fuss if needed. "You know this, Mr. Reed."

His small head wobbled as he looked from Bertie to Fiona. "Isn't that what I said?"

His gaze shifted between the women and, for a moment, he seemed to realize that he sat alone in a cabin thirteen miles away from town. Far enough from his power and influence that he was, finally, stripped to his essence. A little sixty-year-old man whose right ankle often clicked when he walked, because of an old fall off a granary ladder. Bertie Brown was a thin woman in her forties, but he'd seen her wrestle ranchers out her front door, and Fiona Wong was all of twenty-five, but used to tossing full bags of laundry into the back of her wagon and hauling them from town back to the Blind Pig for cleaning. Which is to say he understood, briefly, that these two women could fold him up as easily as a bedsheet, so perhaps he ought to be more thoughtful about the next thing he said.

He watched them and they watched him.

"Shall we play cards?" he asked. "I believe it was your play, Mrs. Wong."

The decision now was Fiona's. The spark of chaos became hers to light. If she reached across the table and throttled this old man, Bertie would only douse the lamp so the deed would be done in the dark. She looked from Mr. Reed to Bertie, then back down at her cards.

"I believe you're correct, Mr. Reed. Let's play."

So they did. And in time the mood returned to something that hovered between friendly and professional. Bertie and Mr. Reed continued to drink hard while Fiona sipped slow. Eventually, round about the time Mrs. Reed and the Busy Bees were singing along to the song playing on the theater organ, almost exactly when Adelaide hurried through the lobby and took Sam to the Grill Cafe, nearly precisely at the moment when Grace Price stopped Finn Kirby to ask him why he'd been so scarce lately, right then the rumble of a car engine played outside the Blind Pig.

"That's a Maxwell," Fiona said to Mr. Reed, peeking out the window through the curtain. "I saw an ad in the paper." She returned to the table, gathering up the cards.

"Brand new," Mr. Reed said, nodding slowly, speaking proudly.

"Expensive," Fiona added, teasing him a bit, knowing a man like Mr. Reed would enjoy such a game.

And he did. The man giggled. Sounding as close to a child as he'd likely done for at least fifty years. He placed his elbows on the table, leaning toward Fiona.

"Would you like a ride?" he asked.

"It's late," Bertie said immediately.

Mr. Reed looked at Bertie quickly, then back to Fiona. "You would both come, of course."

Fiona turned to Bertie, so clearly excited that the decision had already been made.

"Fine, fine," Bertie said. Then, pointing at Mr. Reed, "But you can't drive."

Mr. Reed laughed loudly. "You are *drunk,* Mrs. Brown! My driver does the driving. And while you two are with me, I will sit up front beside him. You ladies will enjoy having the intimacy of the rear seat to yourselves."

Was that some sort of innuendo? By this point, Mr. Reed was in such a state that nearly everything he said felt faintly lecherous. Nevertheless, they were both going. And, though she wouldn't tell anyone else, Bertie planned on bringing her revolver, tucked under her coat. One never can be too careful.

"Come see our horses," Mr. Reed said proudly, proclaiming, not asking. "Out at my stable. Six arrived just this week."

With the decision made, all three rose; two of them needed to place a hand on the backs of their chairs for balance.

A knock at the door and Fiona went to greet the driver.

"I'm here for Mr. Reed," he said.

"You're the driver?" Fiona asked, feeling more at ease already. "You don't look old enough."

He stepped inside, removing his cap so he could tip it.

"I'm young but I've had some experiences," he said.

Mr. Reed clapped for the young man. "He's got a lion's heart. I can tell you that."

Fiona put out her hand and he shook it. "And who are you?"

The young man said, "My name is Joab. Like in the Bible. A man who serves a great king."

33

TWO BOYS, FLEEING ON HORSEBACK, IN THE DEEP NIGHT, THEIR mother bled out before them and their brothers dead in the dark. Joab and Delmus Mudge, riding fast but hardly sure of where their horse headed. Neither Joab nor Delmus had been the one to lead them to Adelaide's cabin. Their mother had been their navigator, in every way. And now she lay dead. Murdered. By a demon. They rode in frenzy, confusion, and chaos, a speck on the endless plains. They had never been so truly lost in all their lives.

Delmus, the older of the two, held the reins, but in all ways Joab was the driver. They rode without speaking for what seemed like an hour, an eon. Their mother, their brothers, were dead. The chill penetrated as deeply as their grief, turning both boys cold from the inside out. They were lost in the night and panicked.

They meant to ride for Rocky Point, a handful of shacks where their mother had been keeping them, up in the Bear Paw Mountains. A wolfer town, that's what people called such places out west. Hideout for rustlers and thieves. Ridiculous to call it a town, five shacks and a barn that tilted to the right. Rocky Point. That's where they meant to go as they fled the horror of what they saw happen to their mother, but in the dark even the mountains disappeared. They might just as easily have galloped off the edge of a coulee, crashed to the bottom and broken their necks.

Eventually—and neither of them could ever say when because they felt as if they'd been riding, running, a lifetime already—Joab raised one hand, catching sight of the faintest flicker to the southwest.

The opera house's pilot light.

They followed it as devoutly as the faithful follow the Lord. By the time they reached town, the boys were barely there, halfway between this world and the Realm Eternal. A pair of ghouls on horseback slumped against one another.

They rode into town when the shop fronts were dark and hardly anywhere remained open. The pilot light burned at the opera house, but the Reeds were most definitely asleep in their large, warm bed next door.

In town, the Bear Paw Cafe advertised itself as "always open," but this proved untrue. Instead, it was George Shibata, another restaurateur, who saw the Mudge boys passing by. He'd been closing up his place, the Grill Cafe, staying late to repair his oven. Then he was locking up the place and walked down the front steps and a horse staggered along carrying two young boys spattered with blood.

Shibata ran to the horse and caught its reins. When he stopped the animal, the two boys fell off the saddle. Even landing on the ground didn't wake them up. Then the horse went down, too. George Shibata considered that they were dead. He was right about the horse. He left the boys where they'd fallen while he went to get Dr. Percy Alkire.

A few would criticize him for this later—saying there could be a heartless quality to the Japanese—but Shibata's conscience remained untroubled. He'd woken Alkire and together they'd carried the boys into the Grill Cafe, warmed them as best they could, and, when the boys woke, fed them. All this while the rest of Big Sandy slept.

Dr. Alkire's specialty lay in animals, not men—he was Big Sandy's veterinarian—but he could see to a wound sure enough. He found none. The blood, it seemed, was not their own. A fact that aroused some suspicion. Nevertheless, Shibata and Alkire tended to the boys until morning and then had them admitted to Worstell's hospital.

This kind of story doesn't happen every day, not even in the wilds of Montana. Soon enough Fred Harnden of the *Bear Paw Mountaineer* arrived at their bedside and asked after their story.

Delmus spoke wildly, of Satan on the plains, but the younger boy, Joab, said his family had been attacked, perhaps by a mountain lion or a wolf pack. Their mother and two older brothers died defending the younger ones, and he hoped the newspaper would record them as heroes. And now Joab and Delmus had no other family. Harnden, tired of making chitchat with Mrs. Reed and the new arrivals at the train station, turned the boys into a story. Not half the town subscribed to the paper, but that half found the tale riveting.

Harnden had aspirations of making the boys into a national story; maybe he could even write a book. But the boys were too modest to sit for photographs. Joab's mother had raised him to put his head down and work, and he said that's all they wanted to do. Joab insisted that this was the only story he wanted to tell, the story of two boys who needed work. Harnden had to suppress the urge to slap the child. How many columns could humility produce? Harnden made a habit of sitting by the boys' bedsides that first week, peppering them for more of their story, but Joab only repeated the most recent events: family attacked, boys orphaned, needing help. And the other one babbled fantasies about monsters.

Harnden's role came to a close when Jack Reed himself reached out to offer the Mudge boys work. He, for one, meant to reward such self-effacement.

Delmus had a harder time than Joab with recovery. He stayed stuck on the wild story of a demon in the night and became fragile, a traumatized hysteric. The death of his family had broken him. Jack Reed gave him work on his ranch. Delmus liked being around the animals, so he became a hand. Nothing too demanding about that.

Joab displayed a different interest. He wanted to remain by Jack Reed's side. Reed flattered himself a father figure to the town, so why not to this orphaned boy as well? He'd just purchased a Maxwell.

"Every road is a Maxwell Road," the advertisements promised. "The Car that Laughs at Hills."

Joab became Reed's driver. This served a special purpose for the boy; in the car he could travel the Badlands much farther than on horseback. Mr. Reed constantly offered others rides in the Maxwell, and this suited Joab just fine. He liked working for the Reeds. What a pleasure not to have to look over one's shoulder for the law, or the relatives of some past victim. Joab liked being legitimate.

But Joab held to a private motive on those drives, too. It can be difficult to express the magnitude of Montana. It isn't vast, it's limitless. And yet he meant to track down a single claim, a lone cabin. Joab might as well try to find a particular crater on the surface of the moon.

But he'd made a promise, a threat: *Mudges never forget*. Maybe his brother had been right. Maybe the Devil did kill their family. If so, Joab would track the beast down and send it back to hell. And the witch who'd summoned it.

34

THE GRILL CAFE'S OWNER, GEORGE SHIBATA, ARRIVED IN CALI-
fornia and followed work east, mostly toiling on the railroads but
quickly figuring out how deadly the labor could be. He hit Havre,
Butte, trying his hand at cooking instead, and ended up in Big Sandy,
a town dominated by a single restaurant, the Bear Paw Cafe. Their
food often went undercooked; their coffee always tasted burnt; the
plates regularly showed faint traces of the last meals served on them.
George Shibata decided he could do better—or, at least, as badly—and
thus the Grill Cafe came to be. And he'd been correct. He did outshine
his competition. Barely. Nearly everyone in town—except maybe the
couple who owned the Bear Paw Cafe—agreed Shibata's Grill Cafe
served marginally better food. But the plates and glasses were cleaner.
To be fair, the man had been trained as an engineer, not a chef. Shibata
just couldn't find such work in America. Or, such work wasn't allowed
for someone like him.

And yet the Grill Cafe and the Bear Paw Cafe had operated at a
standstill. Neither decisively won over the customers in town. If one of
them had been able to serve higher-quality cooking, that might've
done it, but there's no sense in demanding something that will never
come. So imagine Mr. Shibata's surprise when his business soared simply because he'd saved those two boys. People came in to pepper him
with questions, congratulate him on the good deed, and they stayed to
eat their meals.

That's why, after the show at the opera house, the Grill Cafe filled

up. Room for twenty diners, nearly every table taken. Adelaide and
Sam were lucky they'd left early, or else they might have had to join the
line of people along the wall eating from their plates while standing
up. Adelaide and Sam each carried a copy of the *Bear Paw Mountaineer*, given away free—this time—but they went unread because Sam
asked a question first.

"Do you think that lady was right?"

"At the opera house?" she asked. "Mrs. Reed? What part?"

"That we're the wheat, not the chaff."

Adelaide smiled as she squinted at the menu board. Was she going
to need glasses?

"Maybe she meant it, maybe she was just trying to flatter—"

But she stopped talking when she looked at Sam, whose head was
down and whose fingers were laced on the tabletop.

"Why do you ask, Sam?"

Still looking down at his hands, Sam said, "Do you think of yourself as the wheat?"

You had to go up to the counter to make your order, and the line
there continued to grow as more people left the opera house. Adelaide
did feel hungry and had decided she also wanted a beer. But when a
child is thinking seriously, you do well to honor their questions.

"No," Adelaide said. "Most of the time I do not think of myself that
way."

"Why is that, Mrs. Henry?"

And she did not think about where it had gone.

And she did not think about what it might be doing.

And she did not think about—

"I keep secrets," Adelaide said softly, sitting back in her chair.

"So do I," Sam said.

The words came so softly Adelaide hardly heard them. Sam lifted
his eyes to Adelaide from the other side of the table. His young face
suddenly looked tired.

"My mother's secret," Sam offered.

Adelaide sighed. "I know quite a bit about things like that."

Now they were quiet and it felt all right to stay that way. Adelaide wasn't sure if she wanted Sam to share Grace's secret with her. She knew the pain, actual physical pain, it would cause the child to betray the parent. And, of course, by now she cared for Grace immensely. What would be the greater act of compassion, to let the child confess or to quiet Sam so Grace's private concerns remained her own? Though that wasn't quite true, was it? Grace's private concerns were clearly Sam's as well.

"She killed my father," Sam said. Said it so clearly, with such force, that a pair of men at the next table turned fast and then turned away.

Adelaide saw them do it, and saw them secretly listening now.

"A wild horse will do that," Adelaide said. Then she pointed at the men so Sam wouldn't be confused. "I'm sure your daddy tried his best with it."

Instantly the two men became disinterested. They'd been hoping to eavesdrop on gossip, not another boring story of commonplace hardship. They rose from the table and shuffled to the counter to buy more beer.

Adelaide nodded at Sam to indicate they were free to talk again.

"Did you see this happen?" Adelaide asked.

"It was years back," Sam said. "Babies don't have memory."

Adelaide didn't agree, but the child wasn't discussing human development.

"So then how do you know what she did?" Adelaide asked.

"Momma isn't shy about saying it, not when it's just her and me. He was a millstone. *The only work he ever did was how hard he worked to stay in bed.* Those are her words, after a few cups of Bertie's Brew."

"Why are you telling me this, Sam?"

"Because I needed to tell *someone*. And you're the best someone I know."

A touching moment, but Adelaide saw a flash in her mind, that moment when she'd been on Grace's claim, when Bertie took Sam to town to be with Grace as she recovered. When she'd been alone and crept to the second cabin and peeked inside. And there, in the window's reflection, she'd seen—

"Did she ever say where she killed him?" Adelaide asked.

Sam sat up as tall as he could go. "You saw him."

"I saw something," she admitted, looking away to the ceiling to recall the memory. "But then it was gone."

"Sometimes I see him, too," Sam told her.

"Are you scared when that happens?"

Sam looked to the door as it opened.

"Mom's here."

And so she was. Grace Price looking flush from the cold. As she moved toward their table, she slipped off one glove. The glove on her right hand remained on. She'd recovered from the bullet fairly well, but the hand never recovered its color quite the same. The back of the hand showed spiderwebs of veins, and the fingers looked faintly purple and would until the end of time. And Adelaide watched Grace Price feeling shame enough about her wounded hand to hide it, imperfectly, but doing a seemingly perfect job of hiding the fact that she'd murdered her husband.

It wasn't funny of course, but why did it seem so funny right then?

By the time Grace reached the table and sat down, Adelaide felt the tickle in her throat that would become either a cough or a giggle.

"Do you know what Finn Kirby said to me?" Grace asked.

And Adelaide lost it. Of all the sentences she'd expected from Grace, that wasn't even in the top one hundred. She laughed loud enough that it startled Sam, too.

Sam got the giggles next.

Grace sat back in her chair, arms folded, trying to look gruff, but Adelaide took one look at that single gloved hand and lost her composure all over again.

Now Grace just looked confused and then she spied Adelaide's gaze, the glance at her glove, and she slid her hands down to her knees so they were hidden beneath the table.

"Why are you laughing at me, Mrs. Henry?"

Adelaide took a breath, then another. She could see her friend had guessed at the wrong secret but the idea of its exposure hurt her all the same.

"I'm sorry, Mrs. Price," Adelaide said. She placed a hand on her friend's arm and squeezed. "Truly."

Sam went quiet as well, though the child didn't offer apologies. Instead, he glanced at Adelaide, seeming to wonder what she would do with the secret he'd told.

Adelaide looked at the boy directly and hoped he understood her meaning.

I can keep a secret.

Sam settled back into the seat and nodded and said nothing more.

"Finn Kirby said Matthew had an accident on his ride back from your cabin weeks ago."

Now she had Adelaide's full attention.

"He lost the use of his right arm. Finn thinks he was attacked by wolves. Or something larger. He wants to talk with you about that."

Adelaide cleared her throat. "What does Matthew say?"

Grace raised her eyebrows. "Matthew Kirby hasn't spoken a word in more than a month. Somehow, Finn blames you for that, too."

Adelaide considered her options. She might avoid future shows at the opera house. Never come to town again. Grace would be willing to bring her orders to town, and most of the stores were willing to haul them to a claim for a small fee. Maybe she could make that work through this first winter. Then again, Finn Kirby knew where she lived; what would prevent him from riding up to talk with her while she was alone in her cabin? Maybe it would be safer if she spoke with him here, with Grace and Sam to witness it. But then he might say things in front of them that she didn't want said aloud. Which brought her back to secrets and to shame. Thirty-one years of both, nearly thirty-two; her birthday lay days away. There are two kinds of people in this world: those who live with shame, and those who die from it.

Could there be a third kind of person? she wondered. One who overcomes the shame?

"Grace," Adelaide said. "I want to tell you something."

"Did you two order food or is Mr. Shibata especially slow this evening?" Grace asked, looking over her shoulder toward the counter. The line had at least died down.

Adelaide slipped her hand under the table and grabbed her friend's gloved hand.

Grace recoiled at the touch but Adelaide held firm until their eyes met.

Adelaide said, "I didn't come to Montana alone."

35

Prairie dogs sound like birds.
Squeaking and yipping instead of chirping, a sound like
gnats biting the ears.
And too fast to catch. Mountain cottontail just as
tough to grab hold of.
Somehow they're even faster than the prairie dogs.

Hunger isn't the same as appetite.
The first could be controlled, the second had never been satisfied.
Until now.
It crept. It hid. It pounced. It flew.
It was free.

The only things it caught were those two horses in the night.
There were boys riding on them, ones who tried to hurt—her.
Don't think that name. Don't think that name.
Don't think that name.

Think of hunger instead. The more time spent out of the cage,
the stronger the hunger.
Prairie dogs were too fast, and snakes were too fast, and rabbits
were too fast.
But horses. Horses could be caught. Devoured.

It spread its arms and met the wind.
The wind made it light; the wind gave its embrace.
There were only two animals it had ever killed,
horses and humans.
Tonight, it would take whichever it found first.

36

NEW MAN GETS THE WORST TASK. AN OLD RULE AND THERE WAS no point in arguing. Not even if that means you're fifteen years old and left alone to watch a dozen horses overnight.

Delmus Mudge wouldn't have tried to get out of the job even if he could. He wasn't like Joab, who was so much like their mother, the kind who could see three opportunities ahead and position themselves to enjoy them all. Delmus did the work. That's always how he'd been. And in the past, there had been value in such a role. Joab was the planner, and their eldest brother, Edward, had charisma. The second eldest, Jabez, had a way with violence; he'd been the wolf their mother sent when it came time to do the worst. And then came Delmus.

Poor is he who works with a negligent hand, but the hand of the diligent makes rich.

His mother used to whisper this to Delmus whenever he admitted envy about the attributes of his brothers. Think of himself as the *hand of the diligent* and he would always know his purpose within the family. Who picked their next pigeon each time they needed to resupply? Who had the patience to watch and assure the others that this person or that family were safe to pluck? And who erased all signs that the Mudges had ever been there? The hand of the diligent, Delmus Mudge.

She always knew how to make her son feel better.

But now he sat in the stable of Jack and Jerrine Reed and he couldn't smell the horses who'd been put up for the night because days ago, weeks ago, he sank his nose in a can of Havre Special Brew and, as far as he could remember, hadn't stopped inhaling it since. He could buy a whole case for a few dollars. In fact, he'd done exactly that as soon as he'd been told he would be staying the night at the Reeds' stable. He hid it among the square bales up in the loft.

The Mudges hadn't been a family for drinking. Their mother taught them how easily a ruse could fail if you were even just a little drunk. But what did that matter now? All her lessons, all the ways the Mudges felt invulnerable, undefeatable, but today there were only two left and they weren't together very often anymore. And whose fault was that?

Had it been his job as the hand of the diligent to pick out their next target on the train? Yes. He'd picked the Negro woman because she rode alone; and he'd watched her make multiple visits to the luggage car to check on her steamer trunk, so focused on it that something of value must've been kept inside; and who would notice if she disappeared? They'd erased people of much greater value.

He sat at the edge of the loft, looking down on the horses, listening to them snort or snore, opening another Special Brew and remembering how lucky he felt when it turned out they'd be riding together in Mr. Olsen's wagon. No need to ask around town about where the Negro woman's claim lay, the kind of thing someone might remember as strange. Instead, they'd learn where her claim was when Mr. Olsen dropped her off and, at their leisure, stop by for a visit. One woman against five? It was meant to be the easiest hustle of their lives. But it didn't turn out that way.

And whose fault was that?

He fell asleep. Or passed out. At a certain point in a drinker's life, these become one and the same. He woke because one of the horses blew out air, a loud exhale.

No, not one of them, *all* of them.

Even deeply drunk he understood something was happening. He opened his eyes, sat up in the loft, and looked down at the stalls where *something* crept inside.

It could have been a cougar or a gray wolf or even a grizzly bear. It *could* have been any one of those predators. But it wasn't. Delmus knew this instantly. Even in the near dark. You don't forget the sight of the beast that slayed your mother.

If he'd had a gun nearby, he would've drawn it. But the only weapon in the stable—a Winchester Model 1903—was kept in the tack room. Far from this loft where he'd hidden away to drink.

It's hard to say what, exactly, Delmus Mudge meant to do as he got to his feet. He wasn't thinking. Not quickly, not wisely. Or else he'd have scrambled behind the hay and hid. Instead, he tried to climb down; in his sloshy brain he actually thought he might slip over to the tack room for that rifle. Instead, he fell out of the loft and landed at the bottom of the ladder. He lay there huffing from the surprise although he was too drunk to feel the pain. He'd thrown his arms out to stop the fall, and the jolt ran up his left arm and cracked his collarbone.

The demon had been sniffing at the door of a stall, the horse inside already backing away, holding his head high and snorting. But it turned when Delmus landed.

Delmus tried to scramble back up the ladder, but heard the collarbone grinding—a sound more than a feeling—and he collapsed again. He could only rise to his knees as the demon approached.

It smelled of sudden death. He couldn't make out its face yet, it wasn't quite that near, but it salivated as it approached. The droplets so hot they hissed as they landed.

"You took them," he mumbled. "But I'm not ready to go."

Could you plead with a demon? Reason with it? Or, better yet, might he ask God for protection? Fifteen years of crime—he'd been born into the life—but what better time than now to speak with God?

"Give me another chance," he whispered. "Spare me. Spare me . . . and I will do better than I have done."

Delmus closed his eyes because he felt he would lose his way if he had to stare at the Devil as he begged a favor from the Lord.

"I will make it right for all who we have wronged," he said, a little louder now. "I will be the *hand of the diligent* on behalf of those we have killed. Their secret graves will no longer stay secret."

He paused, his throat catching, as he felt *its* breath against his skin.

"I will tell what I have been taught to never reveal. Even if it lands me in the prison cell, even if it shames my family's memory. I will tell it all true."

And with that, the hot breath abated. As if it had backed away.

The stable doors crashed and cracked. The horses squealed and screamed with terrible fear. Delmus listened but he kept his eyes closed in prayer.

"I swear!" he shouted.

Now there came a horrific crashing. The horses were so loud they drowned out every thought Delmus had in his head. But he kept speaking. Shouting.

"I swear! I swear!"

And the stable returned to absolute silence. When he opened his eyes, every stall sat empty. Every door had been thrashed and torn.

All the horses were gone.

He heard them outside, their hooves on the hard ground. Fleeing. Being pursued. But he had not been killed. Delmus had been spared.

He got to his feet though this was difficult. His fear had sobered him, which meant he now felt the pain of his collarbone. The bone grinding against bone as he used the ladder to pull himself up. He staggered out of the stable. He stood in the freezing winds and felt nothing, no cold. He was cloaked in forgiveness. Or boiling with pain. It could be either. It could be both.

Then he saw the lights in the distance and watched as the Maxwell arrived. His brother Joab sat at the wheel and, beside him, their employer, Jack Reed.

In the backseat there were two women—a Negro and a Chinese woman, neither of whom Delmus had ever met.

The car came to a stop where the fence had been smashed through. The sounds of the horses—their hooves—played out in the darkness, but not one of them could be seen. Each one might as well be a spirit already. The stable sat empty, the stalls destroyed, and Delmus Mudge waved to them with his good arm, then fell forward on his face, passed out.

Jack Reed and Joab climbed out of the Maxwell. The man and the boy looked at Delmus, then at each other.

In the backseat, Bertie and Fiona remained quiet, though Bertie did slip her hand around the revolver. Moments like this, one never knew where shock and anger might be redirected.

Joab said, "My brother hasn't been well since our family died."

Jack Reed climbed back into the Maxwell and slapped the door so Joab would climb in, too. "Let's try and salvage my horses!" Mr. Reed shouted.

But Joab had already taken three steps toward the figure on the ground, one for each family member he'd already lost.

Joab turned back. In the headlights of the car, he barely looked twelve.

"My brother ..." he began, but said no more. He didn't dismiss Mr. Reed's command either, but he didn't run to Delmus's side. Joab appeared caught between the two choices.

Fiona leaned forward. Bertie tried to pull her back, keep her quiet, but Fiona pulled away.

"Are you going to leave that boy lying out in the cold? He'll die."

Jack Reed turned. "He should have died defending my property from poachers."

Fiona said, "Is he really Joab's brother? If you abandon him, how will you ever trust your driver again? If you did that to me, I'd stab you the first time you turned away."

Bertie slid the revolver out of her pocket now.

Would she have to shoot this rich white man? Would there be enough time to climb into the front seat and drive the car away before the young man returned to the Maxwell? Probably not, as Bertie had never driven a car before. Which meant she'd have to gun Joab down, too. Then she and Fiona would drive this thing—as best they could— back to the Blind Pig, pack only what they needed most, ride north to the border and over it. In Canada their only recourse would be to find their friend, a Métis trader named Clement Cardinal, who might ferry them even farther north where they might live out their days.

With a single deep breath, Bertie accepted this fate and raised the revolver from her lap.

"You make a point," Jack Reed said. "And I am committed to *Joab's* salvation."

Bertie waited, revolver at the ready.

"Oh, hell," Jack Reed muttered.

He opened the door of the Maxwell and stepped outside.

She would not have to kill him.

Bertie Brown's relief filled the car like birdsong. She and Fiona would not have to flee. She returned the revolver to her pocket. Fiona took Bertie's free hand. The warmth of her touch nearly made Bertie sob.

"I had to say something," Fiona whispered. "Don't be mad at me."

Bertie almost leaned in to kiss her, but Jack Reed and Joab were too close to be at ease. Instead, she gazed at Fiona and squeezed her hand.

"Mad at you?" she asked. "No. That's not what I feel."

37

A HOME IS NEVER FINISHED, IT'S ONLY SAVED FROM DECAY. THAT had been true at the farmhouse in California and only proved more so out here. Maybe the most pressing concern was the wind. Keeping it out, or at least making it tougher for the weather to slip in. Which meant stuffing newspaper between the boards as insulation. This wasn't something done once but regularly as the cold turned the paper brittle or, even more often, simply tore it all away. So it proved a special benefit that Mrs. Reed and the Busy Bees were giving out copies of the *Bear Paw Mountaineer* last night at the opera house. A few people had left theirs at the Grill Cafe, and Adelaide had snatched them up on her way out.

Adelaide had arrived home late, shivering not from the cold but what she'd told Grace and Sam. The truth. That's all it had been. The complete truth.

But Grace hadn't believed it.

No, that's not the right way to explain her friend's reaction. Over their late meal, Grace tried hard to understand the truth, but kept stumbling over it. *There's no such thing as demons, not really.* Grace said this more than once.

And when they separated—Grace and Sam staying in town just a little longer, hoping to make an appointment with Mrs. Reed— Adelaide knew that only the child had listened, only the child understood.

And she did not think about where *it* had gone.

And she did not think about what *it* might be doing.

And she did not think about—

When she woke the next morning, she boiled a pot of water and made tea and read the newspaper and, once done, tore the paper into strips she could tuck into the boards of the home. The subscription might be worth it if only for this use.

It was while she was down on her knees doing this work that the horses arrived outside. Two horses, so she knew it wasn't Grace and Sam, who only ever rode together. Which meant she'd already retrieved her rifle when the knock came at the door.

Adelaide didn't open the door, nor did she peek out the window. Instead, she aimed at what she guessed would be the gut level of nearly any man and said, "State your business."

A snort came afterward, an incredulous laugh.

"I am here to save you from a *raggedy* hairdo."

Adelaide lowered the rifle and opened the door. Bertie and Fiona. Adelaide said, "Took your ass long enough."

ADELAIDE KEPT HAVING TO refrain from stroking Bertie Brown's ankles.

It had become a habit for Adelaide when she sat between her mother's legs, and now more than once she caught her hand right before she touched Bertie Brown's skin. Eleanor Henry had been a small woman, slight, her ankles so thin that Adelaide could loop her thumb and pointer finger around them once she'd grown up. But when she'd been little there was a game she enjoyed, running her fingers over Eleanor's feet, knowing the slightest touch tickled.

This had its bad results at times, of course. Her mother might rap a knuckle on the top of her scalp, and she wouldn't be gentle about it either. Or the tickle might cause her to pull the comb too tough and little Adelaide would yelp and cry. Adelaide wasn't tender headed, at least she didn't think so. It was just that her mother put too much muscle into her work. On this they would always disagree. Meanwhile, if he wasn't out working, Glenville would be over there, reading to them.

You must go back with me to the autumn of 1827.

Now, try as she might, Adelaide forgot herself and her hand ran down Bertie's leg and rested softly on Bertie's gum rubber boot and it was only the feel that reminded her of where and when she was.

Adelaide's eyes returned to focus, back from her sense memories of the past, and she saw her hand stroking Bertie's boot and she lifted it, embarrassed, and when she looked up she saw Fiona Wong watching her closely from the great chair.

The only person who wasn't aware was Bertie, whose boots were too heavy to feel the touch, and who'd become lost in the work she was doing.

"I missed this," she said softly as she rubbed a finger along Adelaide's scalp.

Now Fiona looked away from Adelaide and up to Bertie; for the briefest moment her face sank. Only Adelaide saw this. To keep her hands from wandering again, she reached for the can of pressing oil Bertie had brought with her. It was balanced, expertly, on Bertie's left knee.

Adelaide read the front, out loud. "'Poro Pressing Oil. Made only by Mrs. Annie Turnbo Malone.'"

"That's how you know I'm using the good stuff," Bertie said with a soft laugh. "And believe me, you needed it." She patted Adelaide's neck lightly.

Fiona rose from the great chair, practically leapt from it. "I'm going to be late, Bertie."

Bertie looked up, hardly moving. Maybe there was the slightest shift in her posture, scooting herself an inch or two farther back from Adelaide.

"Look at me, Fiona," Bertie said. "Look at me."

But Fiona had already pulled on her coat.

"I'm nearly done," Bertie said softly.

Fiona slipped the buttons on her coat through the loops.

"And then we'll go to town together," Bertie added, sounding soothing.

Fiona nodded quietly but didn't remove her coat. Instead, she stood there, watching, as Bertie styled Adelaide's hair back to the way it had been. But this was a misstatement. Adelaide's hair had turned so dry it started looking like a straw hat that's been battered by the elements. She'd been keeping it under a scarf but doing little more to protect it. After Bertie Brown's attention, her hair glowed like a crown.

Adelaide rose and looked at herself in the small mirror she'd hung by her bed.

"Yes," she whispered. *"Yes."*

Meanwhile, Bertie rose and quickly packed away her life-saving supplies. She threw on her coat and Fiona yanked the cabin's door open. The two women didn't speak at all. The horses snorted outside, the wind blew and grumbled.

"You're going to town?" Adelaide called to them. She looked away from the mirror, so happy with her hair she felt the whole world had become brighter. She missed any signs of tension between the two women.

"Can I come?" she chirped.

38

IS IT POSSIBLE ADELAIDE HADN'T BEEN TO TOWN EVEN ONCE during the daytime in all these months? It had been daylight on the day she arrived, but other than that? She'd returned to town at night to attend shows at the opera house, but as she rode into town now, a few paces behind Bertie and Fiona, she marveled at how *small* this place seemed.

One road, twelve shops, one hotel, two restaurants.

She'd been used to even less back in Lucerne Valley. There, the nearest "town" was a general store. But this place shrank under the canopy of these skies. A handful of dice left on a large rug.

But if that's how small the town seemed, then what did that say about her cabin?

Adelaide laughed at herself as Bertie and Fiona reached the Gregson Springs Hotel and tied their horses up.

Down the road a crowd of thirty or forty people cheered. The only time that many people gathered was when the trains arrived or for a show at the opera house, so Adelaide had to see what could possibly compete. Bertie and Fiona did not seem interested, though. They walked into the Gregson Springs without even a glance toward the commotion. Adelaide was intrigued. She rode Obadiah closer.

To find Mrs. Jerrine Reed dressed in a black Arabian Lamb Cloth coat that probably cost as much as Adelaide had paid for her horse. Her bluebird pin had been affixed to the lapel of the coat. The Reed family lived right here in town. A home built beside the opera house, as a rectory sits beside its church.

Behind Mrs. Reed stood a tall, meek woman. Thin and hunched forward and wearing a coat that was wrong for the season, but likely all she could afford. She shivered, but whether she felt cold or nervous in front of the crowd it was difficult for Adelaide to decide.

"And that's why," Mrs. Reed continued, "I'm so *proud* to see so many of you here today. And I know Mrs. Sterling and her son Melvin are pleased as well. Isn't that right?"

Mrs. Reed stepped aside, only one step, and Mrs. Sterling leaned forward, tipped her head, and muttered, "Yes, ma'am. So pleased."

Mrs. Reed pivoted back to her place at the center of the audience's attention and applauded, though the sound was muted because of her kidskin gloves. The crowd joined in, Adelaide as much as anyone. A woman starting her own business out here? Adelaide, in her way, felt she was doing much the same.

And just for a moment she felt the flicker of something warm against the back of her neck. A question. *Where is it?* A fear. *What is it doing?*

But she flicked it away like a troublesome horsefly.

"As I mentioned at the opera house," Mrs. Reed said, "the Busy Bees are encouraging all of you that can afford it to bring your soiled fabrics to Mrs. Sterling and her son. I can tell you that every stitch of fabric from our private residence and from the opera house will be taken down the street and deposited with the Sterlings from now on."

As soon as these words were spoken, the rattle of doors called everyone's attention down the street, to the Gregson Springs Hotel, where Fiona and Bertie carried large sacks toward their horses.

"We applaud industry," Mrs. Reed said as she watched Fiona and Bertie.

The crowd turned their gaze to match hers.

And that meant Adelaide turned to watch them, too.

"The promise of this great country is that all of us may find our fortunes through the blessing of freedom this nation promises. But let us all remember that Mrs. Sterling, through no fault of her own, has been left a widow with a son to care for. And that her history with us in this town stretches back more than a decade."

Fiona and Bertie tied the sacks to their horses' saddles, securing them tightly with the ease that comes from experience.

Mrs. Reed returned her gaze to the crowd, and almost all of them turned back to her. A handful, just a few, let their eyes linger on the pair of women, Adelaide's friends.

"Now, some of you live farther out and only visit town occasionally. If, for whatever reason, you are forced to spend the night, you often take a room at the Gregson Springs Hotel. A very fine establishment."

Bertie and Fiona untied their horses and climbed back into their saddles.

"Next time you pay for a room," Mrs. Reed said, "take a moment to inquire about where they have their sheets and pillowcases laundered. Ask *who* is washing the linens *you* will be sleeping on."

Adelaide watched her friends riding off, back toward their home, hauling the sacks filled with the hotel's dirty linens, which would be cleaned by Fiona Wong in a petroleum solvent and then strung up to dry inside the cabin for a day.

Bertie would close the Blind Pig for business while the linens dried, as they would be highly flammable and her customers, many of them smokers, tended to forget this fact. One wall of the Blind Pig had to be rebuilt because of a fire the year before.

"And if, by chance," Mrs. Reed continued, "they aren't supporting Mrs. Sterling and her son Melvin, consider asking them *why*. Let them know how much it would mean to you if one of our own were to enjoy their business. After all, that's how we thrive, by looking out for one another."

With that, Mrs. Reed turned and clapped Mrs. Sterling on the arm. The narrow woman scurried to the door and held it open. Mrs. Reed waved the townspeople into the open doorway.

"Come and see!" Mrs. Reed shouted. "The town's first power laundry! A wonderful day for women's progress."

Adelaide felt tugged in two directions. She knew she ought to ride off with Bertie and Fiona, but, truth be told, she'd never seen a power laundry before. She did want to know what Mrs. Sterling would be using. Was there a machine for washing the clothes? Was it loud? How much could it wash at one time? Was it wrong to be curious?

Adelaide tied Obadiah up and joined the line of townspeople waiting to walk inside. Wasn't she a townsperson? Strange how this suddenly felt like a test.

As others filed out, the line moved forward, and Adelaide couldn't stop herself from trembling. Mrs. Reed had remained at the door, holding it for all. Mrs. Reed smiled at each person and patted them gently on the shoulder as they went in. As Adelaide stepped closer, she tried to decide what she should do if Mrs. Reed barred her entry.

But when she reached the door, Mrs. Reed placed a hand on her elbow (Adelaide was too tall for Mrs. Reed to reach her shoulder comfortably) and said, "It's good to see you. Mrs. Henry, isn't it? I hope you'll visit town more often."

And that was it.

It would be nice to imagine Adelaide storming out of the store, climbing onto Obadiah, and galloping out of town, catching up with Bertie and Fiona and never looking back. But the human animal is a social animal; a lifetime of being treated like an outsider may make a person yearn to finally be let in.

So that's what happened.

Mrs. Reed held the door and Adelaide walked in.

After Adelaide left the power laundry, she spent the rest of the day in town and, to her own constant surprise, every door was opened and every pleasant greeting seemed sincere.

39

"WE'VE GOT WOLFERS."

Mr. Reed said the words from the backseat of the Maxwell, and from the front Joab Mudge called out, "Yes, sir."

They were returning from Reed's barn. In the daylight the damage only appeared more severe. The horses were still just as gone. Delmus now lay in Worstell's hospital, taking up a bed paid for by the Reeds. The "hospital" was just another storefront in town, but it was better than if they'd laid him out to recover in the tack room of the stable.

"A wolfer is worse than a wolf pack," Mr. Reed said. "Those beasts are merely trying to survive."

"Yes, sir."

Joab continued to drive them back toward town. He hadn't been driving the Maxwell but so long and the manual transmission was a novelty. He hadn't yet learned how to have a conversation and drive the car. But it didn't matter, Mr. Reed wasn't the type to do much listening.

"We'll go directly to McNamara & Marlow, right now." He leaned closer to confide in Joab. "I believe Mrs. Reed is having a woman over tonight, she often likes to have a little privacy when they visit. Some ladies speak more freely when men aren't listening."

McNamara & Marlow. The largest general store in Big Sandy. They sold lumber and wool underwear for men, women, and children; furniture and furs. Its founders, McNamara and Marlow, were also Mr. Reed's closest friends. Nearly as wealthy and not talkative at all. One quality shared by the Reeds, mister and missus, was the pleasure they took in an audience.

The Maxwell rattled and roared as it rolled down Main Street. Horses skittered or neighed as the beast rolled past. People who were out on the street stopped to openly stare. In the backseat Mr. Reed leaned forward slightly so his face could be seen through the passenger window, though he pretended he was only adjusting his hat.

Joab parked and Mr. Reed climbed out. He'd taught Joab he should never open the back door for him. That kind of gesture gave off the airs of a king, and this wasn't the land of kings, was it? Mr. Reed opened his own doors.

"Keep the car running," he said as he came around to Joab's window.

"Yes, sir."

And Mr. Reed disappeared inside the general store.

Joab looked back down the street. His brother lay in bed not twenty yards from here. He should go inside and pay a visit, shouldn't he? Yes. He should. But he didn't want to.

When he'd seen Delmus collapsed on the cold ground the night before, he hadn't felt concern. Instead, he'd stiffened with rage. Was this the wrong reaction? Well, fine, but it's how he felt. When he'd knelt by his brother, he'd smelled the liquor. His older brother's pants had been wet with either piss or beer. Both, most likely.

Here's the worse truth: if Mr. Reed had told him to leave Delmus there and go off to find those horses, he would only have asked if he could first drag his brother back inside the stable. He would've left him there rather than refuse their benefactor. And why? Because their mother had taught them only one thing above all: do *whatever* you must to survive.

But what if to survive, one had to betray family?

Thankfully, he hadn't been forced to answer the question and Mr. Reed showed more concern for Delmus than Joab would've guessed he could. Which, of course, only deepened his loyalty to the man. Their mother taught them to believe in no one outside the family unit, but then here was this man, nearly a stranger, who chose to rescue his brother.

So no, Joab wouldn't go check on Delmus now, because Delmus had only made it to that hospital bed thanks to the generosity of Mr. Reed. Joab had agreed to repay the cost of the care from his own salary, but this didn't diminish the kindness of the act, not in Joab's eyes. If Mr. Reed hadn't demanded repayment, it would've marked him as soft, a sucker, in Joab's mind.

All this consideration occurred in the time it took for Mr. Reed to step inside and return again with two more men, McNamara and Marlow themselves. The pair carried heavy sacks, one apiece. Both men wore Burberry trench coats, which had the unnerving effect of making them look like a pair of British officers even though the men had come from no farther than the Dakotas. Nevertheless, those coats looked to keep them warmer than if Joab were wearing every single piece of clothing he owned, all at once.

The three men entered the back of the Maxwell. A tight ride. They whispered to one another and Joab felt the back of his neck go hot. What was it that suddenly made him want to prove his value? Back to his mother's lessons. *Do whatever you must to survive.* If he'd been impressing one wealthy man with his work ethic and loyalty, why not impress two more?

Joab spoke but didn't even presume to turn back to them as he did so.

"You talked about wolfers, sir?"

All three men went quiet. "What about them?" Mr. Reed asked.

"I have an idea," he began, but the words caught in his throat. He tried again. "I have an idea of where they might be hiding."

He thought they'd clap his shoulders and yip with glee, but these weren't children. These were grown men.

"Where would that be?" is all Mr. Reed said.

Here was the moment when Joab might prove himself or damn himself. What to do with the knowledge he held?

"Rocky Point," Joab said. "It's a wolfer town. Up in the mountains."

Long silence. So long that Joab felt the sudden fear one of these men would draw a pistol and shoot him in the back of the head.

How did he know about Rocky Point? His mother had brought him there. Him and his brothers. When they'd stolen horses from a dance, this is where they took them and sold them across the border in Canada, where even the brand of a local rancher meant less than nothing. He knew where the wolfer town lay because he was a wolfer. Joab didn't share that part with the wealthy men in the back seat.

"Which mountains?" One of the other men asked this.

"Bear Paw Mountains, sir."

"That near?" Mr. Reed asked with a shout.

"Yes, sir."

Another silence. Joab listened to his heart, in case these would be the last moments when he heard it beating.

"And how do you know of it?" McNamara asked. He had a deep voice, the deepest Joab had ever heard.

"They're the ones," Joab began, stammering, unsure of what answer would save him from damning himself. "They're the ones who killed my momma and big brothers. We saw them riding off in that direction, at great speed. Nowhere but the mountains for them to hide."

"Didn't you tell that journalist that it was animals who killed your kin?" asked McNamara, that deep voice causing Joab to shiver.

Joab remained quiet for a short while. "They told Delmus and I to lie. Blame the wild rather than them. But I don't want to lie any longer."

Did that work?

Mr. Reed moved in the back seat. He leaned forward, close enough that Joab felt the next words right against his ear.

"Take us there. And let's find the ones that stole my horses, and murdered your family."

Joab, who had turned thirteen only four days ago, an event that went unremarked upon, nodded and drove the car down Main Street.

And it was at that moment when Joab drove right by the tall Negro woman who was tying up a horse outside the Grill Cafe. It was *her*, the woman who'd unleashed the demon that slayed his family three weeks ago.

Three weeks.

Was that all?

Three hundred years, that's how long it felt.

He almost stopped the Maxwell right there, but saved himself from making that mistake. He'd just told these men it was wolfers who murdered his kin. How would it look if he stopped the car right now and went after a lone woman on the street? One job at a time. Get them out to the wolfer town and see about Mr. Reed's horses.

And it was the sight of her horse, a raggedy old thing, that gave him an idea of how he'd track her down. An expense like that most likely came via a loan. Three men in town might contract for such a purchase. They would have her name and the coordinates of her claim.

One of those men wouldn't do business with a Negro, so just two men to check with. And if he told them his inquiries were made on behalf of Mr. Reed, there would be no resistance.

He would find her and live up to the promise he made to her that night.

Mudges never forget.

40

THEY DIDN'T SPEAK ONCE, THE WHOLE RIDE BACK TO THE BLIND
Pig. The sacks of laundry seemed heavier now than any time they'd
hauled them before. The size of that crowd out front of the power
laundry, impossible to unsee it. The wind blew hard and cold but they
did not hurry home. The town receded behind them and Adelaide
Henry stayed back there.

Bertie had built the Blind Pig twice already. Once it had to be re-
done because of a fire, and the second time she expanded the cabin,
adding an extra room when she met Fiona Wong.

They tied the horses up in the corral and hauled the laundry back
to their home. They found a ten-pound sack sitting by the front door.
Bertie opened it, malted barley inside. Not a gift, but a delivery. She
knew who'd left it because he'd left his mark, a small symbol on the
side of the sack. A white figure eight, turned on its side.

Clement Cardinal, the Métis trader, had been here, delivering the
malt she needed for her brew. He hadn't stayed. No doubt he had many
more deliveries to make. On any other day she would've been sad to
miss him. She and Fiona enjoyed his company. But today their mood
felt too sour to entertain. She brought the sack inside, then got back to
hauling the laundry with Fiona.

Once inside, Bertie started a fire on the stove, while Fiona carried
each sack into her workroom. Turpentine spirits, benzene, these were
the solvents of the past. Fiona cleaned her linens strictly with kerosene, as was the modern way.

She opened each sack and dropped all the linens out onto the floor. Then she separated them according to their purpose: bed linens, table linens, napkins, and runners. The Gregson Hotel didn't have their workers' uniforms cleaned for them, preferring to have each man or woman wash those clothes themselves.

Fiona had four large seamless copper buckets stacked in a corner. She set each one out on the floor. The seamless copper prevented stains on the linens; the brass rivets on other copper buckets were the reason yellow stains might appear. And the rivets sometimes caught on the fabric, causing tears. The Gregson had never seen a tear or a stain on a single item she'd cleaned. But would that matter?

She didn't realize she'd gone down on her knees until Bertie walked into the room and knelt beside her. She didn't realize she'd begun crying until Bertie pressed her lips to Fiona's face and kissed her wet cheeks.

Bertie stood and pulled Fiona up as well. She led Fiona out of the wash room and back into the parlor. In the kitchen Bertie had already set a pot of water to boil. It would take nearly thirty minutes for the water to grow warm enough to be of use. Bertie pulled Fiona along to the other room, their bedroom, and drew her in.

They chose this bed together. Bought it in Billings and brought it back on a wagon. Oak with brass accents and big enough for two. Bertie pulled back the knitted counterpane. Then she undressed Fiona.

Older than Fiona by more than a decade, Bertie understood the pleasures of paying attention to the one you love. She started at the bottom, undoing the buttons of Fiona's split skirt and letting it drop to the floor with a soft, plump pop. Beneath the split skirt Fiona wore French Open Drawers; neither Bertie nor Fiona had ever worn a corset in her life.

These French Drawers were an indulgence, white cotton batiste and lace with a pink drawstring ribbon at the waist; not as practical as the split skirt or almost any of the other clothes they owned. But Bertie liked seeing Fiona out in the world, hauling laundry from the hotel or out at the opera or just feeding the horses, and for no one else in the world to know she wore such a luxury. And the fact that Bertie had provided them to Fiona, well, that was its own source of pride.

"I'm cold," Fiona whispered, her bottom half naked while her upper half remained clothed.

Bertie kissed one thigh, from the knee to the top of the hip.

"Better?" Bertie asked.

"Not yet," Fiona said.

Bertie moved to the other thigh, and now she kissed the upper thigh and up toward Fiona's waist.

"Better?" Bertie asked.

"Not yet," Fiona whispered.

Bertie rose and moved Fiona onto their bed. Fiona inched her way backward, until her head rested, partially upright, against the headboard. Then Bertie climbed onto the mattress and crawled beneath the counterpane. Fiona reached down and pulled the counterpane until Bertie could no longer be seen. She lifted the bedspread and peeked into the darkness there. Her breathing slowed and the feelings she'd carried with her since they left town were set down, put away, at least for now.

Fiona opened her legs wider.

She looked down at Bertie, who, at this point, could no longer ask questions because her tongue was doing other things.

"That's better," Fiona whispered.

41

After making a meal of those horses,
After a supper of blood,
Rest.
Even a demon dreams.

In one, its arms and legs fall off and
it's flat in the dirt inside the barn
a chain around the throat that
squeezes tighter and tighter until the end of time.

In another, the girl—don't think that name,
don't think that name—
the girl arrives at night, footsteps outside the barn;
And then her voice, I'm here.
You want me to read to you or sing?
The second dream hurts worse than the first.
Because the second is dream and *memory.*

Awake again.
In the cold; in the night.
No more rest. No more sleep. Alone.
Don't think that name. Don't think that name.
Don't think that name.

42

ADELAIDE HENRY RODE OUT FROM TOWN TOWARD HER HOME.

Didn't take long to realize she'd been followed.

"Telling tales."

It wasn't one of the townsfolk.

"Telling secrets."

Adelaide rode as quickly as Obadiah could go, but the old horse couldn't go but so fast. She leaned back in the saddle even though he trotted across flat ground. She only felt like she was going downhill.

"Hello, Eleanor," Adelaide said.

When she looked to her right, she found her mother walking there. On foot and yet she kept pace with the animal Adelaide rode.

"That's how you address me now?" her mother said.

"I'm grown," Adelaide asserted, but who believed it? Sure didn't sound like Adelaide did.

Eleanor choked or laughed, hard to tell the difference because of the way the sound traveled out of the tear in her throat.

"What kind of grown woman forgets her responsibilities?"

"Not my responsibility," Adelaide snapped back.

"Then whose?" the spirit hissed.

Adelaide slumped in her saddle.

"Let someone else take it up," she begged. "I never wanted it."

Eleanor didn't argue this point. How could she? Or perhaps the spirit had been thinking the same thing about her own existence.

"Why don't I ever see Daddy?" Adelaide asked.

Eleanor Henry clucked softly. "Him you still address with respect."

"I didn't know him like I know you," Adelaide said. "Talking to you is like talking to myself."

"One and the same," Eleanor whispered.

They moved together across the plains. How the wind howled, but Adelaide hardly heard it. It was like a conversation happening in another room. Her mother's voice rang louder.

"It got loose from us one time," Eleanor told her. "Killed cattle, killed sheep. We were lucky that's all it killed. News spread all over about something savage and wild in the Valley, and, sure, we played right along. Your daddy went hunting with the other men. They captured a mountain lion. But did anyone believe that little thing caused so much loss? No. Not really. Suspicions spread between every farm. Lotta ugly feelings all around. If it had happened again, people might've come looking for us. Who knows? But we fixed the problem, best we could. Lashed that demon with a heavier chain. Never got free again."

Obadiah didn't snort or whinny at the sight of Eleanor, nor at the sound of her voice. He only trotted forward and this was how Adelaide knew Eleanor haunted her alone.

"That's why I'm warning you," Eleanor said. "Whatever damage the demon does, they'll come for you. And they will repay you a hundred times."

"I'm not scared of them," Adelaide insisted, sounding more like a stubborn child.

"You should be."

43

THE TRIP TO ROCKY POINT TOOK LONGER THAN EXPECTED. THE Maxwell had more trouble with the hills than advertised, but when Joab drove slower they were fine. While Joab maneuvered the car, the trio in the back talked as if they were at the Blind Pig, trading drinks and talk of business. All three men were armed with pistols but Joab felt sure he was the only one who'd shot anyone or anything. McNamara and Marlow both still carried those sacks in their laps. What was inside? Joab wondered.

"You don't understand how bad it's becoming," McNamara shouted to Reed as they rode.

Marlow added, "The catalogs will kill us, I guarantee!"

Mr. Reed sat between the pair. It was the safest placement in the vehicle and he knew that. It wasn't uncommon for autos to flip.

"What we need," McNamara said, "is a campaign to keep the shoppers local."

"Buy from people you trust," Marlow tried. "Buy from people you know."

"Exactly that," McNamara said. "Support local business, not some scoundrel with a warehouse out in the state of Washington."

"Washington!" Marlow shouted with disbelief.

"They charge so much less," Mr. Reed said to the men. "And ship it right here into town. I see people lining up at the post to pick up their packages."

"It's vexing," McNamara agreed.

Marlow said, "How damn far is this wolfer town?"

Joab bounced in the driver's seat. He did not respond to the question because it wasn't a question. Only a complaint. Better to stay silent around a wealthy man who feels put out. They weren't too far now.

If Joab wished for anything, it was only that his brother Delmus were at his side. How much safer would he feel if his older brother had been beside him in the front? But Delmus must recover. Delmus must go back to work as a ranch hand. They could pool their money and buy a plot of their own. He could qualify for a loan if Mr. Reed were to swear by him at the bank. Delmus would soon be old enough to legally homestead. He thought this way—meaning like his mother; a planner to rival the best of them—as he drove, as the sun set.

TO CALL ROCKY POINT a wolfer town might have been an exaggeration. Not the part about the wolfers, but the part about the town. Five derelict structures, and a well that only offered bad water. Nobody came here for the amenities. Seclusion sold the space. That's why Mrs. Mudge picked it. Hidden in the mountains, and when the land turned wet it became nearly impassible, gumbo mud is what the wolfers called it. An army could be coming to get you and that mud would stop their horses dead.

Ah, but they'd never planned on a vehicle like the Maxwell, slow but stubborn as a tank.

Thirty years earlier Rocky Point had been home to legendary horse thieves like Red Mike and Brocky Gallagher, but by 1915 the quality of its bandits had declined. Joab, Mr. Reed, McNamara, and Marlow found three old men half-heartedly changing the brands on two horses. The job was taking a while because all three were drunk.

"Hello, gentlemen," Mr. Reed said. "We are a community of concerned men from the nearby town of Big Sandy."

The men didn't even try to run.

There's a kind of person who expects the worst to happen to him— has suffered the worst since birth—so when it appears he greets it without surprise. Joab had seen this when his family pulled their guns on others. Many fewer fought back than he would've imagined. That's actually why he shot Grace Price. He'd been so surprised when she came at him; Mrs. Price came at him inside her cabin and he pulled the trigger. He hadn't even realized he fired his gun until the woman went down. Then he stepped out and told the others he'd had to kill her. They were too busy breaking into the other cabin on the property to do more than offer casual nods.

"You men know how this is going to go," Mr. Reed said to the old wolfers.

They weren't putting up a fuss but McNamara and Marlow set down their sacks and pulled their pistols. They seemed whipped, but who could be sure?

Reed sent Joab to search the men for pistols, but they didn't even have one among them. Maybe they'd left them in their cabins, maybe they couldn't afford guns of their own. They hadn't been expecting some posse to show up in the night and overtake them. They'd thought they were safe up here.

Nearby, not ten yards, lay the cabin where Joab and his family had stayed, shuttling back and forth with animals they'd pilfered from one homestead or another.

"I know you."

These words were whispered, slurred. Something muttered as Joab stood close to the last wolfer in the row, checking him for a weapon. The man's face hardly seemed to move when he spoke, his beard becoming a kind of camouflage. Not that much larger than Joab, but likely older by forty years.

"Your momma paid me one whole dollar to retrieve good water for her off the mountain."

This, too, was spoken softly, practically whispered into Joab's ear.

Joab stepped back and the man's face remained alien to him. But why would he remember one wolfer from another?

The man grinned. "Where's your blindfold?"

Joab nearly collapsed right there.

"Out here we call ourselves the Vigilance Committee," Mr. Reed said, stepping closer to the trio, which meant he also stood beside Joab now.

"Look at these three," Reed said to the young man. "Men like this been stealing their whole lives and won't stop until the last of their days."

Mr. Reed leaned even closer to Joab's ear.

"Were these also the men?" he asked. "The ones who slaughtered your dear mother? Your brothers?"

The old man hadn't heard, or wasn't listening. He looked so defeated that it made Joab sick.

"Yes," Joab said. "It was him and his friends."

Marlow moved toward the horses, who appeared nearly as meek as the men. Old things, and poorly fed. Marlow looked close at the brand.

"These aren't even your horses, Jack." He laughed.

"Imagine that," Mr. Reed said, laughing too, but neither sounded pleasant when they did. It was a bit like a hyena's call; it seems like laughter until their jaws are on your throat.

"You want to know something?" the old wolfer said.

He spoke to Mr. Reed this time, not to Joab. But Mr. Reed wasn't listening yet. He had things to say and men like him are not interrupted. He continued.

"I know you didn't come up easy, but I didn't make it here thanks to the help of others either."

McNamara picked up the sack that lay at his feet. Now Joab saw what they'd brought with them. What they'd been intending to do right from the start. A length of rope fell from it, landing on the soil with a sound too soft for its purpose.

Mr. Reed handed his pistol to Joab. Marlow revealed a second length of rope from his sack.

"You want to know something?" the old wolfer said, louder now. He looked from Mr. Reed to Joab and back to Mr. Reed again.

Joab felt the pistol grow lighter in his hand. He would've thought it would be the opposite but desperation drained him of weakness.

They'd brought two lengths of rope to deal with the wolfers of Rocky Point. How would these rich men react if they learned he, too, had been a horse thief? He lifted the revolver and pointed it at the old man's head.

"This boy is a—"

And like that, louder than thunder, the third wolfer's jaw seemed to fall off one of its hinges. It cracked rather than shattered and he actually hopped once, then staggered to his left and fell to the cold ground gasping; the last of him escaped in three short breaths.

"Joab!"

Mr. Reed shouted the name. This should've been enough to make the young man turn to face his employer, but it was the sight of blood leaking from the man's wound that held Joab Mudge's full attention.

"Joab."

Mr. Reed's hand firmly pushed the pistol down. His other hand went more gingerly to the boy's shoulder.

"This is not the way," Mr. Reed said, speaking in a tone that surprised Joab. Not angry, almost soothing.

Joab looked away from the wolfer's body on the ground. Instead of peeking at Mr. Reed, he looked higher, toward the mountains.

"Are you going to fire me, sir?" Joab asked.

"No!" Mr. Reed said, laughing. He turned Joab around so he could see the rest of the scene.

The other two wolfers stood in much the same posture as before, except now each man had a rope noosed around his neck.

"We just have a way of doing this. Bullets cost money but hanging is free."

McNamara and Marlow led the old wolfers to a pair of trees. The trees were as dead as the men were soon to be. They tossed the ropes over tree limbs. One end of each rope had been tied into a large knot. This would be the end they'd pull.

Mr. Reed held Joab close. "Back in Big Sandy we call ourselves the Vigilance Committee," Reed said. "But thieves like this know us by another name as well. Don't you?"

"The Stranglers."

One of the two men said this, but Joab couldn't tell which one.

McNamara and Marlow hooted.

Mr. Reed said, "That's it."

Marlow yanked on his rope and the man rose into the air, as if ascending to heaven. McNamara joined his partner, raising the body even higher.

But as the man lifted from the ground, Joab no longer saw him. Instead, it was his mother in the noose. It was his mother wriggling and writhing and choking. He felt the impulse to cut her down, save her life. But he'd missed that chance, hadn't he?

Mr. Reed leaned close to Joab now and squeezed his arm. "Make no mistake, you're not alone anymore. You survived a horror, lost the woman who raised you, but you're with us, and, Joab, we are with you. You're a Strangler now."

McNamara and Marlow let go of the rope and the body fell. Dead.

"Amen," they said.

The pair grabbed the second rope. They gestured for Joab to join them. Mr. Reed would, too. Joab stood with the men. He held the rope. With their hands so close to his, he could almost pretend these were his three brothers, the Mudge boys working together again. A team. A family.

You're with us, and, Joab, we are with you.

They hung that man and left him up.

He would swing until the rope rotted through.

44

"THANK YOU FOR HAVING US."

Mrs. Reed waved the words off, but Grace suspected the wealthy woman wanted to hear them, needed to hear them. You don't lead assemblies in an opera house because you dislike adoration.

"Please sit," Mrs. Reed told Grace.

They were in the parlor of the Reeds' place. A three-story home that sat right beside the opera house. Both structures seemed hauled in from another landscape, a place where the population rose higher than three digits.

Grace and Sam sat on a sofa that cost more than everything she owned. This didn't intimidate Grace, though; it inspired her. Here was a woman with enough money to fund a teaching program all by herself. The cost of Mrs. Reed's nearby ottoman could probably pay for 151 days of school supplies for every school-age child in Chouteau County; a full school year right underfoot.

"The Busy Bees certainly made a wonderful show of support for Mrs. Sterling today." Grace said this just as she'd practiced in her mind, with a grin that appeared casual rather than overeager. "People have been talking about it all over town."

"We applaud women of ambition."

Mrs. Reed sat in a lady's chair, across from Grace and Sam. The armchair, where only Mr. Reed would be allowed to sit, was adjacent to the lady's chair. There were four parlor chairs here as well. Seven pieces, a full set.

Sam didn't give a shit about any of this back and forth, so instead the kid whipped out the small envelope of newspaper headlines.

"But by this point in the evening," Mrs. Reed said, sighing, "I find myself aching to take off these shoes."

Grace laughed, the first genuine emotion she'd felt since entering this house. Mrs. Reed smiled at her differently now, still a hostess but perhaps no longer wearing the mask of one. To be clear, though, Mrs. Reed did not remove her shoes. Speaking the words was as close as she'd come to undressing in front of anyone but her husband.

"What are we really talking about here, Mrs. Price? I'm sure you didn't ask for this appointment simply to lounge with me."

Sam spoke without looking up from his lap. "She came to ask you for money."

Grace raised one hand and slapped her son on the knee. She realized where they were just before she made contact, so the touch fell far more lightly than it would have if they'd been alone. She'd used her left hand to touch Sam because now the right hand throbbed at night. Every night, no matter what she did, it pulsed with pain until morning.

But Mrs. Reed didn't take it badly. In fact, she laughed so loudly that even Sam looked up to see.

"I love children," Mrs. Reed said. She looked directly at Sam now. "Especially the honest ones."

Sam didn't care much about the compliment. His gaze returned to the articles.

"What has you so engrossed?" Mrs. Reed asked him.

No answer. That's the definition of being engrossed. Grace had to tap him once, lightly, on the forehead before Sam looked up. Mrs. Reed asked the question again.

Sam lifted the article and read, "'Sailor, Steeplejack and Acrobat all in one.'"

He turned the article toward Mrs. Reed, who leaned closer to see the photograph. A crowd gathered in a field to watch a man balanced on the tip of a pole 150 feet in the air.

"That's Mons De Carno," Sam explained. "The greatest pole balancer in the world."

Mrs. Reed clapped her hands. "That's a profession?"

Now that they were talking about something of genuine importance, Sam found a way to stay engaged. "He's a sailor, steeplejack, and acrobat, all in one. That's the whole point of the headline."

"How surprising," Mrs. Reed said. "How strange." She said this as an observation, not an insult.

"There's a lot stranger stuff right here," Sam said. "I could tell you some things."

Grace almost corrected Sam; the tone came across as condescending. Sometimes Sam could sound that way. It might've been part of the reason why the child couldn't hold on to friends, though Sam never meant any harm. Still, Grace understood this wasn't the only reason Sam had often been kept at a distance in Big Sandy.

"Tell me one thing then," Mrs. Reed said playfully. "Even stranger than that pole balancer."

"Mrs. Henry brought a monster to Montana."

Sam said this, then looked back down at the next scrap of newspaper. Might've been reporting on the snowfall so far this season, that's how casual he sounded.

Grace, meanwhile, really did want to squeeze the boy's knee to hush him now.

But Mrs. Reed did exactly what Sam would've expected. She only grinned.

"I saw Mrs. Henry just this afternoon." Now she looked at Grace. "No monsters in sight."

Grace laughed softly. "Of course not."

Nearly under his breath, Sam said, "Okay. I did my best."

Mrs. Reed suddenly hopped up from her chair and, with a gesture, urged them to wait. She left the parlor and from a distance she could be heard rattling dishware in the kitchen. While she was gone, Grace looked down at Sam.

"Monsters," she whispered, deeply embarrassed by such a thing.

Sam did not look up. Grace took this to mean the boy had been properly chastised, but in fact he was only deeply interested in that photo of the pole balancer. Sam wondered if that could be his own profession when he grew up. He had a hard time staying still, though. It was one of the reasons he loved these articles so much. If he cared about a subject, he could focus with an intensity that would shame most adults, but otherwise the body began to tremble and shift.

"I realized you might be hungry," Mrs. Reed said. She spoke to the child more than the mom.

She set down a serving tray. On it was a plate of baked bread, called bannock, two small bowls beside it. One carried butter, the other Saskatoon berry jam.

"It's still warm," Mrs. Reed promised. "Mr. Cardinal makes it for me every time he visits town. I'm trying to have him perform with his fiddle at the opera house. The Métis have their own way of playing. Very spirited."

Sam looked to his mother before pulling at a piece of the bannock. She grinned with relief. Grace wanted Mrs. Reed to see she'd educated him in manners as well, especially with the nonsense he'd said minutes ago. With her nod, Sam prepared the snack for himself and Mrs. Reed turned back to Grace.

"I know you're a teacher, Mrs. Price. This child is a fine example of your expertise."

That meant a great deal. There were more easy days on the plains than there were compliments on Grace's mothering.

"That's kind of you to say, Mrs. Reed."

Mrs. Reed stood and walked closer to the pair. The sofa offered enough room for three. Mrs. Reed slid down on the other side of Sam. The kid looked annoyed at having to shift to accommodate her, but he did it.

"Now you want to open a school, begin teaching," Mrs. Reed said. "But you need help."

"Certainly there's the cost," Grace said. "But also the location. The children didn't like coming to our schoolhouse, it seems."

Mrs. Reed sat close enough that she had to shift her right arm, or else her elbow would've jabbed Sam directly in the face. She lifted the arm and set it on the back of the sofa, nearly resting on Sam's shoulders.

"Their parents had a number of *concerns*, didn't they?"

Grace sat with the question quietly.

"Yes," Grace said.

"Could you understand their . . . misgivings?"

Here it was. What did the answer matter? Grace meant to teach and she would do better at the job than anyone else in this town, including the parents of these kids. But that wasn't enough, was it? Grace understood that what she said next mattered a great deal as Mrs. Reed now considered whether she, and the Busy Bees, ought to throw their support to her. Look what they'd done for Mrs. Sterling.

"I understand they might not agree with some of my choices," Grace began.

Mrs. Reed's hand came to rest on Sam's shoulder, patting it softly. It didn't seem warm, though, or not simply that. Proprietary, too.

"For instance," Mrs. Reed began. "If I was to offer Sam here my support. Perhaps help to adjust the child's *presentation*—"

Mrs. Reed grinned. Here it was, the bargain Grace was being asked to strike if she wanted to be welcomed, accepted.

As if to give her answer, Grace slapped the shit out of Mrs. Jerrine Reed.

She did this with her bad hand. The one that had been shot, that continued to throb every night, and yet she didn't feel any pain.

Grace stood up and crowded over Mrs. Reed. Might've been the first time the rich woman ever felt small.

"Take your fucking hand off my son," Grace said.

That sure caught Sam's attention. The slap had done it, certainly, but hearing his mother swear somehow shocked the kid even more.

"Stand up, Sam."

Sam stood up.

"We are leaving."

Mrs. Reed sat there, too stunned to speak. She watched Grace and Sam gather up their things. They left the parlor. It was only when she heard them unlocking the front door that she composed herself again, hurried out to the entryway.

"I was going to let you sleep in my home tonight!" Mrs. Reed shouted at Grace. "When you asked for this meeting, I assumed it was because you were finally able to embrace reality."

Grace opened the door. She and Sam were already dressed in their coats, hats, and scarves. Mrs. Reed felt the cold air pummel her as it entered the house, but she refused to shiver. Her face still burned from that slap.

"You have closed a door that can never be reopened, Mrs. Price."

Grace placed a hand on Sam's shoulder. "I heard you bore a child once, but it didn't survive."

Mrs. Reed looked as shocked by the statement as she had been by the slap. That such stories were circulating about her, somewhere beyond her control, and that it was true. Grace could see that on the woman's face.

"I speak to you now as a mother," Grace said. "Mother to mother. If you ask me to pick between my child and your approval, I will pick this boy every time."

So much for that plan. Grace and Sam left and Sam began asking why in the world his mother had assaulted Mrs. Reed and Grace said she'd explain when Sam was older. The sensible thing to do would be riding back to the homestead, but Grace didn't have the willpower, not tonight. Instead, she suggested they spend the night at the Gregson Springs Hotel. It would mean spending all the money she had with her, which meant all the money she had in the world. But they went in anyway. Grace only had enough for a room with a single bed. Good enough. She and Sam would find a way to fit.

Elsewhere, Joab drove back down from the Bear Paw Mountains with the other Stranglers.

Adelaide Henry rode home with her mother by her side, and the spirit didn't leave her until she'd made tea and fallen asleep.

And on the plains two old, scraggly horses had been sent running from Rocky Point. They weren't Mr. Reed's and hardly looked like they'd survive the journey back. He'd slapped them each once and left them to their fates. The demon found them on the plains, but didn't devour them. It passed them over.

It was seeking something else that night.

45

The mountains.
A home high enough to hide away,
Maybe even dreams wouldn't make it this far.

It climbed the mountain, going past the trees.
A light nearby. A home. Small, but not empty.
The scent of human beings inside.
Ignore them. Go higher. Higher.

Near the peak, under the eye of the moon.
Dark and quiet. A cave.
No scents within, neither human nor animal.
Make a home here. So high up you will never be found.

You want me to read to you or sing?
Neither. Neither.
Outside the cave, the sun begins to rise.
Best to lie in darkness.

46

THE FIRST HEAVY SNOW FELL ON THE THIRTEENTH OF NOVEM-ber, five days after Adelaide's birthday, which she did not celebrate. Twenty-two inches before it let up. The first death followed soon after.

Frank Baluca, three years old, got up from bed in the night and tried to walk to the outhouse by himself. Too sleepy to realize the snow stood as tall as him. In the morning his father found him, halfway between the well and the home; he'd been wearing only a nightshirt. There was blood in the snow, a side effect of his struggle to stay warm. That's what his parents thought. They wouldn't be able to bury him until the spring thaw.

Two days later the *Mountaineer* reported that a schoolteacher arrived on the day of that November snow. Her wagon driver, Mr. Oskar Olsen, hurried to get her to her cabin despite the weather. She'd been determined to reach her claim. When Mr. Olsen left her at her new home, she'd been unpacking. A neighbor arrived, having heard of the new resident, only to discover the cabin empty. The front door looked as if it had been torn in half.

Then Carl Gunderson was found, nearly frozen to death. He'd been thrown from his horse and almost died in the cold. No evidence of his horse remained. Not even tracks indicating it had run off. Gunderson said the horse had flown off. Literally. The town doctor diagnosed him with ptomaine poisoning and profound drunkenness.

Such stories became more common that November, shared in the newspaper, in church, and at restaurants. "Hard luck" is what they called it out here, and of course this land could be unforgiving. But after the fifth death, the seventh, all within a week, luck seemed less involved. A sense of doom descended on Big Sandy, shrouding the land just as surely as the snow.

47

FIONA WONG COULDN'T FIND HER FATHER'S GRAVE.

She'd been searching, without success, for three years.

"If I'd known how slow your horse was," she said, "I would've offered to let you ride Bertie's."

Adelaide Henry took offense on the horse's behalf. She patted a gloved hand on his crest as if to soothe him.

"Obadiah does take his time," Adelaide said. "But he's a tough old thing."

A joke, but Fiona wasn't listening.

One thousand ninety-three days.

That's how long Fiona had been searching.

Glendale, Montana, this time. Two days' ride from Big Sandy and still not the farthest Fiona had traveled as she tracked her father down.

"Why didn't Mrs. Brown come with you?" Adelaide asked.

"She's tired of these trips," Fiona said. "Been on too many with me."

Glendale. In 1875 this town had grown up around a forty-ton smelter nearby, on Trapper Creek. Mining made the men come, all to work for the Hecla Consolidated Mining Company. In the 1880s there had been about two thousand people living here.

But by 1900 the mines had closed and the town withered. The death of industry killed the town. That forty-ton smelter had been reduced to little more than a foundation the land had already begun to reclaim. After the mines were gone, the only job left in Glendale was to work ore from the enormous old slag piles left behind. That hadn't lasted long.

Towns died out here, as sure as any living thing. Husks left to rot and return to the earth. So Adelaide and Fiona rode toward what *used* to be Glendale. Adelaide remembered her night at the old hotel, how Mr. Olsen told her there had once been an entire town there. But the land took it back.

"Bertie suggested I make this trip now because I was sitting around the cabin just fuming," Fiona said. "That's the honest answer. You saw me at dinner last night. I'm afraid I wasn't good company. Gregson Hotel sent word yesterday morning, they won't hire me out for laundry again. They've decided to give the job to Mrs. Sterling's power laundry."

Fiona turned to look back at Adelaide. Fiona stood a foot shorter than Adelaide, but their builds were so similar. Wide across the back and shoulders.

"But now you need to tell me why you volunteered to come with me, Mrs. Henry."

Adelaide turned away. She'd noted the many deaths in the past week. She feared she'd unleashed something hellish on this town. That it was her curse, that monster, picking off people in Big Sandy. But she couldn't be sure. Most of the deaths sounded like the horrible but relatively commonplace ends people met in this unforgiving land.

"If I'm alone," Adelaide offered, "I think too much. That's why I offered to join you."

FIVE MILES OUT OF Glendale they passed fifteen charcoal kilns. Each stood twenty feet tall and just as wide, all made of red brick, looking like the hives of a gargantuan race of bees. The kilns were eerier because no fires burned in them anymore and hadn't for at least a season.

"Plus I'd hate to think of you out on these plains alone," Adelaide said.

Glendale had been even more populated than Big Sandy at one time, but it had been a place for passing through, not for settling. Adelaide could see the difference between this town and her own: plenty of saloons, no opera houses.

The town ran along a single street that curled up from the bottom of this slight valley and into the surrounding hills. A racetrack lay in disrepair. Storefronts sat shuttered. The snowstorm hit Big Sandy, two days' ride north, much harder than Glendale. Not even a foot of snow here. For this part of Montana, that counted as a dusting.

"Your father was a miner?" Adelaide asked. "Is that why he came here?"

"He ran a laundry in Helena," Fiona said softly, looking into every corner as if she might catch sight of the man peeking out. "That's when he still lived with us. But some of the women in town raised a protest against Chinese laundries. When I was born, there were seventeen Chinese laundries in Helena. By the time I could walk, there were three."

Adelaide watched both sides of the street as well, but she wasn't searching for Fiona's father. She felt warier of wild dogs. Or wild men.

"My family didn't choose the Lucerne Valley as a place to farm," Adelaide said. "It was all the government would offer. Negro farmers got the worst land, tried to make the best of it."

"How'd it go?" Fiona asked, slowing her horse and peeking into a saloon. The faint sound of voices filtered out.

"We did all right, for a time," Adelaide said, surprised by the new tightness in her throat.

Fiona dismounted and Adelaide followed. They walked their horses to the saloon and tied them up outside. Obadiah snorted twice and, without thinking, Adelaide went into her bag for some sugar beets. Adelaide had discovered he loved them and they'd helped him put on some weight.

"You bringing a gun inside?" Adelaide asked Fiona.

Fiona smiled. "All I'll need is this."

Fiona revealed a black umbrella that was stowed beside her saddle-bags.

"What's that going to do?" Adelaide asked.

"I've been doing this a while," Fiona said. "Believe me, this will work better than the gun."

"You may be right," Adelaide said. "But I'm taking my pistol with me anyway."

MORE ACCURATE TO CALL this place a watering hole; to describe it as a business would insult businessmen. The bar itself had been dismantled more than a decade ago. All that remained now was a long iron pipe where miners had once set their boots as they leaned forward to shout their orders. There had been a mirror on the wall behind the bar once, but it had shattered and been ground down. The only proof that it once existed was a sort of sparkle to the wood boards. When Adelaide and Fiona entered, the bits of glass caught the daylight and for a moment the inside of the saloon seemed to shine. Adelaide and Fiona had to cover their eyes.

When they lowered their hands, they found five men sitting inside, gathered around the only intact table left in the place. The men looked up to find a Black woman, nearly six feet tall, and a Chinese woman holding a black umbrella.

"That's a surprise," one of them said.

The other four nodded their agreement and said nothing.

"Gentlemen," Fiona began. She didn't smile; she spoke slowly. "My name is Fiona Wong. And I am looking for my father's grave."

Each man looked wrung out by life, wrinkled and dry.

The man who'd spoken earlier pointed. "You're expecting rain?"

Fiona held out the black umbrella. "When we open the coffin, I must open the umbrella."

A long pause from all of them; even Adelaide cocked an eyebrow.

"Why?" one of the other men finally asked.

"This is what we do," Fiona said. "The Chinese. Then I will collect his bones, wrap them in a yellow cloth, and send him home to China."

The men sat quietly with this new information. Adelaide realized not one of them had a drink before him. No bottle on the table. This worried her more than if they'd all been lousy with liquor. Why would five men sit together in a saloon if not to imbibe? It was as if they'd just been waiting for someone to walk in. She knew that couldn't be true, and yet she couldn't stop thinking it.

And what had they been planning to do to that visitor?

"Warm in here," said one of the other men, looking at the women.

"Getting hotter by the minute," said another, looking at his hands.

"There's a cemetery up the hill," the first man finally said. "You won't miss it."

The same man pushed back from his chair and rose from the table. That's about all Adelaide needed to pull out her Colt. *Mrs. Mudge's Colt.* Adelaide wondered whose it had been before that woman got it.

The man stopped moving when he saw the firearm.

"I was just going to point the way," he said. It would have been better if he'd smiled when he spoke. The smile would've been a lie but at least it would've shown he was willing to pretend.

The other four men looked to Adelaide now with a new coldness, as if they felt insulted on their friend's behalf.

Fiona tapped the bottom of her umbrella on the boards. "I'm sure we can find it," she said. "I want to thank you all and wish you well."

Now Fiona reached over and put her hand on Adelaide's, lowering the Colt and urging her friend backward through the saloon doors and into the sun.

Adelaide made Fiona mount her horse first, keeping herself—and her revolver—aimed toward the saloon doors. Before Adelaide climbed onto Obadiah, she handed the gun to Fiona.

"You're not too big on trust," Fiona said, smiling.

"You don't approve?" Adelaide asked.

"Oh no," Fiona said. "Now I'm even happier you came."

———

"AT LEAST HE WASN'T lying," Adelaide said as they reached the top of the low hill. They rode their horses into the cemetery. This didn't feel disrespectful, as the grounds hardly seemed maintained.

Below them Glendale took on the look of a skeleton—scavenged, then scorched by the sun. From here they could see the saloon had been the only intact structure in the whole town. If others stood, they lacked a roof or rear walls. Maybe that's why the men had been sitting inside. It was the only shelter left. The only place where the snow hadn't crept in.

The graves, those that could be identified as such, were scattered without apparent design. No orderly rows. It would be easy to step on one plot while searching for another, especially after the storm, so to guard against this, many were surrounded by fencing, wooden slats or metal rails. The women dismounted and walked among the markers and tombstones, pulling their horses behind them.

"What was your father's name?" Adelaide said.

"Hum Tong," Fiona answered. "But that won't help."

When Fiona said this, Adelaide had already crouched down to peek at a marker, doing the math in her head. "This one is a child."

"This one, too," Fiona said.

"Why won't knowing his name help?" Adelaide asked as she moved on to the next plot.

Another child.

"My father left Helena and took on work at mining camps. He went all over Montana, following the miners. He tried to do laundry for them, but they had more need of a cook. So he became a cook. My mother never could believe they hired him," Fiona said, smiling softly. "She said he was the worst cook she ever met in her life. But he worked cheap. That was good enough in a mining town."

Fiona and Adelaide stopped searching and scanned the graveyard. It wasn't terribly big, not considering the town had once held nearly two thousand souls.

"Do you know what they called my father?" Fiona asked. "When they hired him and logged his name in their record books?"

"Not Hum Tong?"

"John Chinaman."

"I'm sorry," Adelaide said. "That is just the most ridiculous thing I have ever heard."

Fiona pressed the bottom of her umbrella into the dirt.

"When he moved on to other jobs in other towns, they listed him as Joe Chinaman. One mining town might have three Joe Chinamans and two John Chinamans."

Adelaide looked around the graveyard. "Even if you were to find one of those graves, could you tell if it was your father?"

"Yes," Fiona said. "Yes."

They walked past three gravestones, all at cockeyed angles, not a John Chinaman in the bunch.

"You must have loved him very much," Adelaide finally said.

"I didn't know him. I don't remember him at all. He left right after I was born. I never saw him in person, not that I can remember. All I have is a photograph."

Fiona stopped and went into her saddlebag. She revealed a photo of a thin man wearing a black silk shirt with a tiny collar. He wore a straw boater and looked away from the camera, as if about to pick up and go.

"He's handsome."

"Right?" Fiona said. "I always thought so."

She held the picture a moment more, then slipped it back into the bag.

"I've been through so many camps. There are pictures of the miners. Men outside the mines, men standing in town. Maybe the company took them. Maybe some worker had a camera, I don't know. But I never saw one picture of the Chinese men who worked in these camps. You could almost believe they'd never been here. Easier to forget they were a part of all this, if you never have to look at them. Or maybe they

just didn't think men like my father were worth the expense of a photograph."

Adelaide and Fiona surveyed the cemetery. To Fiona it seemed as
if her father had been swallowed up by the state.

"Could you let yourself . . ." Adelaide began, but felt afraid to finish.

"Stop?" Fiona asked, looking up at her.

"Yes. Stop."

"Did you grow up with your family?" Fiona asked. "All of them
close?"

"I never got away from them." Adelaide sighed. "Not even now."

Fiona slipped the umbrella back into its place in the straps of the
saddle.

"Maybe it's easier to remain devoted to someone you never knew,"
Fiona said.

Adelaide nodded to this, but Fiona's campaign—crisscrossing
Montana looking for one grave—wrenched at her own sense of guilt.

"Was it just you and your parents?" Fiona asked. She meant nothing by it, how could she? It was the most casual of questions.

Adelaide turned away from Fiona. She mounted Obadiah quietly.
She'd told Sam some of the truth. Why not tell Fiona the rest?

She turned to Fiona, who hadn't mounted her horse yet, and that's
when she saw them: the five men from the saloon, standing at the edge
of the graveyard.

"Warm in here," one yelled over, looking at Adelaide directly.

"Getting hotter by the minute," said the next, looking at his hands.

"Mount your horse," Adelaide said to Fiona. "Now."

"We just wanted to make sure you found the place," said the man
who'd given them directions.

The five men threaded into the graveyard, one by one, all in a row.

"Didn't find what we needed," Fiona said from horseback. "But we
thank you."

No fencing around the graveyard itself, so the women trotted to the
edge of the grounds. The men did not seem deterred.

"It didn't rain," a fourth man said, pointing at her stowed umbrella.

The fifth, the largest, had yet to say anything.

"Warm in here," another repeated.

"Getting hotter by the minute."

"Stop saying that!" Adelaide shouted.

She reached into her saddlebag and retrieved that Colt, and the line of men turned to move toward her, like a river changing course, and for the first time in her experience Obadiah rose on his hind legs, startled, and she nearly slipped off. It was hold on to the reins or hold on to the gun.

The Colt fell out of her hands, landing in the dirt.

Fiona shouted, "Let's go! Let's just go!"

The women guided their horses and Obadiah offered a pleasant surprise. He raced downhill, sure-footed, toward the road that snaked through town. Fiona rode fast beside her, wearing an expression of frenzy, delirious terror.

Though they rode much faster than men could run, Adelaide and Fiona both felt sure the men would be right behind them if they dared to look back. They didn't slow until they'd made it five miles out of Glendale, passing those enormous charcoal kilns.

Finally, they slowed the horses; the pinch of fear at the backs of their necks had gone. They watched the road, breathing as heavily as their horses. They scanned the enormous abandoned kilns; each looked as ominous as an open grave.

Then, very softly, a sound that somehow played *underneath* the wind seemed to emanate from the abandoned kilns, like some kind of residual heat. Voices.

Warm in here.

Getting hotter by the minute.

They heard it.

They both heard it.

Adelaide and Fiona stared at the abandoned kilns. A shadow seemed to move within one of them and Adelaide swore she saw silhouettes inside. Five, in fact.

Adelaide Henry and Fiona Wong took the fuck off.

Each rose in her seat and leaned forward, shortening the reins with a swift, simple shift of the wrists. Two days' ride back to Big Sandy. They got those horses galloping and did not stop until Glendale, Montana, disappeared from sight and memory.

THEY MIGHT NOT HAVE spoken the whole ride back. The strangeness of Glendale remained on them like a foul scent. At least that's what Adelaide thought was haunting her. But the farther they rode, the more Adelaide understood it wasn't just the place—those men—that had unsettled her.

A month without her burden. Thirty-two days free of the family curse.

And here was the worst of it: she had never felt happier.

But then here was Fiona, riding across the state to find a grave, to dig up bones and send them to another nation. She didn't seem overjoyed with the responsibility but she didn't shirk it either. Who would understand the situation any better? Adelaide had tried with Grace but the problem had been that she still spoke too vaguely. She told Grace and Sam she'd brought a demon with her to Montana, and only the child believed her. But that's because she hadn't said the truest thing.

"Fiona," Adelaide began.

Fiona's reaction was an interesting one. She didn't ask questions, but she did pay close attention. They rode side by side by this point and the younger woman watched Adelaide expectantly, as if she'd been aware there was a secret but not what the secret might be.

"I didn't come to Montana alone."

Adelaide had the stray thought that Bertie and Fiona had, perhaps, shown up at her cabin not only to offer a bit of hair care but also to learn more, to see inside her home. And why not? They were trying to decide if they could trust her. Would that change after she confessed?

Was she really going to say it? What had never once been said out loud beyond the confines of the farmhouse where she was raised? The one she'd burned down?

"I came here," she began, but the last three words caught in her throat and she turned her head away from Fiona, looking away from her horse, thinking she'd vomit. But it was only fear making her gag. Fear and shame.

"I came here with my sister."

THREE

48

THE DAY THEIR PARENTS DIED BEGAN WITH A BIG LUNCH. UNUSUAL
to eat that much with half a day's work still to be done. Adelaide had
remarked upon it when she ran into the house from working the field.
Eleanor ignored her. This wasn't completely uncommon when her
mother had lots of work to do.

By any standard, though, the feast awaiting Adelaide and Glenville
would've been surprising: clear soup, fried smelts with butter sauce,
chicken patties, rice croquettes, sweet potatoes, green corn pudding,
and cranberry jelly; pumpkin pie, mince pie, and coffee.

"Mom," Adelaide said, "how much company you expecting?"

"Just sit," Eleanor said.

Glenville didn't seem at all thrown by the size of the spread. The
man simply took up a plate and filled it, overfilled it. Eleanor did the
same. Adelaide felt so startled she hardly put anything on hers. Instead, she sat and watched her parents chew the food. They might as
well be cows with cud.

"Found a gopher snake near the well," Adelaide said.

Even as the words came out, she knew they weren't interesting, but
it felt so much odder to sit in silence. Near silence. Eleanor and Glenville didn't even keep their mouths shut as they gobbled. A rule they'd
taught Adelaide ever since she was tiny. Now it was like they'd forgotten it completely.

"I watched the snake for a bit," she continued. "It was stalking a scrub jay but the jay figured him out, hopped up into a tree and would not stop squawking at it."

This brought no response either and Adelaide felt herself ready to shout.

Then Glenville looked up at Eleanor and said, "I can't taste a thing."

Eleanor stopped chewing. "Me neither."

"Adelaide," her father said. "I need you to go to your room."

Adelaide frowned, then laughed. "Daddy, I am thirty-one."

"And stay there," Eleanor said. "You been working hard all morning. Rest a while."

Adelaide looked from her mother to her father. She had a childish thought. *Is it my birthday?* Of course it wasn't. But why else would her often despairingly plain parents suddenly seem as batty as the Bundren family who'd once worked a farm not so far away?

"Now," Eleanor Henry said. "Go on."

And thirty-one years old or not, Adelaide rose from the table, took her plate into the kitchen even though she hadn't eaten anything, set it by the sink, then climbed the stairs and entered her room.

She pulled a book from the shelf, as if her mother might open the door and check on her. Then she sat on the edge of the bed and waited.

For what, she didn't know.

Soon she heard the sound of the farmhouse door opening, then slamming shut.

She rose from the bed and crept to one of her windows. She didn't even have the courage to pull the curtains aside. Thirty-one years old and she only peeked.

Glenville Henry, her father, walked toward the barn with his shotgun in his hand.

Eleanor Henry followed behind him, carrying the Bible close to her chest.

Together they walked toward the barn, as somber as when they'd been eating. Glenville held the shotgun in his left hand, the barrel facing the sky. At the door to the barn, he broke the gun, then turned it so he could feed it two shells. In the pocket of his jacket, she could tell, he carried more rounds.

As he did this Eleanor held the handle of the barn door and the pair locked eyes with one another. Adelaide had spent her whole life with them but she'd never seen them exchange a look quite like this one. Resolve and resignation.

And now Adelaide understood.

They were going inside to kill the demon.

No. That wasn't right. Her mother and father wouldn't wear such an expression if the task was as clear as that.

They were going inside to kill Adelaide's sister. And her sister had a name.

Elizabeth.

They're going to kill Elizabeth.

In that moment—it seemed to happen exactly then—Eleanor looked from Glenville and up toward Adelaide's window. This would be the last time she saw her mother alive. Adelaide didn't know that yet, but she felt it. As sure as she still held that book in her hands. Why was she holding on to that book? With that thought, that question, it fell from her hands. She didn't even hear it land on the floor.

Eleanor kept her gaze trained on Adelaide's window. Was she hoping Adelaide would stick her head out and beg her not to do it? Was she searching for one last moment of connection with her child?

She got neither. Adelaide stepped back from the window. She let the curtains close and returned to her place on the edge of the bed.

From inside the barn the shotgun sounded like a short round of applause.

The screaming that came afterward played much louder.

Her father first—low-pitched and startled—and then her mother, higher and anguished and continuous. Adelaide rose from her bed and she ran for her door—she had to help.

But then she stopped.

She squeezed the handle of the door so tight she'd have bruises in her palm by morning. Eleanor and Glenville wailed in the barn, and she heard Elizabeth's growl, the voice of a storm. All of them out there, all caterwauling, and Adelaide Henry let go of the door handle.

She stood still a moment; from the barn the sound of slaughter.

In this moment maybe she still had a chance to save someone, to do *something*. But what did she do instead?

Adelaide picked the book up from the floor, and she sat back down.

Why don't we stop playing now? No more self-delusion.

Adelaide sat on that bed and hoped—in the ugliest part of her heart—that given enough time all three of them would die. Eleanor, Glenville, and Elizabeth. She didn't feel good about this wish, but that didn't change the truth of it.

Thirty-one years of living on this farm, a literal lifetime raised apart from the community around them. Taught by her mother and father that they couldn't let anyone in, couldn't share of themselves, for fear that others would learn of their monstrous child, Adelaide's inhuman sibling.

Look at that, even there, Adelaide was still lying to herself.

Elizabeth was Adelaide's twin. Born together, first Adelaide, then Elizabeth minutes after. The midwife set Adelaide on her mother's chest, but when the second child was birthed, the midwife ran out of the room. She wasn't empty-handed. She carried the second child in her hands. What was she going to do? Throw the child in a well? Dash its skull against a rock?

Yes. Both.

Glenville Henry was the one who'd stopped her. He'd been down in the parlor, waiting on the good news. When the midwife ran past, her face slick with sweat and tears, he rose based on nothing but instinct. Something was *off*. He reached her at the threshold of the farmhouse and found her carrying something in her arms and when she showed it to him—explained that this *thing* had been in his wife's womb—the man went down on both knees at the truth.

But.

But when she told him what she wanted to do—*end this abomination*—he grabbed her shoulder tightly and said, *You are talking about my child.*

And he took that child from the midwife's arms even as she cursed him and told him she would not step back into that farmhouse to help Eleanor. *What did they do,* she demanded, *to cause such a demon to be born?* Glenville thanked her for her labor. He went into the kitchen and found her payment where he'd been keeping it in an empty Atlas jar. He carried the child, whom they would name Elizabeth, tucked in one arm. He paid the midwife and said, *We'll do our best.*

Then he shut the front door on her and, in a sense, the Henry family never opened that door to outsiders again.

ADELAIDE CLEARED HER THROAT. She'd told that whole story—that family history and then all that had happened here in Montana—with her head down. Now she finally looked up at the others, all gathered together in the kitchen of the Blind Pig.

Fiona, Bertie, Grace, and Sam.

They didn't speak and Adelaide mustered all her courage to keep from looking away. She wanted to cry, but refused to cry. Hearing it out loud, she didn't deserve the solace of tears. She felt hot with the shame of it all, every part of it. The shame threatened to burst her heart.

The kitchen of the Blind Pig was large enough for a medium-sized table. Normally this would be where Bertie might prepare meals for, at times, half a dozen men who'd come through for drinks and card games. More than enough space for the five of them. Bertie had prepared coffee for all, including Sam.

Adelaide didn't know what to do with her hands, and with the silence of the other women, so she lifted her cup and sipped the coffee, though she didn't register the taste.

Finally, Bertie sat back in her chair and her features softened, nearing a state of tears. She patted her belly softly, an unconscious gesture. She looked away from Adelaide, then back again.

"You can say it," Adelaide told her. "Say whatever you feel."

Bertie took a deep breath and patted her belly one more time.

"Your poor sister," Bertie whispered.

Adelaide sat up at this, as if she'd been jabbed, but she deflated again because of course it was true. Adelaide used to sneak out to Elizabeth in the night. She would offer to read a book, or to sing. Young enough, naïve enough, to believe she and her sister understood each other and that she could parse out the growls or grunts as if they shared a language. Maybe they did. Maybe back then, they actually were sisters rather than what they became, Adelaide just one more jailer. Elizabeth's favorite song—at least Adelaide believed it was her favorite—was "O Rocks Don't Fall on Me."

But eventually Adelaide was caught. It was the only time her mother ever beat her. Adelaide tried to be craftier about getting out to the barn, but Eleanor stayed up waiting and caught her. A beating every time. Eventually Adelaide stopped going.

"And you," Fiona said, reaching across the table to take Adelaide's hand. "I'm sorry for what you went through."

Who better understood the role of the dutiful child than Fiona? Who could sympathize more with the one who had gone on and done what was expected of them?

"And *them*," Grace said.

"My mother and father?" Adelaide asked, surprised by the rush of anger she felt.

Even Bertie and Fiona looked to Grace with repulsion.

"All three of you can feel however you like," she said. Grace looked to her child, touched Sam's back lightly with an open hand, resting it there. "But you don't know what it is to do *this* work. How it can drain the best out of you."

Grace looked at all three women with an unblinking gaze. "So yes, I pity them, too."

Each woman slipped into silence. All of them scrolling through memory and personal history.

It was Sam who spoke next.

"Shouldn't we go find her?"

49

Elizabeth Henry.

That had been its name. But no more.
What use is a name when you are alone?

Second night in the cave and it smelled them.
Humans approaching.
If they were human, then what was it?

Elizabeth Henry? *No. That meant nothing.*

They came closer. Scents and footfalls in the snow.
It wanted to rest in solitude. But it rose to its feet.
Killing could work, too.

They appeared at the cave mouth. Two shadows.
Two new scents.
They left something behind.
It listened. The shadows crept back down the mountain.

It heard the door of a cabin creak.
That small cabin halfway down the mountain.
It still waited until the night had gone quiet again.

It crept to the mouth of the cave.
Moonlight made a show of something there in the dirt.
Three prairie dogs. Caught and killed. And left.
Like a gift.
Like an offering.

50

"CALAMITY."

Mrs. Jerrine Reed stood center stage at the opera house. Even more homesteaders had left when the truly heavy winter snows began. The town's population had shrunk by a quarter from the last time they'd all been here, when Mrs. Reed read out women's triumphs from around the world.

This made the already empty plains feel even lonelier. Even with all of the remaining population of Big Sandy in attendance, the opera house only sat less than one-third full. The bell clanged outside even though the show had begun. Considering the state of the weather, some folks might be lost in the night if they didn't have that sound, and the pilot light, to draw them into town.

"I'd hoped to hold tonight's meeting as we'd done before," Mrs. Reed continued. "Read off some inspiring bits of news, hand out newspapers, greet one another as neighbors. But tonight will be different. Nevertheless, on behalf of the local chapter of the Busy Bees, I welcome all of you here."

She looked toward the curtains, where the other Busy Bees were gathered.

"Our small community is no stranger to hardship," Mrs. Reed began. Though she'd said she wasn't going along with the usual program, two copies of the *Mountaineer* lay on the stage, by her feet. "None of us trekked to this grand land expecting to put up our feet and rest."

Mrs. Reed looked down into the floor seats, to the faces there.

"But even for us, these past weeks have been a test."

Mrs. Reed looked to the side of the stage again. Now there were two men standing with the Busy Bees. The pair were expected. She turned back to the audience.

"Chouteau County is named for a pair of fur traders," Mrs. Reed said, "Augusta and Pierre, who owned the trading post out of Fort Benton. When Mr. Reed and I first came here, we stayed at the fort, but soon enough we got out to Big Sandy.

"If you can believe it, there weren't enough people here to fill the stage I'm standing on. When it's as empty as all that, you make friends wherever you can. That's how we came to know Rocky Boy, the Chippewa chief. We even had him into our home.

"He explained that his people had come to Montana because of a prophecy. Westward from Pennsylvania until they reached this land about twenty-five years ago. Along the way his people faced hardship and rejection from settlers and red men alike. Their only kindred turned out to be the Cree, led by another chief, Little Bear.

"In 1902 Rocky Boy asked President Roosevelt to establish a reservation for his people. He was rejected. In 1904 he tried again, but met the same response. In 1909 Rocky Boy and his people were thrown on trains and moved like steerage to the Blackfeet Reservation, but conditions for them there were so poor they had to fashion an escape past the armed guards who surrounded the reservation.

"They hope that President Wilson will finally grant their petition. It hasn't happened this year, but perhaps it will come to be in 1916. It would be a great gift if Rocky Boy were able to do what even Moses wasn't. To walk his people into the promised land and prosper with them there."

Mrs. Reed walked along the edge of the stage as she spoke, looking into the shadowed upper tier, then down to the seats on the floor. The upper tier sat empty.

"One of the stories Rocky Boy told me was about Old Snowbird and Lady Snowbird, a pair of wolves they say are the mother and father of all the wolves on this continent. He said they were majestic, but fierce. And always hungry. Rocky Boy's people believed that when a Chippewa died on their long journey west, it was Old Snowbird and Lady Snowbird who had caught up to them on the trail and snatched them away to the Realm Eternal."

Mrs. Reed put her hand up to the audience as if to wave off any skepticism.

"I know," she said. "I thought the same when Rocky Boy spoke of such things. Magic wolves. The kind of story one loves from such people, but hardly to be taken seriously. *Local color,* as they say."

Mrs. Reed looked back toward the curtain, waved once.

"But recently, as our town has been thrown under a cloak of fear and lethality, I was visited by two men with a story I wanted all of you to hear."

Out from the curtains walked Finn Kirby.

A moment later Matthew Kirby appeared.

51

"YOU CAME."

"I had to be here."

Joab touched his brother's shoulder. So good to see him upright, out of the hospital. He remembered the sight of Delmus waving at the mouth of the barn and then toppling to the ground. Out here, at the back entrance of the Reeds' home in town, he stepped close and hugged his brother.

"Come in," Joab said.

Mr. Reed waited inside. Not in the parlor but the kitchen. The lack of the usual hospitality suggested the importance of this meeting. The kitchen couldn't be reached by accident. No one simply strolled in.

"There he is," Mr. Reed announced as Delmus walked inside. "Don't you two look alike?"

"We do," Joab said. "Brothers for sure."

"You're even the same height," Mr. Reed said. Short men were quickest to notice such things, always calculating, comparing. "And how old are you again, Delmus?"

"Sixteen now," the boy said, still not having moved from the threshold, even as Joab closed the door behind them. "Just last week."

Joab went into his pocket and handed a small wrapped package to him.

"I remembered," Joab said.

Though of course he hadn't. If he had, why wouldn't he have come to Delmus's hospital bed to deliver it to him? In the past Delmus would've been angry with his younger brother. For forgetting and, now, for lying. In the past, Delmus had always been overlooked. But what did it matter if Joab forgot the day? Delmus had been seen by something mightier than even the rich man, Mr. Reed. Seen, and spared.

"Come and sit," Mr. Reed ordered, so that's what Delmus did.

A plate of bannock, just pieces of it now, sat in a bowl on the table. No butter or jam to accompany it. The pieces of bread were hard and cold. This would've felt insulting if Delmus were capable of feeling insulted anymore.

"Feeling healed up by now?" Mr. Reed asked.

"Much better than I was," Delmus answered, though in truth you don't heal up from a cracked collarbone that quickly. His left arm hung in a sling and the doctor had prescribed morphine, injected with a hypodermic, twice a day until he healed. He'd already had his second shot for the day, so he arrived feeling at ease.

A long silence followed Delmus's answer. He looked from Mr. Reed to Joab. Joab communicated an imperative with his eyes. Delmus understood and looked back to the wealthy man.

"Thank you for putting me up there," Delmus added.

Now Mr. Reed waved a hand as if this were unimportant to say. But it had been important. Still, Delmus could see this man needed to hear the thanks and also dismiss it; both were required for this show.

"I will repay you with my labor," Delmus said.

Mr. Reed looked to Joab. "Your brother has already paid off your debt," he said. "Three times over."

Delmus looked to Joab, who blushed, looking so much like the proud son.

"We didn't know our father," Delmus said. "Your words mean the world to him."

"To him," Mr. Reed said. He looked at Delmus more evenly. "But not to you."

"No," Delmus agreed. "Not to me."

Why did he say that? Because it was true. But when had that ever mattered to a Mudge? It mattered now, didn't it? *I will tell it all true!* That's what he told the demon and it spared him. One lie would be all it took for the thing to return and drag him into the hell where he feared his mother and brothers were cast.

"Delmus had my mother's heart," Joab said in a surprised, stuttering gulp.

What did that even mean? Also, Joab knew it wasn't true. He'd stammered the words out, trying to avoid insulting this man.

"I'm drinking," Mr. Reed said, rising from the table. He found a bottle of Monogram rye and poured out three glasses. "We need to have a conversation about my horses."

Delmus lifted his glass and sipped the rye. His first time enjoying alcohol since the attack at the stable; this rye was—without question—the highest-quality alcohol he'd ever tasted.

"Seven of my horses disappeared while you were on watch," Mr. Reed began. "I couldn't have this talk at the hospital. Wasn't enough space in there for a fart, let alone a private conversation."

"You want to know what happened," Delmus said.

Mr. Reed lifted the bottle and slammed the bottom on the table. "I just told you what happened! Seven of my horses went missing. And you, as far as I can tell, fell over drunk while they were stolen."

Delmus looked back at his brother, but Joab wouldn't return the gaze.

"Don't look to your kin," Mr. Reed said. "He's already proven his value to me. You, on the other hand, remain merely a draw on my funds."

"How did he prove it?" Delmus asked, finishing the rye in his glass.

"He rode me out to Rocky Point and we found wolfers hiding there."

Delmus stayed quiet. Heard his voice in his own head. *I will tell it all true!*

"Did Joab tell you how he knew about Rocky Point?"

Mr. Reed nearly choked with strained anger. Geography lessons weren't the point of this talk. He drank his rye just to kill the taste of his sudden rage.

And what about Joab?

He didn't speak. But now he came around the table so he stood at the left shoulder of Mr. Jack Reed. Together, the man and the boy became a portrait of fealty. Delmus didn't need to see much more.

Delmus Mudge rose from his seat and grabbed the top of the Monogram rye. He lifted the bottle and swung it like a sledgehammer, connecting with the side of Mr. Reed's head.

The bottle didn't break, but it sounded like Mr. Reed's skull might have. Not a crack, but a popping sound, and the small man fell from the chair to the ground and his eyes went white with confusion. He flopped and gasped on the ground, not unconscious but lost in the shock of what just happened.

Joab shouted his brother's name, but Delmus ignored him.

"I made a promise!" Delmus called. "I will tell it all true! And what I see is that *you*, Mr. Reed, are a devil determined to steal my brother from me!"

Delmus stooped over Mr. Reed, who had pulled himself into a ball on the floor. Delmus raised the bottle to bash out the rich man's brains.

"And you don't even know what *he* is, what *we* are. The ruin we've caused in seven states!"

Delmus felt the spirit of true confession overtake him. It was a kind of frenzy. He felt every evil deed the Mudges had ever committed like hives appearing across his skin. The only way to ease the itch was to disclose them all.

"Keep quiet!" Joab shouted. "Hold your tongue!"

Joab said these words but he knew. He knew. He'd known ever since those horses went missing. Since they found Delmus facedown outside the stables. Joab would never become some new version of himself so long as the old one lingered. In all the world there had been four people familiar with Joab Mudge and all the bad he had done. And now there was only one.

Joab fell upon Delmus.

The younger brother felt a fury for new life, whereas the older brother had only been surviving. They were the same size, everyone agreed. Thrashing on the ground now, they might as well have been the same man. Joab might as well be killing his old self.

Delmus scrambled, surprised, trying to push Joab off his back, get his arm from around his throat, but this proved difficult to do with one arm in a sling. And the weight of his brother made it feel like his collarbone had been dipped in flames. Delmus coughed for breath, squeaking and wheezing, and Joab wanted to let him go but knew he couldn't.

Joab chanted to himself, *I'm a Strangler now. I'm a Strangler now.*

This was the only way he could keep throttling his brother, the last of his family.

He held on because if he let go, Joab knew the truth would come out. All of it. Mr. Reed and the other men had shown what they did with thieves and criminals. If he let Delmus go and the pair ran off into the night, how long before Mr. Reed recovered and called in the others? Those two men and more besides. A whole town coming after him. And him with nowhere else to go. No refuge but this house and that man, Mr. Reed.

Earlier that year, a homesteader found petrified fish and shells fifteen feet down inside his well. According to the newspaper this suggested that once all of Montana had been covered in water. An ocean where now there were only plains. Wasn't this evidence that worlds, and lives, could transform so dramatically that one could never imagine how different they had once been? The great ocean and the desert plain; Joab's life three months ago and his life today.

"Joab. Joab, listen to my voice."

Mr. Reed had recovered enough to get on his knees. He leaned close enough that Joab could smell the rye on Mr. Reed's breath.

Joab looked into his eyes.

"Relax your arm now," Mr. Reed said. "Relax it."

Joab pulled his arm away but did not look down at the figure that rested against him.

Mr. Reed was not telling Joab to spare his brother.

Mr. Reed was only letting Joab know his brother was already dead.

"I'm going to help you up now," Mr. Reed said.

He took Joab's hand and guided him to his feet. Something lay at his feet, but Joab couldn't make himself name it.

"I was only trying . . ." Joab began.

"You protected me," Mr. Reed said, leading the boy out of the kitchen and into the parlor. He sat Joab in the armchair. "Now let me protect you."

52

The prairie dogs hardly filled the belly,
But the act of giving,
That satisfied.

It came down the mountain. Curious.
But cautious.
To find the door of the small cabin lay open.
The warmth of a fire inside.

It entered slowly. Thick rugs on the floor.
Before the fire.
Like a bed of pelts, on which it settled.

"Ah, pobrecito."
A voice. A woman. Very small. Easy to break.
It watched her. She spoke again, but it didn't understand.

"It's too bad," the woman said, in a tongue it grasped.
"You don't even know your true language."
Behind her, the second shadow. A man. The same size.

Their hands were empty, open, as they moved closer.
It bared its teeth to show how badly this could go.
They did not run. The man sat on the floor,

whispering in that unknown language.
The woman stood by the fire. Above it, on a mantel,
Something small, strange to see.
"This is you," the woman whispered. "Don't you know
your own face?"

It lifted its head to see the figure more closely.
"We brought this with us," the man whispered.
"From Tepoztlán."
The woman smiled at it. The woman smiled. At it.
"You are a long way from home, goddess."

53

NOT FAR FROM THE BEAR PAW MOUNTAINS, JOAB MUDGE HAD just killed his brother and Mr. Reed pulled the body out of the house, stowing it inside the Maxwell.

At the Blind Pig, Adelaide, Bertie, Fiona, Grace, and Sam were mounting their horses. Elizabeth didn't know it yet, but they were coming to find her.

But they weren't the only ones out searching that night.

SAM HAD A WAY of showing his frustration while riding with his mother. He would lean his chin into Grace's left shoulder and press there. If she asked what he was doing, he could easily explain it away as an accident of posture. He'd been doing this, now and then, since he was old enough to ride behind her instead of in front.

"What is it then?" Grace shouted as they traveled.

Sam didn't even have to pull his chin away to speak. He was an old pro.

"I want to ride out with the others," Sam shouted. "I want to see Mrs. Henry's sister for myself!"

"I know you do," Grace said, not shouting anymore. "But what kind of mother would I be if I took you?"

Sam lifted his chin now. His mother wasn't going to be swayed. He'd never believed she would, not really. He was old enough to know a plan destined for chaos when he heard it.

"Now understand me, Sam, *I* am going to help Mrs. Henry but *you* are going to bed."

Sam went quiet. Why did it make him happy to hear those words? He would miss it, but his mother would go. Which meant he would hear about it later, firsthand. Better even than a headline in the newspaper. Eyewitness testimony. Okay, fine, that would have to do. Sam leaned into Grace then. No chin.

"Tell me something else then," Sam asked. "Another town."

Grace gave a little laugh. "I'm about to leave you at the cabin by yourself and you want me to tell you one of those? You'll complain of nightmares."

"Tell it anyway," Sam said.

"All right then," Grace said. "Where from?"

"Someplace close this time. Montana."

The wind at night served as a third participant in their conversation. If they hadn't spent years shouting to one another on horseback, this would've all been lost in the howls and shrieks of that endless Montana turbine. But when Sam and Grace spoke, it almost seemed as if they were always inside a small, cozy room, talking directly into each other's ears; the chamber of mother and child.

"Did I ever tell you about Glendale?" Grace asked.

They'd been riding at a gallop, then had slowed to a canter, and now their horse moved at a trot, tiring as they neared their homestead. They hadn't spoken at the higher speeds.

"Glendale used to be a mining town," Grace began. "Over a thousand men lived there, mining silver and lead. But by 1900 or so the mines all died and nearly everyone left, chasing the next claim.

"Weren't more than one hundred men left by 1910, and then, one day, there weren't any men in Glendale at all."

"They all left?"

"That's what some people thought. But then, one day, someone went down to the charcoal kilns, not five miles from Glendale. They opened up those big old kilns and what did they find?"

Sam didn't speak but the closeness of his face, the way he tilted his ear to hear her better, all made his question clear. *What? What?*

"Had a real cold winter going that year," Grace said. "A killing frost. Twenty, thirty below zero. Most of the remaining men had the right idea, forget the town and find someplace safe to bed down. But five men made a different choice. Five men stayed.

"Hid themselves inside the kilns, hoping for a little protection. And someone had the foolish idea to start the fires going. Must've got real warm in there. Lot of smoke, too."

"They burned up?" Sam asked.

"More likely they choked to death on the smoke," Grace said. "The fire just burned the flesh. That's your ghost town story for tonight," Grace said.

She might've asked, for the hundredth time, why the child liked to hear such things, since his imagination was so rich it always kept him up. But he insisted. Wheedled and whined. So she told him about all those disappeared towns and the tall tales associated with each one. Zortman. Alder Gulch. Now add Glendale. Maybe she did it because it tickled at her teacher's heart as well.

"Oh," Sam said, hardly a whisper.

She thought it was a delayed reaction to the idea of five men burning up inside that kiln, trying to decide which would be worse, the heat or the cold.

But that wasn't what Sam had been reacting to.

They reached the homestead, but others were already there. Eight riders, all on horseback. She couldn't tell who they were at first because they all wore scarves wrapped high over their faces and hats pulled down tight.

They might as well be wearing masks, Grace thought. Eight bandits at her home.

She rode up and one lowered the scarf and revealed themself.

"Mrs. Reed," Grace said.

Looking to the others, seven other women.

The Busy Bees.

"I hoped we would find you," Mrs. Reed said. "The men have gone after your friends."

54

THEY SAW GRACE AND SAM OFF FROM THE BLIND PIG, THEN
mounted their horses without speaking a word. Adelaide had finally
said it all—shared it all—but had the world changed? Had the uni-
verse turned upside down at the truths she'd shared?

No.

Make no mistake, everything was different—Adelaide, Fiona, and
Bertie were riding off to search for Elizabeth; Grace had taken Sam
back to their cabin and she would be joining them on this hunt soon—
but this wasn't what she'd imagined when she'd told the other women
about her family.

Keeping a family secret, one of this scale, the kind of secret that
shaped four lives for decades, there is no way to measure the propor-
tions of it within a person's mind. There is no moment when the secret
recedes. It's a sound that never stops playing in one's ear; a pain in the
body that never quite seems to heal. The keepers of that secret—
meaning every member of the family—each one hides it differently,
but they are always hiding. The idea that you would ever stop is as
impossible to imagine as all the stars falling from the sky. Better to
take the secret to your grave.

But she'd done it. And the stars hadn't fallen. Now she felt a deeper
shock, a different revelation. Maybe she'd never had to keep the secret
at all.

It was this that pulled her from her thoughts; it was this idea that
made her collapse on Obadiah, leaning forward and slipping to the

side, not fainting but blacking out, losing herself entirely. The old horse, Obadiah, sensed the shift in her weight and he slowed, whinnied. It seems ridiculous to suggest the animal meant to catch her, to save her, and anyway, it wasn't enough.

But Bertie was there.

Catching at Adelaide's shoulder and tugging her back upright.

And Fiona was there.

Riding along the other side of Obadiah and snatching at the horse's reins.

It was the slap of the cold that woke Adelaide. She looked down, as if surprised to find herself so far from the ground. It occurred to both Bertie and Fiona that Adelaide seemed disappointed to find herself upright. To find herself still alive perhaps.

"Mrs. Brown?" Adelaide said. "Mrs. Wong?"

Bertie, of all the women at that table, felt the deepest sting at the story Adelaide told. To put it another way, she felt angriest, at Adelaide, at Eleanor and Glenville. How does a family do that to one of their own? But for this moment she tucked that feeling elsewhere. It would come out, but not here, not yet. Instead, she held firm to Adelaide's right arm.

"Mrs. Henry," Bertie said. "We are with you."

Adelaide guessed how Bertie felt about her. And what Bertie said at that table—*Your poor sister*—the tone with which she said it, that had been important to hear, necessary. She kept her gaze locked with Bertie's now though every instinct told her to look away with shame. But what use was shame? Shame solved nothing.

"Thank you, Mrs. Brown."

"Look here," Fiona said, gesturing to the west.

There in the darkness, they saw a light—a lantern most likely—bobbing with movement.

"Someone's coming," Fiona said.

55

"I ADMIRE YOUR MOTHER."

No response from the child. Mrs. Reed didn't mind. She knew she could be intimidating. How many grown men came to her with their heads bowed? Most. She liked to believe it wasn't simply her wealth that steered their eyes toward the floor. The Busy Bees often addressed her in the same manner, no matter how many times she urged them to treat her like a peer, like a friend. As a woman of authority, she felt there was a particular loneliness to her position. Her husband never seemed to suffer from it. He had more friends than fingers and toes. McNamara and Marlow might as well be appendages. Had she started the weekly gatherings at the opera house simply to enjoy the company of others? Why bother with questions whose answers would only sting?

"Well, where is she then?" Sam asked. "My mother. Are you giving her a medal?"

Mrs. Reed led Sam from the first floor of her home up to the second. She couldn't help herself, she liked this child.

"You don't hide your feelings for anything, do you?" she asked.

Sam trailed one step behind Mrs. Reed on the stairs.

"My mother says I risk sounding rude."

Mrs. Reed reached the second-floor landing and waited on Sam. Right down this hallway lay a bedroom where Sam might stay, the bedsheets freshly made. But it would be too easy for Mrs. Price to find the child there, so Mrs. Reed meant to take Sam a little higher up.

Sam reached the landing, and when he did, Mrs. Reed continued on.

"Where *is* my mother?" Sam asked.

Mrs. Reed waved for Sam and Sam followed. They reached the stairs leading up to the third floor. Mrs. Reed ascended the stairs. There was no landing at the top, just a single door. Mrs. Reed waved Sam up and again Sam followed. Far below, on the first floor, a door opened and shut. The sound of footsteps on the stairs.

Mrs. Reed found a key in her coat pocket. The key was tied, with a bit of old leather, to a small baby's rattle. She unlocked the door, opened it.

"You don't hide your feelings," Mrs. Reed said. "But there's something else you've been trying to conceal."

THE THIRD FLOOR WAS an attic. A single room, long and low. Even this space had been fitted for gas lamps, and much like the opera house next door, the work hadn't been done perfectly. No one had been to this attic for quite some time, so the gas lamps hadn't been updated, as they'd been in the floors below. When Mrs. Reed turned on the lamp, a faint leak began. But this was undetectable at the moment, though eventually it would become quite clear. Mrs. Reed walked into the dark space with ease, authority, familiarity.

Sam stayed at the threshold. It seemed for a moment as if Mrs. Reed had disappeared; only the sounds of her shoes, thumping on the wood floor, told Sam any different. Then the rattle of a matchbox, the soft scratch that led to a flame. There she was. Mrs. Reed lifted a small glass globe on the wall and touched the match to the gas jet.

Light.

She slipped the glass globe back over the flame to tame it. Then she replaced the matchbox on a side table along the wall, turned to Sam. Sam remained at the threshold. Were those really footsteps on the stairs behind him? Someone reaching the second-floor landing? It wasn't his mother's step; he could recognize the sound of her anywhere. So who was it? It was this that made the child quick-step into the room. Choosing Mrs. Reed over the faceless figure below.

"It's been some time," Mrs. Reed said. "I used to come up here more often."

The attic was large, bigger than the cabin Sam shared with Grace, but there were only a few items inside. A bed and a trunk pressed together at the far end. And closer, one item. Mrs. Reed stood beside it.

"A crib?" Sam asked.

"Cast iron," Mrs. Reed said. "Brass knobs on the corners."

"I didn't know you had a kid."

"I didn't."

The crib had no mattress, no pillow or blanket; it looked closer to a cage than a bed. Mrs. Reed touched one of the brass knobs, then pulled her hand away quickly.

"We had a wicker basket ready, but then McNamara and Marlow got this into the store and Jack had to have the first one."

Sam moved around the crib slowly, having never seen one of these either. Grace had slept him in the bed with her until he'd graduated to a bed of his own.

"I gave birth in this house," Mrs. Reed said. "In our bedroom. That's what made it easier."

"Made what easier?"

"To hide it."

On the second floor, footsteps. One person. Would they climb the stairs to the attic?

"Not but three women in the room. One was my mother and the other my sister. Both of them long dead now. I do miss them."

Sam watched her face, shadowed despite the gaslight.

"They showed Jack before they showed me," Mrs. Reed said, looking off toward the nearby bed, as if into the past. And for a moment Sam could almost see two women, holding a small bundle, arms extended toward its father, Jack Reed.

"Did you have a boy or a girl?" Sam asked, beginning to understand Mrs. Reed's expression as grief.

"I don't know," Mrs. Reed said.

Sam felt confused now. "How could you not know?"

Mrs. Reed looked at Sam closely. "I said I admired your mother and I meant it. She ended up with such a wonderful, healthy child. I'm glad for her good fortune."

She took one of the child's hands in her own and tapped each finger lightly, counting them.

"Mine didn't have fingers," Mrs. Reed whispered. "It had claws."

Mrs. Reed let go of Sam's hand and Sam struggled to grasp what the woman had just said. In that moment Sam remembered the women at the table, listening to Mrs. Henry tell her story. Sam wanted to tell Mrs. Reed, *You're not the only one.* But then Mrs. Reed said something else.

"Jack took it from my mother and throttled it in the corner. I heard it die."

Sam stepped closer to Mrs. Reed, pressing against her in the way Grace found so welcome at times. The child's embrace.

"I'm sorry," Sam said.

But Mrs. Reed pushed Sam away. "Sorry?" Mrs. Reed said. "He did what was necessary."

Sam turned and put a hand on the crib for balance.

She said, "He did what was right."

Mrs. Reed had already composed herself. She moved now to the other side of the attic, to the bed.

"I want to speak with you now about what's necessary, my dear. About what's right. All of us in town knew your father, and no one judged your mother for the decision she made. He was a man of low quality."

She leaned over the mattress and lifted something that had been lying there.

Sam took three steps away from the crib; it would be more accurate to say Sam stumbled back.

"But we couldn't be quite as forgiving about some of her other choices."

Mrs. Reed held up a dress.

Dark blue silk and Irish crochet.

"I had this made for you, the day after you were in my home."

"The day my mother slapped you?" Sam asked, feeling scared and angry. "That day?"

Mrs. Reed's hands gripped the dress fabric tightly, shaking it, but she said nothing.

Sam looked back toward the door. "Where's my mother?"

Sam reached the door and grabbed its handle.

Mrs. Reed spoke firmly, *"Samantha Price."*

Sam stiffened at the door. It took a moment to respond, so Mrs. Reed said it again.

"Samantha Price. *That* is your name."

"Princess Volonsky," Sam said.

Mrs. Reed said, "What are you talking about?"

Sam turned back. "Princess Volonsky, the Russian, who dressed as a man so she could fight in the war. Do you remember reading to us about that? You said she was brave. You asked us all to say a prayer for a person like that."

Mrs. Reed laughed to dismiss him. "You aren't comparing a woman in a war to me asking you to wear this dress, are you? Please now, you're a smart child."

Before Sam could say anything more, someone knocked, from the outside, and Sam let go of the door handle as if it burned.

"Come in," Mrs. Reed called, and the door opened, softly.

A boy peeked inside.

"Am I too late?" he asked.

"No," Mrs. Reed said. "You're exactly on time."

The boy stepped inside. He wasn't much larger than Sam. Sam couldn't speak because he recognized the face.

"Samantha Price," Mrs. Reed said. "I want you to meet Joab Reed."

The boy startled as if he'd been slapped, paying no attention to Sam.

"Joab Reed?" he said. "Really?"

"Yes," Mrs. Reed said. "It was Mr. Reed's idea. And I agreed with him."

Mrs. Reed started toward Sam and Joab, carrying the dress in two hands. She handed it to Sam and Sam felt compelled to take it. Too stunned to do anything else.

Mrs. Reed opened the door now and stepped outside, waving Joab out, too. She'd said they had no children, none that lived, so was this boy her nephew? Was it her nephew who shot Sam's mother?

"You took my shoes," Sam said.

Mrs. Reed didn't understand the significance to the words, but that boy sure did. He looked at Sam with a sudden coldness, worse than if the roof came off this home and the Montana wind blew in. Mrs. Reed only seemed confused.

"But you're wearing shoes, dear," Mrs. Reed said.

Did that woman ever look stupider than she did just now? Sam almost laughed at her but couldn't find enough air in his lungs to do it.

"You will change into proper attire now," Mrs. Reed said, poking the dress Sam still held with one finger. "Then I'll send Joab back inside. He'll keep you company tonight."

Joab watched Sam coolly.

"What would you like me to do?" he asked Mrs. Reed.

"Just welcome Samantha to the family."

"I already have a family!" Sam shouted.

Mrs. Reed pulled the door closed. Sam heard the pair out there, waiting for him to put on the dress. Mrs. Reed pressed her face to the door and spoke softly, even warmly.

"You have a better one now," she said.

56

A HORSE PULLING A CART. A LANTERN HANGING ON THE CART. That's what Fiona had seen. One rider. Bundled up so that only the eyes were visible. The most recognizable thing about him was the cart. They heard it long before the rider reached them. A loud screeching noise that, at first, Adelaide assumed was the wind. Instead, it was the unlubricated axles of this, a Red River cart. The rider slowed their horse and stopped before the women.

Bertie Brown lowered her scarf. Adelaide looked her way. Bertie was smiling.

"Mr. Cardinal," she said. "I thought I'd missed you this time."

"Did you find your barley?" he asked, his voice coming out muffled through the cloth covering his face. "I left it on your doorstep."

"It was there," Bertie assured him.

She lost her breath for a moment. When was that? A year ago? A day ago? How would she mark time now? Before Adelaide's story and after it. Did Bertie Brown believe the story? That was a better question. The answer was yes. But only in the abstract. What Bertie did believe in, felt it deeply, was that Adelaide had a sister and that woman had been mistreated, abandoned, and needed to be found. This was all she really needed to know, or believe in.

Fiona said, "I thought you'd be back in Saskatchewan already."

Clement Cardinal lowered his face covering. He had a thick mustache but no beard. His thin face looked drawn. He wondered if he

looked as tired as he felt. He'd been sorry to miss the hospitality of the
Blind Pig, one of the few places on his routes where he felt truly safe.

"Saw six white men headed west on horseback," Clement said. "I
decided to head the other way."

"Headed west?" Adelaide asked. "Where?"

He turned and gestured behind him. There were, quite possibly, a
thousand destinations in that direction, but one of them, most definitely, was familiar.

"My cabin," Adelaide said.

Clement focused on this new woman now. New to him. Larger
than the others, larger than him. Both Bertie and Fiona stared at her,
and Clement quickly understood who that posse of white men were
after.

"I don't know your name," he said.

"That's Mrs. Henry," Bertie told him.

"Hello, Mrs. Henry. I'm sorry to bring what sounds like bad news."

All four of them remained quiet for a moment. The growl of the
wind was like their minds grinding collectively.

"My cart is nearly empty," Clement offered. "Only a few furs I
couldn't sell."

He looked at Adelaide.

"You could climb inside, tuck under them, I'll have you across the
border by morning."

"You would do that?" Adelaide asked. "You don't even know me."

He used two fingers to tip just the edge of his wide-brimmed hat.
"A woman in trouble can always count on me. Come live with the
Métis, we're more civilized than the Americans and the Canadians."

Bertie shook her head. "Stop flirting with her, Mr. Cardinal."

"I'm not flirting!" he shouted.

Was he flirting?

In the middle of the night on the plains of Montana, with a posse
of white men seemingly hunting for this woman? No. He wasn't flirting. Yet.

But would he flirt once he helped her reach safety? Definitely yes.

"I'm grateful, Mr. Cardinal, but I can't accept your offer."

Adelaide looked away from her cabin, scanning the landscape. Elizabeth hadn't been back to the cabin since the death of the Mudges. She doubted her sister would be there now. But where else then?

She tried to know her sister, meaning to capture some essence of how she might be thinking. It hurt to do this, because it required admitting Elizabeth was a thinking being, and any thinking being that had been locked away for so long would be filled with rage. Elizabeth had already released some of that rage on their parents, but Adelaide doubted that would absolve her. She understood what was waiting for her when she greeted her sister. Vengeance, rage, retribution. All of it well deserved. *Did I do enough?* Why even ask the question when the answer was so clear? Nowhere near enough.

When she saw the mountains, she knew the answer. Felt it. Where else could Elizabeth go? She pointed so the others would look.

"You don't have to come with me," she told them.

Bertie and Fiona tugged their reins to turn their horses.

Clement Cardinal raised one hand. "I don't know what's happening, but I'm *not* going up on a mountain in the middle of the night."

Adelaide laughed; it felt good to do that just now. "I don't blame you."

Bertie waved for Clement's attention. "Will you go back to the Blind Pig and wait there? You can rest, eat and drink whatever you like."

"I would love to sit by a fire for a little while," Clement admitted. "But what if that posse comes to your establishment after they don't find Mrs. Henry at her place? They must know you all are friends."

Fiona looked to him. "Then we will meet you in Saskatchewan."

57

JACK REED, MCNAMARA AND MARLOW, FINN AND MATTHEW KIRBY, Mrs. Sterling's son—these were the six riders Clement Cardinal saw. Jack Reed could hardly stomach the rage he felt at having to ride another man's horse since his were all gone. A quarter horse, one of Marlow's. At least it outpaced the other horses. At least this meant Jack Reed would be the first to the Negro woman's cabin.

No one spoke as they rode. What would be the point? They knew where they were going and the two Kirby men could always call out if Jack Reed lost the path. The men didn't speak, but the wind had much to say. It seemed to rake Jack Reed's face and find its way into the hidden corners of his mind. One moment, in particular, had been tucked so far away he thought it would never surface again.

A small thing in his hands. He didn't call it a baby. He'd *never* called it a baby. A small thing in his hands and the words of his mother-in-law. *Jack, do your job.* The woman's hands had been bleeding because the skin had been so rough to the touch. *Jack, do your job.*

He never questioned it. Something strange had come to his home, had inflicted sadness and pain on Jerrine, who mattered more to him than his lost horses and his opera house and the whole town of Big Sandy. The way she'd wept when she saw it. That was part of the reason he'd been able to fulfill the task. His wife's desperate cries. Anything that harmed Jerrine became his enemy.

Then this morning Matthew Kirby told his story to Jack and Jerrine, sitting in their parlor beside his stoic uncle; and again, in the evening, to the whole town at the opera house. A tale of the horror he endured. Of a demon being kept by a Negro woman, who therefore must be some sort of witch. All kinds of backward nonsense that had certainly worked on the others. Even McNamara and Marlow, who he'd thought would be too educated to be roped in. But now he understood they were only acting on the amount of evidence the world had ever made available to them. How else could something so monstrous and strange appear except by the workings of the Devil himself? Meanwhile he and Jerrine had been through different schooling. What frightened the two of them more was understanding this meant there had been at least *two* monstrous children born into this world. This idea hadn't brought them comfort.

There had been some solace in thinking the experience had been theirs alone. That in all of human history only they were subjected to that predicament. And so they never tried to have children again and, instead, poured all that energy into this town, these people. The opera house, the Busy Bees, all of it grew in that spoiled soil. Good things that they tended to with sincere care. And if they blamed themselves, or considered themselves cursed in some way, they never spoke of it. They never spoke of it. They never spoke of it.

For all their certainty that they'd done the right thing, Jack Reed listened to Matthew Kirby and had only one thought. *They raised it?* This idea crushed him. It meant that others had done what he and Jerrine couldn't. Some Negro family had been made of sterner stuff.

"Here it is," Finn Kirby shouted.

Jack Reed returned to the moment, to the territory outside of himself. As vast as the land could seem, it shrank in comparison to all that he—that anyone—kept within.

He would've missed the cabin if not for Mr. Kirby's guidance.

"Doesn't seem like she's here," Jack Reed said to the others as they gathered around him. The horses snorted and coughed and caught their breath. Animals riding animals, that's all they were.

"Should we go in?" one of the men asked.

Jack Reed climbed down from his horse and handed the reins to

Marlow. He walked toward the cabin and with each step he felt a rage boiling over. He didn't knock on the door, he kicked it in. The door gave him no resistance. It fell apart so easily that he actually stumbled inside.

It was all so ordinary. Bed, stove, utensils, and books. What did he expect? He couldn't say. Whatever he found would've enraged him. Jack Reed turned the bed over and he kicked over the stove and he saw the trunk, opened it, but it was empty. This only enraged him more. Nothing satisfied him.

The other men gathered in the doorway, watching Jack Reed losing his shit.

"Burn it!" Jack Reed shouted. "Burn everything she owns!"

He said this, then looked out at the other men.

Finn Kirby said, "You're the one right next to the stove."

Jack, do your job.

They gathered outside the cabin as it began to burn. The newspaper Adelaide Henry used for insulation proved especially useful as kindling. Before the cabin was lost entirely, Matthew hopped from his horse and ran inside. The other men started; Finn Kirby shouted out. Quickly they heard a scraping sound.

Matthew Kirby reappeared, pulling the steamer trunk behind him. He could do it even with only one hand. Much lighter now that it was empty.

In the faint moonlight, the men watched Matthew, clucking with exasperation. It was late, they were cold, and the woman wasn't even here. And now this numbskull was worried about a trunk?

Finn climbed off his horse, pulling a length of rope from a saddlebag.

"We'll pull it," Finn said. Assuring the other men this wasn't their concern.

"If it slows you down, we'll leave you behind," Jack Reed said.

Finn crouched as he tied a knot to one handle. "We're big boys. We'll find our way."

"If she's not here, then where?" McNamara asked, getting them back to the point.

"Blind Pig maybe," Marlow offered, looking to Jack Reed to see if he'd be willing to bring this chaos there as well.

"The Blind Pig," Jack Reed said. "Fine. If she's not there, we'll make them tell us where she is."

They mounted their horses. For just a moment Jack Reed sagged in his saddle. He could feel the anger in him and knew it wouldn't be enough to ask questions of Bertie Brown. The Celestial no longer had work in town and the Busy Bees were pushing hard for Prohibition. The movement had enthusiasm all over the state. Bertie would be out of work soon, too. He knew this even if she didn't. The Blind Pig would not last. If it burned down, it would not be rebuilt. The county was enormous, but soon there would be no room for those women. He would miss them but he would not fight for them.

"Look there." It was Mrs. Sterling's son. What was his name? Who could remember?

He pointed toward the Bear Paw Mountains. The three-quarter moon offered the only light. It was enough.

"What is that?" the Sterling boy asked. Strange to call him a boy, he was the same age as Matthew Kirby.

"Too big to be a bird," McNamara said.

"And too late at night for a bird to take flight," Marlow added.

"You know what it is," Finn Kirby said. "My nephew already said."

Those words silenced them for a moment. It's one thing to hear about a monster, but another thing entirely to see it.

"Look at the size of it," Marlow whispered. "Even from this distance."

"Is it hunting?" the Sterling boy asked, scared. And who could blame him?

All six men sat on their horses but did not urge them forward. Now they had seen it, but still hadn't faced it. It could remain a trick of the light, a spot across their eyes, a mass delusion. But the moment they rode toward it was the moment they crossed the threshold. Now they would know the world held more mystery than their minds previously understood. Most people don't want to know. Most people avoid knowing more than the simple stories their parents told to explain the world when they were young.

"Look now," Finn said, speaking softly. "It's diving."

"You see," the Sterling boy told them. "It *is* hunting."

"Hunting what?" Matthew Kirby asked, the first words he'd said on the ride.

Jack Reed gave his horse a kick. "Let's find out."

58

"MRS. BROWN, WHY WON'T YOU LOOK AT ME?"

Adelaide rode alongside Bertie; Fiona trailed just behind.

"You can't tell what I'm looking at in the middle of the night," Bertie said.

They approached the Bear Paw Mountains and all that might be hiding there. Why did Bertie's opinion matter to Adelaide at all? But it did.

"I can tell," Adelaide said.

Bertie rode quietly and Adelaide thought they would reach the base of the mountains soon. There were trails up ahead, accessible only by foot. They would have to tie the horses up. She wondered if the trader, Mr. Cardinal, had been right about the white men on horseback and the direction they'd been headed. If so, maybe they were already at her cabin.

"I was born in Perry County," Bertie said, catching Adelaide's attention, drawing her out from her own thoughts. "This is Missouri I'm talking about. The first job I remember having was to stand by Master Joseph's bed at night, keeping the flies off him with a fan. There was a punishment if I fell asleep and the flies bothered him. I believe I was six years old. By that point the Great Rebellion had been over for five years. We were emancipated. Slavery had ended, but I was still enslaved.

"The problem is that I had no people left. My mother had been raising us kids on one plantation and our father lived on another, not too far away. But he died, then she died, then Master Joseph sold off every other child. I was the last born. Don't even have a memory of my mother's face, not any of my sisters or brothers. Master Joseph kept me on out of loyalty to my mother. That's what he said. But I think he needed someone to work the house. Still, he was the one who taught me how to make a home brew. He was too impatient, though, never fermented the mash for quite long enough. I improved on his recipe."

Fiona had caught up to the pair and then rode past them, ahead of them. Adelaide saw her look up at the summit of the mountains and then, for a moment, slightly higher and to the west. What had she seen?

"Maybe you're right, Mrs. Henry. I have held on to conflicted feelings ever since you told us about your family, about that sister of yours. Now, I don't know what we're going to find when we track her down. To be as honest as I can, I'm not expecting no creature with claws and wings. I'm expecting a child of God, who has been abandoned and neglected. Whose family didn't pull her into their warm embrace. And why? Because she was born in some way that troubled the rest of you? Is her leg game? Or her mind not quite calm and collected? For that you would hide her away? For that you would lock her up?

"You have to excuse me, Mrs. Henry, because I'm becoming angrier with every breath. And maybe it hurts me most because I would have loved the chance to know any one of my siblings. No matter how they were, no matter who they were, I like to think I would've embraced them. I needed someone on my side, let me tell you. It's why I'm so grateful for Mrs. Wong now. I needed someone on my side. And it sounds to me like your sister could've used the same thing."

Adelaide might've said something, looked like she was about to speak, but then choked back the words instead.

Ahead of them, Fiona now turned backward in her saddle, shouting, waving, but it hardly had time to register.

"What are you on about?" Bertie shouted to Fiona.

That's all Bertie had time to say and then she got an answer, of a kind, as Adelaide Henry flew off her horse.

To be clear: Adelaide Henry flew. Her horse, on the other hand, went flying.

Obadiah cracked in half, folded over himself. Not even enough time to whinny or cough. Where there had been one horse, the old gelding called Obadiah, there were now two large portions of flesh that would soon fill the bellies of a nearby pack of wolves.

And there was Mrs. Henry.

Aloft.

Receding into the distance.

Bertie stared upward without comprehension. Something had happened, but it existed so far outside her understanding that it was difficult to believe. Mrs. Henry's arms and legs dangled, about twenty yards ahead of them, and ten yards above.

Mrs. Henry wasn't flying; she was being carried.

"Fiona!" Bertie shouted. She wasn't calling for help, but out of concern.

"I'm here," Fiona said, closer than Bertie realized. "I'm—"

They both watched the shape moving up through the night sky, headed toward the summit of the nearest mountain.

"I thought she was telling tales," Bertie whispered.

The enormous wings. They beat louder than the sound of Bertie Brown's own heart. Were they supposed to go up there and rescue Adelaide? Did they have a fucking choice after the speech Bertie had just made to Mrs. Henry?

Fiona reached out and grabbed Bertie's wrist.

"I know," Bertie said. "We'll go up. We'll do it."

"No," Fiona said. "I don't think we will."

Six men appeared on horseback. They surrounded Fiona and Bertie.

Bertie found her composure as she focused on their leader.

"Mr. Reed," Bertie said, steadying her voice. "Can I interest you in a night of cards and all the brew you boys can drink?"

Jack Reed took a deep breath; a decade of patronage, one would even dare to call it friendship, passed between them in that glance.

"No time for games, Mrs. Brown."

59

THE TREES SWAYED. SHE'D NEVER SEEN THEM DO SO FROM THIS angle. From above.

She wasn't fully awake but she had become aware. She'd been sitting on her horse, talking with Bertie, Fiona pointed to the sky . . . and now here she was. Looking at the trees. They swayed. She heard nothing but ringing in her ears. Maybe she'd been shot. And this was what she saw as she ascended to heaven. Wouldn't that be nice? To imagine she deserved heaven.

A woman is a mule.

She heard her mother clearly. Might as well be with her there in the air. More proof that she'd left the plane of the living and was now approaching the Realm Eternal.

A woman is a mule.

Adelaide shook her body, wriggled and squirmed. Something held her. The hand of God perhaps. She couldn't tell because she couldn't see. She blinked but her eyes wouldn't focus on anything but those trees.

A woman is a mule.

She heard her mother, saying the phrase spoken more often than *I love you*—and Adelaide's entire being reacted with revulsion, with terror. If she was heading somewhere to meet that woman again and to hear that mantra, that explanation for the meaning of life, then she didn't want to go. If that was what eternity had to offer, she'd rather turn to dust. So she kicked and flailed and kicked some more and she succeeded. Adelaide fell back to Earth.

Hurt like hell.

She came down through those trees. They didn't seem so soft and swaying as she tumbled down those branches. They slowed her fall, but it wasn't gentle. By the time she landed on the frozen ground, she was awake but wished she wasn't.

Adelaide remembered why she'd come to these mountains. The thought of Elizabeth made her rise. Or, to be more precise, it made her crawl. Toward something nearby. Lights? How could there be lights up here? Had Elizabeth learned how to build fires?

She dragged herself forward. Barely rising from her hands and knees.

Adelaide found herself at the door of the small hut; a tiny man and woman stood inside. The woman spoke, the man watched. She introduced them as Carlota and Francisco. They had been running the fire in their hearth all night.

"You missed her."

"My sister," Adelaide said. "Where is she?"

Those two words—*my sister*—caused the pair to stoop lower and peer closer at Adelaide's face. They looked to one another. They'd been blocking the doorway, but now they stepped back. They didn't help her up, but Carlota gestured her inside. Adelaide rose, though it took effort. She snorted and groaned. She stepped into the glow of the firelight.

"I see the resemblance now," Carlota said.

"Is that a joke? I'm too tired for jokes."

Francisco, already moving toward the kitchen, said, "You're looking in the wrong place."

"The resemblance is here," Carlota said. She patted her heart.

Why did this make Adelaide's legs tremble? She collapsed into a squat.

Francisco arrived holding a cup of coffee for Adelaide. She took the mug in her hands and tried to leach the warmth through her palms, send it throughout her body.

Francisco held up a smaller cup, thimble-sized. "Sheep's milk," he said.

Adelaide nodded and he poured. She began drinking before he'd emptied the small cup. She slurped and gulped and this was the only sound inside the home. Carlota and Francisco watched her.

"Where is she?" Adelaide asked again.

She couldn't understand the irony of what she'd asked. That she'd been with Elizabeth only moments ago. Carlota walked to the open door of the cabin and pointed out, upward, to the top of this mountain.

"I'll go now," Adelaide said softly. She returned the cup to Francisco. "Thank you."

She got to her feet a bit too quickly and her head went light. She stood tall enough to place a hand on the ceiling to right herself. She was still in pain from the fall, of course, but this was something else. Her vision had changed. The colors of the world seemed brighter, the edges of her vision blurred. She looked again at the two cups in Francisco's hands.

"Was that really sheep milk?" she asked.

"Yes," Francisco said.

"And no," Carlota added.

"What did you do?" Adelaide asked.

"What we gave you," Carlota began. "It will help you when you get there."

Adelaide moved one foot toward the door. At the threshold, Carlota handed her a lantern, the light inside already burning.

"Help me how?" Adelaide asked.

"Help you see more clearly," Carlota said. "See what you must do."

ADELAIDE TROUBLED HERSELF ALONG the path from the cabin, trying to figure out how she might make it to the peak. Without the lantern she would never have made progress, lost in these woods forever. But finally, she found a place where the snow showed tracks that hadn't been covered by new snowfall yet. At first she'd taken them for bear or moose tracks. Something four-legged and large and wild. But they could belong to Elizabeth, too.

Once she'd started following the tracks, she noticed the trees.

They didn't sway anymore, they rippled. Like curtains. She knew it wasn't possible but then remembered Carlota and Francisco and that drink. Adelaide stopped walking and watched them. If they were curtains, then soon they would part. And what would they reveal?

Through the trees, peeking out, she caught sight of a farmhouse.

Their farmhouse. Back in the Lucerne Valley.

Sunlight. Without question she saw sunlight. She took two steps toward the trees, thinking she might actually feel the warmth, but when she did this the trees only seemed to drift farther away. Another two steps and she caught herself. What if she ran after that vision until she lost the path altogether? Easy to chase the past and lose the present.

She turned and shone the lantern back on the ground and returned to the tracks and only glanced back once more; the Lucerne Valley was still there—sunny day, farmhouse—close enough to touch but forever out of reach.

The tree line broke and the vision disappeared and she felt its loss as a pain in her throat. Too cold to cry. She saw the peak now. Behind it the night sky opened like a throat. Adelaide continued upward.

She reached the mouth of a cave.

A wave of heat warmed her face. Coming from inside the cave mouth. Was she hallucinating again? No.

The warmth she felt was the heat of Elizabeth's breath.

ELIZABETH HAD GROWN.

Adelaide had to tilt her head back to see the scale of her sister. Her head loomed high above and she stared down at Adelaide with great silver eyes. Adelaide didn't understand how she could see anything; it took a moment to grasp that she still held the lantern in one hand. It didn't do much, but just enough to see that the cave was vast and yawned around them, seemingly larger within than the mountain itself.

Adelaide understood this couldn't be true, but like the vision of the farmhouse, that didn't make it untrue.

Now those silver eyes moved, graceful as twin sharks. They descended and Adelaide watched them. Three steps and she would've been back outside, but it seemed too far to go. Instead, she waited for her sister's approach. Beneath those eyes would be the mouth, the teeth. While Elizabeth had become enormous, Adelaide felt shrunken down.

"I knew what was happening in the barn," Adelaide shouted. "I knew and I stayed away."

The eyes approached. The silhouette of Elizabeth's incredible head.

"I wanted them to kill you," Adelaide said. "And I wanted you to kill them."

She went down on her knees, felt the cold of the cave in her bones.

"I wished you all were dead," she muttered. "I hoped you'd kill each other. And I would finally be free of my family."

There it was.

Everything would have to be said.

"For as long as I can remember," she said, "it's been you we worshipped. You who ruled. There's not a day of my life that hasn't been about you. You spent your life locked away in a barn. I've spent my life like a servant."

Elizabeth crept close enough for Adelaide to smell her breath, hot and fetid.

"But I never thought of you," Adelaide whispered. She breathed in and out. "Of you outside of me, I mean. My suffering helped me forget yours."

Elizabeth perched so close now she could tear Adelaide's neck open with no effort at all.

"You needed a sister," Adelaide said. "But instead, you got me."

Adelaide lifted her chin and exposed her throat.

"If you kill me right here, I won't blame you."

Closer now. How was there any distance between them anymore?

"I just want you to know I'm sorry, Elizabeth. Don't know if that's worth much. But I'm sorry I wasn't better to you. I'm sorry."

Elizabeth's breath spread across Adelaide's neck, her face. It felt as if her sister had learned to breathe fire.

Or was that a feeling burning from within? All that shame, so combustible.

Adelaide wept as Elizabeth's flames consumed her.

60

"HISTORY IS SIMPLE," MRS. REED SAID. "THE PAST IS COMPLICATED."

The opera house. Of course they'd all gathered there tonight. Thirty-four residents of Big Sandy. The hardest and the heartiest. The ones who were dug in for winter. Twenty of them filled the seats in the orchestra. It was them that Mrs. Reed addressed.

"When we look back on this experiment, by which I mean this town though I could also mean our nation, what will we say about its ambitions? It seemed all of us arrived in Montana and agreed to a certain compact. Perhaps this was naïve of me, but if so, I don't mind. Let me be called naïve. Let me be labeled an optimist."

Mrs. Reed looked offstage and waved someone out from behind the curtains. One of the Busy Bees—Mrs. Mitchell—walked out carrying a sack, filled with something that appeared bulky, but not too heavy. She handed it to Mrs. Reed, then walked back off the stage.

"A town like ours is a shared dream. Call it vanity if you like, but there are days when I imagine journalists and historians will write about us. They will want to know how we made it when so many towns scattered across this state simply disappeared, gobbled up by the endless appetite of this environment. It's so hard to survive in this place, it's almost taken for granted that most towns, and most people, just won't. Which is one more reason why, when I look out and see you there, I thank my God and my husband that we settled in Big Sandy."

Mrs. Reed dropped the sack to the stage floor. The audience sat so silently they all heard the thump it made when it landed. The top of the sack had been tied off with twine. Mrs. Reed untied it slowly because her hands were still stiff from the cold they'd endured when they rode out to Grace Price's homestead. She finally got it open and reached inside. But she kept her hand there. She looked at the audience. They were all leaning forward, wanting to see what was inside.

Mrs. Reed crouched down instead, hand still hidden.

"When Mrs. Sterling came to the Busy Bees and explained her business plan, we couldn't wait to support her. Of course, this meant there would be changes to how things had been done in Big Sandy. I hope you'll understand that, much as we wished otherwise, we had to throw our support to a fellow American.

"Mrs. Wong and her *dear friend,* Mrs. Brown, were both offering services our town no longer required, or desired, but that didn't mean we felt any hostility toward them. But you can tell a lot about a person by the company they keep. I like to think the Busy Bees do well by this town. And I know each of you by name; I meet every newcomer with warmth. Even now I wonder if I greeted this woman, Mrs. Henry, when she arrived. Did I offer hospitality to someone who brought evil to our town?

"I saw some of your faces when the younger Mr. Kirby told his tale, explained what he'd endured. I could hardly blame you for skepticism. I can only add that as he spoke, I knew his words to be true. Knew them out of my own lived experience. I can't be the only one here who understands the world contains both the righteous and the damned. And it is for each of us to decide which one holds our salvation. I know which side I'm on. I know which side you're on. I believe Mrs. Henry has chosen the opposite path. And these women, it seems, have decided on damnation as well."

She looked toward the wings of the stage again and Mrs. Mitchell came back out, but now she was trailed by three others. Bertie Brown, Fiona Wong, and Grace Price. And behind them walked Finn and

Matthew Kirby, McNamara and Marlow. Mrs. Sterling's son had joined her down in the orchestra seats.

Fiona looked directly at Mrs. Reed. "I was born in Butte, you bitch."

Bertie and Grace would've laughed if they could've, but their throats were both too dry.

"It brings me no joy to say this," Mrs. Reed told the crowd, speaking louder as if to drown Fiona out. "But I believe there is a poison in our town. One we have ignored for too long. We have looked the other way, politely, but no more. The deaths we have suffered, the terrible fear we've been living through. I have asked these women to tell me where Mrs. Henry can be found, to help us now in our late hour of need. But each woman has refused. There is right and there is right."

Mrs. Reed rose to her feet and now they could all see what she held: a length of rope. With her free hand she pointed at the women.

"And none of these women is right."

She reached into the sack again.

"Now, I am a firm believer that a family, or a town, can do some things in daylight and others must be kept in the dark. My dear husband and his associates have served the latter role. Some of you might not even have known of their labor in service of this town. But tonight, we must work together, refusing the impulse to keep secrets, and feeling no shame. This night, and maybe only this night, we are all . . ."

She stopped there, touched her free hand to her chest.

"I find myself breathing heavily. I don't mind admitting I feel nervous even saying it."

Mrs. Reed looked offstage; the last person back there stepped out into full view. Mr. Reed, he walked toward her, wearing a soft grin of understanding. She looked, to him, as beautiful as the day they met, the day they married. Think of all they'd been through together and their connection never wavered.

"If I may, Mrs. Reed," he began.

She made the moment into a show, almost curtsying toward her husband. The moment made only more strange because she had to tuck the four lengths of hanging rope under one arm to do so. Down in the sack, hidden from view for the moment, were the other ends of those ropes. The Busy Bees had already fashioned them into nooses.

"For the sake of our town . . ." Mr. Reed began. He swept his arm to the orchestra seats. "We are all Stranglers now."

61

"YOU DON'T LOOK COMFORTABLE."

Joab said this with a smile as he entered the attic room again, but Sam didn't grin back. Sam stood stiffly, wearing the dress and looking as if it were a snake that might bite him if he moved.

"Where's Mrs. Reed?" Sam asked.

"Next door," Joab said. "At the opera house."

"Is my mother with her?"

"I don't know," Joab told him.

Sam looked up from the awful dress. "You're lying."

"Your mother's next door, too," Joab admitted. "It's true."

"When can I see her?" Sam asked.

Joab looked away and back again. "That, I truly don't know."

There wasn't much in the attic. The old crib, the sagging bed.

"How come your mother lets you dress like a boy?" Joab asked.

"Because it makes me happy," Sam said.

Joab frowned. "What does that have to do with anything?"

"Your mother doesn't want you to be happy?"

"My mother's dead. Killed."

"My father, too."

"Dead?"

"Killed."

"You know who did it?"

A silence lingered in the room. Finally, Sam sighed. "Yes. I know. My mother did it."

Joab blew out a breath. "I was not expecting you to say that. I thought you were some kind of little princess."

"No," Sam said. "That's not what I am."

"All right, all right, don't get offended. I feel stupid just standing around in some empty room."

"Let's leave then."

"No, I'm sorry, Mrs. Reed told me we should wait here till she's back. Let's sit down, at least."

Sam scanned the room—only one comfortable option, that bed. Sam did not want to sit on a bed with this boy. Instead, he sat cross-legged on the floor.

Joab did the same. "Good enough," he said. "I've been in worse conditions."

"You're wearing a pistol," Sam said.

"Yes, I am."

"You weren't before."

"That's true," Joab agreed. "Mrs. Reed gave it to me."

"Is it for me?" Sam asked, unable to look up from the floor.

"It's for whoever needs it," Joab told him.

Sam nodded, eyes still focused on the ground, his face turning red. Joab realized the kid was trying not to cry. One of his brothers would've slapped him the moment the flush appeared on his cheeks. Mudges don't cry.

But he wasn't a Mudge anymore, was he? He was a Reed. The missus had said so.

What would a Reed do at the sight of a nine-year-old stifling a cry? Joab didn't know for sure. He watched Sam, trying to figure out what the right reaction would be. This slowed him down more than he realized; his trains of thoughts were being rerouted.

His brothers would've slapped him. His mother would've lectured him, telling him the reason he shouldn't cry is because the world would see his weakness and take advantage of it. She thought the world only existed to feed on the soft and dumb. And she'd been right, in a sense. Except they'd been the ones doing the feeding, hadn't they? How many people had taken them in out of sympathy, a mother and four blind boys. And how many of those people woke to find a pillow over their faces, those boys holding them down? All of them.

And Delmus.

Dying in the kitchen, two floors below.

No. Not dying. Killed.

Murdered. By Joab.

And discarded, somewhere, by someone who wasn't even his blood. Shouldn't Mr. Reed have stopped him from strangling Delmus? Joab hadn't been raised with the same compass as most others, but he felt pretty sure the answer was yes. Even stunned on the ground, he should have commanded Joab to stop. Would he have listened? Who could say, but all Mr. Reed offered to do was hide the body.

Joab had been lost in those thoughts for more than a minute, because when he focused on the child again Sam had his newspaper clippings out. There were more than a dozen in all. He lay them out on the ground, spreading them into a grid, like a quilt. Headlines and photographs. Joab leaned closer.

"'Sailor, Steeplejack and Acrobat all in one,'" Joab read aloud.

The Russian victory over Austria in the Carpathians.

Mr. Johannes Leafedlt. Founder and heaviest stockholder of the Mackton Coal Mine.

Portable Montana Exhibit Interests Virginians.

Tammany Brave Meets Real Indians. Mayor Gaynor of New York Has Pow Wow with Blackfeet Indians from Montana.

Tango Step from the "Three in One."

The Sistine Madonna.

"What is all this?" Joab whispered.

Sam said, "It's the world."

Joab scanned more headlines and photos. "There's so much of it."

Sam smiled, for the first time since Joab had come around. He shuffled more of the clippings, revealing others as well.

"Why are you showing me all this?" Joab asked.

"This isn't for you," Sam said. "It's for me. If you shoot me dead, I want to be looking at something that makes me happy."

Joab's throat closed up. The pistol on his hip dug into his side. Joab didn't realize he was crying, but he was. Did he want to shoot this girl who liked to dress as a boy? The child whose mother only wanted him to be happy? Imagine that. *Imagine that.*

"Or we could just sit here," Sam said. "And I could show you more of these pictures."

Joab didn't look up. He couldn't.

"Do you want to look at them with me?" Sam asked.

Joab inhaled deeply, composed himself. He spoke.

He said, "Yes, please."

62

THE HANGING WOULD BE ACCOMPANIED BY MUSIC.

As they were on the theater stage, the batten was lowered from the fly loft above so the nooses could be tossed over the metal bar. This had the strange effect of lowering a piece of painted scenery from the last show that had been staged at the opera house. A hit from England, brought over by the ambition and good taste of Mrs. Jerrine Reed herself. The play was called *Pygmalion.*

But the nooses hung too high in the air. Even with the batten lowered, the women were too far below them. Mrs. Reed looked perturbed. A moment afterward a scraping sound echoed in the opera house. Matthew Kirby appeared, dragging Adelaide's steamer trunk. It had survived the trip back from her cabin. His uncle stepped out and lifted the back end of the trunk so it wouldn't scrape the floorboards any longer. They didn't want to damage the stage.

The men lifted it together and set it down in front of Grace, Fiona, and Bertie, whose hands were tied behind their backs. Then they hefted each woman up onto the trunk. Grace cursed Finn without reservation. Now the women were high enough for the nooses to reach. One of the Busy Bees climbed up as well, though this much combined weight made the trunk groan. The woman quickly slipped all three nooses on, then hopped down with the help of Finn Kirby, who offered his hand.

All this happened in silence and it proved too grim. Mrs. Reed looked to one of the other Busy Bees.

"Mrs. Thomas," she said, "won't you play something on the organ? Something with energy."

Mrs. Thomas walked to the theater organ and played, singing along with the music as well.

"By the sea, by the sea, by the beautiful sea. You and I, you and I, oh, how happy we'll be!"

Bertie, Fiona, and Grace balanced with nooses around their necks; behind them hung the lab of Professor Henry Higgins.

"When each wave comes a rolling in," Mrs. Thomas sang. *"We will duck or swim, and we'll float and fool around the water."*

Mrs. Reed sent the other Busy Bees to the wings, offstage. All they had to do next was raise the batten again and the three women would be lifted from the lid of the trunk and choked until dead.

But before she could give them a nod or gesture, the front doors of the opera house opened. They all heard this rather than saw it. The front entrance sat outside the theater ring. The doors opened and the wind announced itself and then cut off just as quickly. Doors being opened and then closed.

Mrs. Reed turned to watch for the new arrival. Her heart thrilled at the idea it would be Joab and Samantha, her two children coming to see their mother's work. Her attention turned every other head in the audience. Except for Bertie, Fiona, and Grace. This is because the Busy Bees had been too eager. They thought Mrs. Reed gave the signal to lower the sandbags. So that's what they did.

The set began to rise.

The three women in nooses did, too.

"Over and under, and then up for air," Mrs. Thomas sang, getting even louder now as she watched the women hang. *"Pa is rich, Ma is rich, so now what do we care?"*

And now the door that led into the theater opened and there she was.

"Mrs. Henry!" Mrs. Reed shouted.

Instantly Mrs. Thomas stopped playing, turned from the theater organ, and rose to her feet, as if she might tackle Mrs. Henry herself and drag her to their makeshift gallows. But then she hesitated. Mrs. Reed looked just as taken aback. Because this body staggering into the theater barely appeared human.

The coat soaked in blood and dirt; the hair torn out in patches; the eyes looking large and crazed, visible even from up here onstage. Not a woman. Not a man. Something dug up from a grave and reanimated, maybe. A creature. A thing.

"Yes," Adelaide croaked. "That's me. I'm here for a second chance."

Behind Mrs. Reed all three women were now in the air, straightening their feet to try to stop their air from being cut off. The ropes could be heard, straining under the weight, and the women, too, made soft noises, panting, trying to limit their loss of air.

"A second chance," Mrs. Reed said. "You're all out of those."

Adelaide shuffled forward. One of her legs appeared injured. The townspeople rose from their seats and moved toward the stage, as if Mrs. Reed would serve to shelter them.

"Not for me," Adelaide corrected. "For you. You let those women down now. Forgiveness is possible. But you have to mean it. You still have time."

Adelaide leaned forward and spat blood on the floor. She took gulping breaths.

Mrs. Reed turned back and seemed surprised to find the three women now a foot above the trunk. Had she given the order? Maybe it didn't matter.

"It is my sincere hope," Mrs. Reed began, "that when we rid ourselves of you, we save ourselves from your corruption."

Matthew Kirby stepped forward. "You can see I saved your trunk," he said. "We'll bury you in it."

"Then we'll find your demon," Jack Reed shouted. "I'll snap its neck myself."

Adelaide stood tall again. She looked at these people. Most were clearly terrified. And most, down in the audience, had been kind enough to her since she'd moved there. It was the people onstage—the Reeds, the Kirbys, the Busy Bees and Stranglers—these were the ones who had caused all this harm. The twenty people in the audience had arrived in Montana and simply tried to survive. They should have protested when they saw three women being hung, but Adelaide didn't think they deserved quite the same treatment as the people who were gathered on that stage. They would be spared.

Adelaide looked up now. From the upper tier of the theater came the sound of wood snapping and groaning, as if under a great weight.

"That wasn't a demon," Adelaide said.

Mrs. Reed followed the tilt of Adelaide's head. Matthew and Finn Kirby narrowed their eyes in that direction, too. The second level of the theater remained shrouded in darkness, but there was a new quality to the shadows. They seemed to gather and shift. One might almost imagine they had come to life.

"That is my sister."

And with that, Elizabeth Henry introduced herself.

63

THE DOORS OF THE REEDS' MANSION WEREN'T LOCKED. WHY would they be?

Grace threw the front door open with such force that it barely held to its hinges. She tried to cry out for her child, but couldn't. Her throat hurt too much. She could barely breathe through her mouth. She staggered into the mansion.

Bertie and Fiona followed behind her.

They staggered through the parlor and the kitchen. Grace moved like a golem, heavy and unstoppable. The chairs flipped over, the tables too. It's not that she thought Sam might be hiding underneath them; instead it was impossible to contain her worry and her rage. She didn't even remember overturning the furniture. It was as if the pieces were afraid of her and leapt out of the way.

Grace climbed the stairs to the second-floor landing. Bertie and Fiona followed. They held each other's hands. They, too, might've been trembling at the sight of Grace unleashed.

Grace kicked open bedroom doors. Her voice had recovered enough now that she could howl and moan. Was she calling Sam's name? She sounded like a bear. Moved like one, too.

Bertie and Fiona wanted to stop her, to help her, but they didn't dare get in the way. The two of them had removed their nooses once they were cut down, but Grace hadn't delayed. As soon as she was free she ran for the exit, out into the cold. They barely caught up to her when she bashed open the mansion door. Now they watched her moving toward another landing, leading up to the third floor, the noose still around her neck, the length of remaining rope dragging behind her like a tail.

She howled again and began up that flight of stairs. A closed door stood at the top. And as she approached, her feet stamping so hard their echoes filled the home, a cry came through the door. A wail of mortal fear. Which only made Grace move faster. She recognized the voice as surely as any animal knows the mewling of its cub.

But before she could reach the doorway, Bertie and Fiona reached her. They tackled her halfway up the stairs and she turned on them. She showed them the face revealed to those who would deny a mother her child, and when they saw it they were terrified by her fury, but because they loved her they did not let go.

"Not like this," Fiona whispered. "Not like this."

Fiona had to say it six or seven times before Grace could recognize language, understand the meaning. She looked down at herself on the stairs, the noose loose on her neck.

"Don't let Sam see you with this," Bertie said, talking as calmly as she could.

Grace looked from Bertie to Fiona. These were her friends. They weren't trying to stop her. They wanted to help. She had to explain this to herself just to keep from clawing out their eyes for slowing her down. After a moment she nodded and Fiona slipped the noose over her head. She threw it down the second-floor hall so Sam wouldn't see it at all. Fiona almost expected it to come alive and slither away.

Now they released Grace and she turned and rose and tried to arrange her hair so she looked more like the mother she'd been only an hour ago. She got to her feet.

And then six pistol shots rang out.

Six rounds punched through the door.

She looked down at Fiona and Bertie, who were just as stunned. If they hadn't stopped her, she would've had six holes in her, too.

Now the door opened slowly and there stood the boy, the one who'd shot her in the hand.

"What are you doing in there with my child?" Grace shouted.

The woman flew faster up the last few stairs than the bullets had left Joab's gun. She went over him, damn near through him. Joab went staggering backward and Grace crouched above him. She snarled and snapped. If he'd shot at her, what had he done to Sam?

"Mom?"

Grace turned her head to find Sam there, crouched behind what looked to be an old, sturdy brass crib. Grace didn't get to her feet; instead she scrambled across the floor, running on all fours to reach her one and only.

"Sam!" Grace purred as she held him.

Bertie and Fiona entered the room and stood between Joab and the scene.

Grace held Sam close and couldn't imagine letting go again, though the child squirmed a bit in the embrace. Grace finally pulled away and realized there was something different about her kid.

"Why are you wearing a dress?" Grace asked. "And why is it so dirty?"

But Sam didn't answer.

"Answer me now," Grace said. She touched the front of the dress. "Is this blood? Why is there blood on this dress?"

Sam only stared at Grace, top to bottom. He looked at his mother's face, her hair, her hands, her clothes.

"It wasn't there until you hugged me," Sam said. He touched Grace's face gently. "Did you get cut up?"

Grace frowned, confused. She looked back at Bertie and Fiona. They'd made a fuss about the noose, but all three of them were bathed in blood. Why hadn't she noticed—or understood—how they looked until now?

Shock. That's the reason. Grace didn't understand it, but she'd been in shock for a little while now. She finally looked down at herself. You would never know the original color of her clothing. Her hands were so red they looked as if they were covered in dry mud. She touched her hair, which felt heavy with the stuff.

"I'm okay, dear heart," she said. "This isn't my blood."

Sam said, "Then whose blood is it?"

64

THEY TOOK JOAB'S PISTOL AND LED HIM OUTSIDE. DIDN'T EVEN leave him time to put on a coat. They marched him over to the opera house, but then just stood there waiting outside. Why didn't they take him in? Sam asked.

Soon enough, as if called to, the doors of the opera house opened and out stepped the Negro woman, Mrs. Henry, who played a part in killing his mother. Instinctively he reached to his side for his pistol. They were smart to have taken it from him. Even without the rounds in the chamber, he would've run at her and tried to split her skull. Though it looked like someone else had done that work for him already.

"I want to see Mr. and Mrs. Reed," he finally said.

They all stood quiet for a long minute.

"No you don't," Mrs. Henry finally said.

He stepped forward now, half her size but unafraid. "I saw my mother's arm torn clear off her body, the blood shot as high as my face. You were there, too. Do you remember it?"

The women looked to Mrs. Henry but she'd already turned, starting for the opera house doors. She knew she couldn't tell this young man shit.

"Let him come," Mrs. Henry said.

Mrs. Henry opened the door and held it. She waved for Joab and Mrs. Wong and Mrs. Brown. Mrs. Price moved only to put her arms around her child.

"Not Sam," she said.

Mrs. Henry nodded. "Not Sam."

"I'm going to get him fed," Mrs. Price said, leading Sam across the street, toward the Grill Cafe. Mr. Shibata had closed down for the winter season, but there might be something stored that they could eat.

Sam took two steps with Mrs. Price but then turned again, broke loose and ran to Mrs. Henry, who leaned down close. She thought Sam had come in for a hug, but instead Sam whispered in Mrs. Henry's ear, then returned to his mother.

The women led Joab inside.

JOAB DIDN'T RECOGNIZE THE opera house.

The walls still stood, but many of the seats were missing. Not missing, but moved. Hadn't they been bolted down? He was sure they were, but now they lay scattered in piles the way the Montana winds sometimes overturned cabins and wagons, turning them into toys.

But that wasn't the only difference.

"Walk carefully now," Mrs. Henry said. "Don't slip."

The floors were dark and slick. The gaslights didn't illuminate the ground well enough to understand why. Mrs. Brown and Mrs. Wong no longer held on to him, so he wandered ahead of them by a step or three. He had to move slowly because Mrs. Henry had been right, the floor was slippery and it would be easy to fall.

As his mind adjusted to the wrecked orchestra seats, the slick floor, after he had a chance to comprehend these things, he then registered the smell, a scent really, and he knew it right away. His mother appeared before him, there on the floor of the opera house, the blood flushing from the torn arm socket; even out there at the cabin he'd understood the aroma of an ending. Damp and overwhelming. But if that had been the smell of one death, then the opera house stank of a dozen more.

Something moved on the stage, behind the curtains. This was what drew his eye to the stage, where the theater organ had been toppled over. It lay at an angle on the stage.

Joab felt no fear because, truly, he felt nothing. He pulled himself up on the stage, looking to the curtains that billowed. He looked backward and the women were not approaching him. They weren't even paying attention to him. They, too, looked around at all this chaos and struggled to understand it, even as they had been *in* it before they came for him and Sam.

Standing on the stage gave Joab greater perspective. Now he could see the orchestra seating a little better. He saw two men. They couldn't see him. They couldn't see anything. They were, at this point, only parts of people, flung about as wildly as the chairs. These were Matthew and Finn Kirby.

Joab and his brothers had held people down while their mother smothered them. He'd seen death plenty of times before now. But he'd never seen slaughter. It looked as if someone had released rage from a bottle and let it loose on the town.

"My whole life," Mrs. Brown said, down in the orchestra. "My whole life I've felt like doing this. But it wasn't allowed."

Joab turned away from her when she said this. On the stage he could see the blood better. It made the floor here as slick as it had down in the orchestra. Blood all over.

He walked closer to the theater organ to see why it sat at an angle. He crouched to find people underneath it. Was it Mr. Reed? Or Mrs. Reed? The Busy Bees?

Yes.

Parts of them.

Then the curtains shook again and out it came.

"Demon," Joab said.

Bigger now. Or had he shrunk it in his memory just so he could tuck it away into a small corner of his mind? No words could do it justice. In that moment, it appeared to be five stories high and twice as wide. Why wasn't he scared? Maybe he'd been expecting this. Something like this. Maybe he even welcomed it.

"All right then," he said.

The creature stalked closer. When it stepped on the theater organ, it finally cracked in half. In two more steps the demon was here. The mouth seemed large enough to swallow him.

"All right then," he said again. It might've been a kind of final prayer.

But then someone else joined them on the stage. Mrs. Henry stood beside Joab.

"Elizabeth," Mrs. Henry said. "Please let this boy live."

Elizabeth? What the hell kind of demon was named Elizabeth?

The creature looked from Joab to Mrs. Henry. Something strange occurred to him as he watched the pair up close. He couldn't explain it, but was there a . . . resemblance?

"Please," Mrs. Henry said.

A moment. A request. A decision.

Elizabeth snorted and turned and stomped to the lip of the stage and leapt down. Mrs. Brown and Mrs. Wong stood close to each other, but they didn't run. Elizabeth approached them and, to his shock, they held their hands out and touched *Elizabeth's* face. With tenderness. He looked away, back to Mrs. Henry.

"Why?" he asked. He said this with anger, not appreciation. He didn't care for pity, or even sympathy, from this woman.

Mrs. Henry looked at him for a long moment.

"Sam said you deserve another chance, too."

65

What she is, is not what she was.
Maybe she never was what they called her.
Each time her sister spoke the name
It became more and more her own.
Elizabeth. Elizabeth. Elizabeth. That was me.

Her new name was hers alone.
A secret sound,
One that only the wind whispered
When Elizabeth took to the sky.
Unknown to others, a private pride.

She spared her sister. Saved her sister.
The other women, too. And the child.
She chose to do that. Because of her, they had survived.
And her? Yes, her too.
Elizabeth had survived.

66

CLEMENT CARDINAL COULD BRING THEM TO CANADA. HE RODE into town to find them eating breakfast in the mansion once owned by the Reeds. He'd shown up because the pilot light above the opera house had gone out. First time he'd ever seen that happen. He knew it meant something disruptive had occurred. What a relief when it turned out it was his friends who made it through the night. Did he ask what happened? No, he did not. What good are questions if the answers will only drag you in the middle of someone else's trouble?

They were eating breakfast in the kitchen and offered him a cup of coffee. Sam lay in the parlor, sleeping on the couch. Grace didn't want him out of eyesight.

They asked Mr. Cardinal if they would find, in Canada, a nation vastly different from the one they'd be leaving. Someplace better for them?

Mr. Cardinal quoted Canada's interior minister, Frank Oliver, from memory. "'The purpose in giving free land to homesteaders is that the land may be made productive, and giving homesteads to single women would tend directly against that idea.'"

If a woman wanted to homestead in the North-West, she'd better get a man to come along. That was Canada.

"Not to mention," Mr. Cardinal added, "whose land do you think you'd be getting for free?"

He drained his coffee and wished them all well, walked out and mounted his horse. The Red River cart sat empty now; someone had swiped those last few furs he hadn't been able to sell. *No bother,* he thought. Stranger things than a few missing furs happened out here on the plains. Much stranger.

Back in the kitchen, the Lone Women discussed the future. If not Canada, then where? Points west, like Washington or Oregon? California? They considered a dozen directions, but all had their flaws.

"Then let's stay," Adelaide said.

"Here?" Grace asked. "You let about twenty people leave the theater before Elizabeth got to work. I think it was the right thing to do, but they'll be back with the law. How will we explain . . . any of this?"

"Montana is big," Bertie said. "We get away from here, but stay in Montana. Where, though?"

Fiona leaned in, elbows on the table, smiling. "Wouldn't it be amazing if one of us had spent the last few years visiting abandoned towns across the state?"

67

JOAB STOLE THE FURS. THAT'S PROBABLY OBVIOUS. BUT WHY?

Because he went to find the Maxwell, figuring he'd drive himself far from this town, this life, and into something entirely new. It's not like Mr. Reed would still need the car. But when he found the vehicle—pretty easy to do since it was parked behind the mansion—he found where Mr. Reed had discarded his brother, Delmus. The backseat.

Seeing the body, Joab's first thought—as irrational as could be, he knew that—was that Delmus must be cold. He meant to break into McNamara and Marlow's store—they, too, wouldn't need the items inside anymore—but found the Red River cart out front, Clement Cardinal's furs right there. He stole them all and covered his brother and swore taking those furs would be the last crime he'd ever commit.

He drove west with his brother in the back. The ground had become too cold to dig into, or he would've buried him. Instead, the corpse kept him company. That may sound morbid, but it didn't feel that way to Joab. Mr. Reed had refilled the car with gasoline the night before, and Joab carried all the money he'd ever earned with him. Mudges don't believe in banks. And that is who he was, for all the good and the bad. Joab Mudge. He wouldn't forget it again.

He drove to Great Falls, arriving as the sun set, and parked the Maxwell in the tony Lower North Side of the city. There, among the mansions of the wealthy, he set the car on fire and watched, from a distance, as the residents ran out to find the blaze. They worried for the vehicle; Joab felt it was the next best thing to burying his brother.

While these men, women, and children crowded in the road—servants arriving with bucket after bucket of water—Joab thought to enter each home and take whatever valuables he could find. Call it an instinct, or learned behavior. He only stopped himself at the kitchen entrance to a particularly large Queen Anne mansion. Reminded himself he wasn't doing crime anymore and, with that, he walked away.

The next morning he enlisted in the Navy, just thirteen years old.

In England, a boy named Sidney Lewis had already enlisted with the East Surrey Regiment in August. Sidney was twelve when he joined the British military, and by age thirteen he was fighting in the Somme.

So Joab became a squid. In 1917 the United States joined the war. Joab joined the German blockade, saw both Spain and Ireland. At those times he wished he could've written to Sam to explain how vivid, how enormous, the world turned out to be. He wished he could've told Sam thank you.

68

WHERE DID THEY GO?

The Lone Women were wise ones; they didn't have to go far, just far enough.

A town tucked down between a set of tall hills—you could hardly call them mountains—the hills cupped the territory like a pair of protective hands. For this reason more than two dozen structures remained standing, though almost all needed some form of repair. A county courthouse, a Methodist church, and, to Grace's profound joy, a schoolhouse.

Why had this town been abandoned? Three diseases ran through it: scarlet fever, whooping cough, and diphtheria, all at once. The original residents—those who survived—came to believe the town had been cursed. But it had been nine years since the last holdout moved away, nine years of dormancy. Those plagues had passed but its infernal reputation remained. A town considered so vile that its coordinates had been erased from the maps of memory. What better place for these women to settle in?

Behind the old saloon they found gallows. It was the only thing they tore down.

They spent the winter traveling between Big Sandy and their new home. They cleaned out the Gregson Hotel for beds, bedding, and tables. They took everything stocked in McNamara and Marlow's well-stocked general store. They didn't want to take anything from the Reeds' mansion but Bertie pointed out how stupid it would be to leave their well-heeled home with nothing and the women came to their senses. They took everything.

The last thing they did was turn up the faulty gas lighting in the opera house and let it run for a day. Adelaide threw an Atlas jar full of gasoline into the lobby—making sure to toss it from across the road; the opera house lit up like it was opening night. The bad gas in the top floor of the Reed home had been leaking for days by that point, and it went up just as quickly.

The street was so tightly packed that each structure caught fire as well. The power laundry, the Bear Paw Cafe, and so on down the row. If, by chance, someone was to call these women thieves and arsonists, well, at least they weren't a fucking lynch mob.

In this new town, their new home, Elizabeth occupied the old county courthouse and Adelaide lived in a cabin that sat behind it. Bertie and Fiona took over the saloon. There was a second floor to the schoolhouse—formerly a Masonic lodge up there—where Grace and Sam took residence. They thought it would be the six of them and no more, but that's not how it worked out.

More women arrived. Their appearance so startling that, at first, Adelaide and Elizabeth met them with a grimace and a snarl. Try to imagine a moment more intimidating than the Henry sisters squaring up against you. There ain't one.

So imagine Adelaide and Elizabeth's surprise when the first woman to appear didn't flee or shiver. Instead, she said, *I've been looking for this place.*

That's what the next woman said, too. And the ones that came afterward. As if they'd been drawn there—across the state or across the continent—by an instinct. Some looked like they'd come straight here, while others seemed like they'd been wandering the plains for half their lives. Nevertheless, this is where they settled.

I've been looking for this place. This is what each of them said.

A town of six became sixteen. Thirty. Sixty-five. Some came alone, others with their children. Adelaide welcomed the adults; Elizabeth greeted the kids. The little ones adored her—every child wants to learn that dragons are real—and each day she basked in their love. She had never dared to imagine a life outside that wretched barn, but here it was anyway.

They stayed on and survived, even though the days turned rougher as the years passed. In 1916 the state started to go dry, and the Dust Bowl era waited just ahead. Hard times for everyone, not just them. But they remained. They endured. And at times they thrived. Adelaide and Elizabeth, the Henry sisters, led the populace so well the people came to name the place after them. The town of Two Sisters, Montana.

You can scour the maps of the state if you like, but there's so much of the territory, even now, that escapes the eye. When you think you've surveyed it all, there's more. A town like that, it's easy to miss. Even more so if they don't want to be found. You might read histories about this time and place and never find mention of these women, any testimony that folks like them were here at all. But that's only because history is simple.

And the past?

The past is complicated.

ACKNOWLEDGMENTS

SOMETIMES I GET INVITED TO DO READINGS AROUND THE COUNTRY, and when I go, if it's a place I doubt I'll visit again, I buy a book about local history so I can better understand the place where I've just been. In 2012 I was invited to the University of Montana in Missoula. I went there, read and met with students, had a real good time. Then I hit the university bookstore and looked through the books about Montana. One book, in particular, caught my attention: *Montana Women Homesteaders: A Field of One's Own,* edited by Dr. Sarah Carter.

Did I know there had been lone women homesteaders? Women who didn't need a man to cosign for their tracts of land? Did I know this right wasn't reserved solely for white women?

No, no, and no. And that was only the beginning of what I didn't know.

Dr. Carter's book served as an entry point to a period of history that surprised me a little more, pretty much every day. I reached out to some of the friends I'd made in Montana, asking if they knew about all this stuff. Most of the people I asked were born and raised in the state and *they had absolutely no idea.* If even they didn't grow up hearing about these women, I thought maybe I had found a story worth telling, history that deserved a much larger audience.

After I finished Dr. Carter's book, I dove into so many more: *African Americans on the Western Frontier,* edited and with an introduction by Monroe Lee Billington and Roger D. Hardaway; *Vigilante Woman,* by Virginia Rowe Towle; *The Montana Frontier: One Woman's West,* by

Joyce Litz; *African American Women Confront the West, 1600–2000*, edited by Quintard Taylor and Shirley Ann Wilson Moore; and *Letters of a Woman Homesteader* by Elinore Pruitt Stewart. If this history seems interesting to you, I would recommend every single one of these books. Highly.

I also need to clarify that I chose Big Sandy, Montana, a real town, because of its location and history, but I want to emphasize that I have fictionalized this story—adding elements that never existed there, like the opera house, among many other things. The good people of Big Sandy are not the same as the people who tried to kill Bertie, Fiona, Grace, and Adelaide. It's a lovely town. If you're ever in the area, it's a real nice place to visit.

This novel began as a story I wrote for an anthology called *Long Hidden: Speculative Fiction from the Margins of History,* edited by Rose Fox and Daniel José Older. When I finished the story for that wonderful anthology (worth picking up, there's so much good work in it), I realized I'd only told part of Adelaide and Elizabeth's story. A novel's worth of story to tell. I'm grateful to Daniel and Rose for their invitation to submit something, and for the editing they did on the piece way back then.

I'm grateful, as always, for my agents, Gloria Loomis and Julia Masnik, and my editor, Chris Jackson. Thanks also to the whole big One World/Random House team: Sun Robinson-Smith, Carla Bruce-Eddings, Andrea Pura, Barbara Fillon, Tiffani Ren, Lulu Martinez, and Avideh Bashirrad. I'm grateful to all of you for your hard work bringing this book to readers.

Last, I thank my wife, Emily Raboteau, for helping me figure out the conclusion of the book. I discussed all the possibilities with her before bed. This is how we help each other with writing projects all the time. Should some of the Lone Women die? I wondered. If so, how many? Which ones? Should the Lone Women flee to Canada? Emily said, *None of the above. Women are losing enough in the real world these days. I want the Lone Women to win.*

It would be a happy ending, but boy, would they go through a lot to get there. That seemed right to me. Here's to hard-won happy endings. For them and for you.

—VICTOR LAVALLE

BRONX, NY

OCTOBER 24, 2022

ABOUT THE AUTHOR

VICTOR LAVALLE is the author of eight works of fiction: five novels, two novellas, and a collection of short stories. He has also written two graphic novel series. His novels have been included in best-of-the-year lists by *The New York Times Book Review*, *Los Angeles Times*, *The Washington Post*, *Chicago Tribune*, *The Nation*, and *Publishers Weekly*, among others. He has been the recipient of a Guggenheim Fellowship, an American Book Award, the Shirley Jackson Award, the World Fantasy Award, and the Key to Southeast Queens, among many others. He lives in the Bronx with his wife, the writer Emily Raboteau, and their kids. He teaches writing at Columbia University.

ABOUT THE TYPE

This book was set in Caslon, a typeface first designed in 1722 by William Caslon (1692–1766). Its widespread use by most English printers in the early eighteenth century soon supplanted the Dutch typefaces that had formerly prevailed. The roman is considered a "workhorse" typeface due to its pleasant, open appearance, while the italic is exceedingly decorative.